JACK OF HEARTS

BY

KEN SCOTT

A BOOTLEG BOOK

A BOOTLEG BOOK
Published by
Bootleg Press
2431 NE Halsey, Suite A
Portland, Oregon 97232

Bootleg Books may be purchased for educational, business, or sales promotional use. For information please e-mail, Kelly Irish at: kellyirish@bootlegpress.com.

First Bootleg Press Trade Paperback Edition.

December 2005

10 9 7 6 5 4 3 2 1

ISBN: 0976277913

Cover by Compass Graphics

For my children, Emily and Callum.
For Hayley, who is always there for me.
And for my parents, Tommy & Irene, who never stopped
believing.

JACK OF HEARTS

Rules are for the obedience of fools and the guidance of wise men.
Douglas Bader

CHAPTER ONE

HANNAH HART CHECKED HER WATCH, 8:30. Damn. If she was late again, she'd be in trouble. Sure the job was temporary and she wasn't getting paid, but she needed positive reviews from her superiors, one of whom was her Uncle Harrison, before she would be allowed to take her exams. Sometimes she thought it wasn't fair, she was expected to keep up with her studies, while she held down this glorified gopher job. She clenched a fist. If she had to go for one more cup of coffee, she swore she'd dump it into the sender's lap.

She sighed, of course she wouldn't do that. She was lucky enough her uncle gave her the position at the National, the bank that "Tries harder for you!" if you believe their commercials.

Sigh over, she took in a deep breath, inhaled the misty Newcastle air. It looked like rain. She stopped in front of the cold concrete steps that led up to both the National and Martin's, the bank next door. Soon she'd be through with her exams and she'd start her first real job, but at Martin's, not at the bank where she'd done her training.

She could train at the branch managed by her uncle, but she couldn't work there, because of the National's rules about nepotism, but she'd always assumed she'd be employed by them in another branch. She never dreamed Martin's would come through with such a generous offer. Now her only problem was how to tell Uncle Harry. She'd been putting it off, but now that the National had finally come through with a job in their Edinburgh branch, she was going to have to come clean and tell him she wasn't going to take it, that she was going to work for the competition.

He wasn't going to like that.

She stiffened her resolve. Today was the day. She bit her lower lip, started up the steps, stopped at the top. Part of her wanted to tell him just before quitting time, but her better part was telling her to march straight into his office and get it over with.

She was just about to push through the great double doors when she heard tires screeching. She turned, saw a black cab leaving rubber on the road as it braked to a stop in front of the two banks. Four men, wearing Disney cartoon masks, burst out of the cab and charged toward her.

Mind working on high speed she recognized the four, Mickey Mouse, Donald Duck, Goofy and Pluto, characters every child loved. However, she didn't think they were going to be so lovable this morning. Mickey, Donald and Goofy were brandishing guns. Pluto had an American aluminum baseball bat. The first three pushed past her, forcing their way inside, but Goofy grabbed her by her long hair, put a gun to her head, dragged her into the bank and demanded access to the secure area.

It had happened so fast, Hannah hardly had time to be scared. Goofy jammed the gun at her head, hurting her ear.

"Take it easy." She tried not to shout, tried to stay calm.

"Shut up!"

Everybody looked afraid. Some of the staff seemed on the verge of tears. Didn't they know you were supposed to stay calm during a robbery and give the criminals whatever they wanted?

Reginald Swaggart, a teller who had been with the bank longer than anybody could remember, seemed to be the only calm person in the face of the gun and, much to the horror of those behind the protective screens, let the robbers in. What was wrong with them? He was doing what he was supposed to do. Didn't they see the gun pointed to her head?

"On the floor!" Donald shouted.

No one moved. They seemed stunned.

"Now!" The duck grabbed Louise Adler, a silver-haired teller who had been with the bank almost as long as Swaggart, pulled her into a hug, as if he were going to dance, wrapped a leg behind her knees, pushed and she went down with a thud.

She screamed, a banshee sound that chilled up

Hannah's spine.

Pluto turned on Betty Wilson, Louise's best friend, Who'd hired on with the National the same day as Louise, and smashed her in the shoulder with the bat.

"Home run!" Pluto shouted as she fell.

"Bloody Christ, you didn't have to do that," Goofy said. Hannah tasted the garlic on his breath as he talked. He had her in a tight grip.

"Just get the fucking money, so we can get out of here," Pluto said.

"Everybody down!" Donald waved the gun, but he needn't have bothered, because now everybody, except Swaggart, was diving for the floor.

"Hurry," Pluto said, "we don't have much time."

And now, working at a speed Hannah thought would be impossible, unless they had some kind of inside knowledge, they filled two rucksacks with the cash from the tills that had just been prepared for the new day.

"See here!" Reginald Swaggart said. "You can't treat women like that."

"Get down, Reggie!" Louise shouted.

"Listen, you," Reggie said, "I'm trying to co-operate. Just get the money and go."

"Shoulda listened to the lady." Pluto set upon him as if he were a rabid dog, smashing him again and again with the bat, until he lay still. It was uncalled for. "Any other heroes?" he said when he was finished.

No one spoke up, but Betty crawled over to try to help Swaggart and got clubbed again for her effort. Pluto raised the bat for still another blow, but she scurried away on hands and knees, screaming and crying, out of the bat's reach, luckily the maniac dog didn't come after her.

By this time many of the women were crying and the situation appeared to be spiraling out of control. And now Hannah was afraid.

* * *

Bob Heggie stepped off the train, tucked the paper under his arm. Ten minutes from now and he'd be at work. Just another day wasted away at the bank. He sighed, but the train covered the sound as it rumbled out of the central station.

The twenty minute ride from Monkseaton was uneventful, as usual. He'd spent the time reading yesterdays evening's Chronicle. He bought it on his way home everyday, but usually worked on his laptop on the ride, thus cutting down on the amount of work he'd have to do the next day, allowing him extra time for lunch.

Like every morning, he tried to find a bit of good news in the paper to brighten the beginning of his day and, like every morning, there was almost none to be found. A murder, that was rare, even for Newcastle. A mugging, an elderly woman pushed around by a couple of young toughs, her purse stolen. No, nothing good in the news. He flipped to the sports section where he found a bright spot in all the gloom. An editorial writer waxed prolific on the game he'd been to Saturday last with his son. His beloved Newcastle United had won a last minute victory, which sent his son into the clouds and Bob enjoyed reading about it and reliving the game.

At the station he took the escalator upward, ignoring the other passengers. At ground level, he tossed the Chronicle into a bin and made for the exit, where he found Old Tom, the paper-seller, who had the morning

Journal in his hand and a smile for Bob, even though he was waiting on another customer, an American youth who was asking directions to the student union at the college. Bob wanted a word, so he decided to wait a bit.

"Look, it's easy peasy," Tom said to the pimply faced kid. "Nip to the other side of the road at the pedestrian crossing." Tom pointed. "The university is just there." He was still pointing. "You'll pass Blackwell's Bookshop, then turn left at the Campus Coffee House on the corner and that'll be King's Walk, take the steps up and the Student Union will be on your left."

The kid thanked Tom and left. Ah, youth, try as he might, Bob couldn't remember his. Sometimes it seemed like he'd been born straight into the rut his life had become.

"What can I do for you, Bob?" Tom scratched what looked like a two day beard. Bob had never seen Tom clean shaven and that beard never seemed to grow. Old Tom was always the same, scruffy looking coat, faded, but clean jeans, shoes that had seen better days, silver hair, badly in need of a comb, just touching his shoulders.

"I was wondering if you'd do me a favor? My soon to be ex-wife heard about this horror writer who did that book signing last week at Blackwell's. She called and they have some copies left over. If I give you a tenner, do you think you could pick me up one?"

Debra had come by this morning to pick up a few things she'd forgotten when she'd turned the house over to him and, in typical fashion, asked him to pick up the book for her, because the bookstore was close to the bank, never mind that it wouldn't be open yet when he walked by on his way to work. Ah well, what could he do? It seemed he was still running errands for her.

She was an avid reader, King, Koontz, Grisham and Crighton, she read them all. Bob envied her that. The newspapers and the racing forms were the extent of his reading, those and the endless amount of crap he had to go through at the bank.

He tried to keep Debra sweet, anything she wanted really, ever since the separation. Bob was a bit bitter, but bitterness didn't get him days out with the kids. Debra controlled his visiting rights and could cancel planned days out and stopovers at the drop of a hat. "Sorry, Bob" she'd say, "I'm not sending them over if you're in that mood." And the line would go dead. He'd ring back of course, but it was always engaged. Left off the hook.

She had a new man now, Stephen, who sad to say, was actually a pretty nice guy. He liked Bob's kids, Stephen did. Debra couldn't stop talking about how good he was to them. The children talked too and that broke his heart. "Is he our new Daddy?" Cameron asked one afternoon. Bob just about cried himself to sleep that night. He'd learned to play the game with her now, didn't even ask about Stephen anymore.

"That'd be Jack Priest," Tom said, bringing Bob back to the present. "Nice young man. Bought a couple of papers from me. Left a tip both times. A bloody tip, Bob, can you believe it? Nobody tips Old Tom for a paper, it's well seen he's a Yankee."

Bob laughed as he handed over the money.

"I'll have the book with your evening paper."

"Thanks." Bob waved goodbye and started the five minute walk to the bank.

* * *

The thugs demanded access to the safe and Mickey took nineteen-year-old Gloria Alan, who had only been with the bank for two weeks, hostage. Now the robbers held two women with a gun to their heads. And for some reason that made no sense, Hannah was more afraid for Gloria than she was for herself.

Mickey dragged Gloria to the exit, preventing anyone gaining access and also giving himself, what looked to Hannah, a good view of the street. The other robbers knew where to go, and this reaffirmed Hannah's belief that this was an inside job. They were in the safe for only a minute, maybe two, then they rushed out with full rucksacks.

It was at that point that the raid began to go wrong.

Somehow, against all odds, Reggie was back on his feet, trying to block Donald's way, but his heroics were short lived as Pluto reacted with a crazed yell, attacking Reggie with a madman's fury, battering him back to the floor. A normal man would have screamed, but today Reginald Swaggart seemed far from normal and Hannah was impressed. His courage was contagious, giving her strength. Reggie grit his teeth and said, "Bastard!"

Pluto turned back round, stood over the wounded man.

"Don't swear at me, Granddad!" he said with a cigarette tuned voice. "I know who my father is." He raised a foot, stomped on Reggie's knee.

"Cunt!" Reggie grit out in defiance.

"Oh, that was not smart!" Pluto took a step back, aimed a heavy kick at Reggie's head and let fly, sending Reggie straight into unconsciousness.

Hannah had to do something and, as if he had second sight, Goofy wrapped his arm tighter around her neck, stuck the gun in her ear.

"Don't make me hurt you, sweetheart!"

* * *

Bob stopped in front of the Starbucks a couple doors down from the bank. Every now and then he went in and spent too much for one of their specials. It was an extravagance, but it was much better than what they tried to pass off as coffee at work.

Sometimes he took his lunch at the coffee shop, as he could go online there, but he favored the Starbucks at Eldon Square. He preferred the hustle bustle of the shoppers and students. Eager young kids about to step into the wide world of work. Tomorrow's teachers, engineers, doctors and dentists or, God help them, bankers. He needed the smiling faces to remind him that not everybody was as depressed as he'd become.

And he needed to be away from the bank when he went online. He liked to check on the vacation spots in the sun. Mallorca, St. Martin, Thailand, someday he'd be going to those places. Someday. But mostly he went online to check the ponies. Everyday he checked the stats. He doubted there was anybody in England who knew the ponies as well as he did. However, even though this wasn't a private passion, it wouldn't do to be caught checking up on the horses at work.

This morning, having spent his extra money on the book for Debra, he was a little short, but he couldn't tell her no, because he wanted to see his kids more than she was letting him. But he sure hated that he couldn't afford the price of a cup of coffee.

He was about to continue his short trek toward the bank, when he caught his reflection in the coffee shop window. Double damn, he had food or something on his chin. What was that? Egg yolk from breakfast? He wiped it off. Hadn't Debra seen it when he'd stopped by to see the kids this morning? Was she so caught up in her new life she hadn't noticed? Had she been thinking about Stephen?

Bob shivered. That really ate at him, thinking of her with someone else. And he hated it that the bastard was such a nice guy, so good with the children. A natural father the man was. The kind of father Bob had always wanted to be, but couldn't. Someone had to work, to support the family. It wasn't his fault.

It wasn't.

He scraped the yolk off with his thumbnail. It had hardened, set in, didn't come off easily. What a right lousy start for the day and he hadn't even set foot in the bank yet. Debra, the boyfriend, egg yolk, what else could possible go wrong before he got to work?

Yolk gone, he resumed his trek, wondering if anyone had noticed. One thing for certain, the other passengers on the train must have seen. Old Tom must have seen it as well, but then he was far too polite to say anything about it. What a dilemma it must have posed to him. Should he point out the yellow stuff on his customer's chin, thus saving him embarrassment later on, or should he pretend he hadn't seen it?

He shook his head. He wondered if anybody at the bank would have said anything. He wondered if they'd have even noticed. The customers would have. John

Mackenzie, the shit he worked for, he'd have noticed as well. But everybody else seemed to be caught up in the same kind of humdrum existence he'd been spinning around in for the last couple years. Like him, they kept their heads down and did just enough to get through the day, without losing their jobs.

He forced a smile at his window reflection. He wasn't the best looking man on God's polluted planet, but he wasn't the worst either. Still, much as he hated to admit it, he didn't have the kind of looks the ladies went for. His mass of graying hair that refused to be regulated, combined with a nose that had been broken in a confrontation with an Iraqi soldier during the first Gulf War, gave him sort of an aging, beat up boxer appearance.

That and his cheap suit made him look almost like a man on the skids, a man on a fast track to a dung hill, not the under manager of a bank. Yeah, when you saw Bob Heggie for the first time, banker wasn't the first thought that flashed through your head, not the tenth either, it didn't even make the list.

He turned away from his reflected self, continued on, just a short way now and all of a sudden it started raining. Well, why should he be surprised, it was just one more thing gone wrong before he got to the bank. He felt like he should quicken his step, but it was only a drizzle and besides, he wasn't in a hurry to get to work, not ever in a hurry for that.

The rain started to come harder, but still he moved along at his turtle's pace. He shook the wet mop of unruly hair out of his eyes. By the time he got to the bank it was raining ropes, as the French would say, had been for about a minute. He might have been able to get up those steps and into the bank before it started, but he'd spent that few extra minutes with Old Tom and now he was paying for it, as he'd left home without an umbrella.

Lightning flashed in the distance, thunder roared. It was going to be a stormy morning. Bob sighed, gave a thought to Old Tom as he remembered their conversation and wished his day was over and he was picking up that book for Debra from the paper-seller. Wouldn't it be great if he could just move eight hours into the future. Skip the workday altogether.

* * *

Someone hit the alarm as the gang moved out of the secure area and the screeching sound panicked Donald. He turned and fired four shots into the bullet-proof glass as someone screamed.

Mickey apparently had all he could take, he pushed Gloria away, waved his gun in the air, as if he were trying to signal his compatriots, but for some reason he stayed silent, a frightened man waving, signaling a crazed crew, who were beyond paying any attention.

"Come on!" he shouted, but no one seemed to hear. "We gotta go!" he shouted louder, still no one heard.

He fired the gun into the ceiling.

That got their attention, then he turned and, quick as the Flash, was out the door. Donald, seeing Mickey flee, decided it was time for him to go as well and in blur he took off after the mouse.

"What the fuck?" Goofy said, grip still strong around Hannah's neck.

"They're going," she said. "You should go too."

* * *

It started to come down even harder as Bob approached the bank. Had he been going anywhere else, he would have dashed through the rain in a mad run for shelter. But he was going to work and he'd just as soon arrive drenched as not. So he shuffled along, in spite of the downpour, head down, left arm stiff as a pipe, anchored by a briefcase that felt as if it were stuffed with bricks instead of paperwork and his laptop. He looked up for an instant at the doorways to Martin's, the bank where he worked, and the National, the Bank next door. He took the first step. God he hated this job, his boss, his life. One step, two, three, he climbed, eyes on the wet concrete. At the top he started toward his bank when he heard an explosion.

"What-" his explanation was cut short as Mickey Mouse, with a pistol big as his ears, burst out of the National. Mickey was wearing an expensive suit, Bob saw that straightaway. And the blue silk tie that flew over the mouse's shoulder, flapping like the Union Jack, looked like it cost more than all of the ones he had stacked neatly in his tie drawer back home put together.

Thunder roared off in the distance and if Bob hadn't seen the gun in the mouse's right hand, he might have thought the explosion he'd heard a few seconds ago was thunder as well, but he did see it, a forty-five automatic that looked like an old American military issue.

And he saw the mouse's trembling hands. Had he just shot someone in the National? Was this a raid? Was he robbing the bank, this odd looking mouse in the expensive suit?

"Out of the way!" Mickey roared.

Bob jumped back, not about to argue with a mouse

brandishing a forty-five.

Mickey turned, pointed the automatic straight at Bob's heart and for a flash of a second, that seemed a lifetime, the two men stared at each other. Even through the rain Bob registered the bluest eyes he'd ever seen behind that mask. Frightened blue eyes. Unforgettable. The man was terrified and all of a sudden, Bob realized he was not.

For an instant he almost wished the man would pull the trigger and put him out of his misery. Just put him down the way you did a dying dog, because that's what he felt like, a mortally wounded animal. Life had boarded the train and left Bob Heggie at the station, without a ticket.

"The rain," Bob said, "it's not good for the suit." As soon as he'd uttered the words, he knew it had been a stupid thing to say.

"What?" Now it was Mickey's turn to be surprised.

Bob shook his head.

And Mickey's hand started shaking. He was going to pull the trigger. Quicker than a wink of God's eye, it was all going to be over and Bob would learn the answer to life's ultimate question.

"Get it over with," Bob, beyond caring, spit the words.

"You stupid mother-"

"Fuck, fuck, fuck," Donald Duck squawked as he shot out through the National's double doors, colliding with Mickey, just as the mouse pulled the trigger.

"Jesus," Bob said, but he didn't hear the words. The blast had been so loud his ears seemed on fire.

"Come on, Mickey Mouse, move it!" the duck shouted, loud enough for Bob to hear, despite the ringing in his ears.

Donald too had a gun in his hand and his mask was

askew, threatening to come off. Instantly Bob noted he was dressed as well as his rodent pal. Something he'd want to remember for the police, if these Disney desperados didn't kill him first.

"Yeah, yeah," the mouse said, not as loud, but Bob's hearing was coming back.

"No killing, remember?" The duck pushed the mouse away from Bob, toward the steps leading down to the street. He was angry, any idiot could see that, and Bob was no idiot. "Get going!" He gave Mickey a second shove, then took off at a run.

"Arrrgh," Bob heard Mickey scream as he stumbled halfway down the steps, crashing to the ground. But his adrenaline must have been kicking into overdrive, because he was up in an instant.

* * *

Inside the National, Pluto gave the downed Reggie another kick.

"Stop!" Hannah said. "He's had enough."

Pluto raised his bat.

"No, she's right," Goofy, with an arm still around Hannah's neck, said, then he made his way toward the door, dragging Hannah along with him.

Gloria had frozen in fear, rooted to the spot where she had been released. Hannah saw her, Goofy did not and just as he put on a final push toward the door, he collided into her and went down, taking Hannah and Gloria along with him.

They hit the floor hard. Gloria cried out in panic. Goofy panicked too, letting go of Hannah and firing two shots in no particular direction. The first round hit the plaster ceiling with a dull thud and an explosion of cloudy powder cascaded down. The second struck Gloria below the chin, exiting through the top of her skull.

"No!" Hannah shouted.

Goofy grabbed a fistful of Hannah's hair.

"You shot her." Hannah tried to get away.

"Shut up!" He jerked her to her feet, wrapped a hand around her neck again.

"You shot her," Hannah repeated, brain numb.

"Come along, or you're next!" He shoved the gun into her cheek.

"Get out of here, go! Go!" Pluto shouted.

"Yeah, right." Goofy dragged Hannah toward the door.

* * *

Bob jumped back as door to the National burst open again. Goofy this time. He had a gun too. He also had an arm snaked around Hannah Hart's neck, dragging the unwilling woman in his wake. Hostage or cover, was Bob's first thought as the Disney dog released her with a shove.

Hannah stumbled, fought to stay on her feet, grabbing onto Goofy's gun hand to keep from falling.

"Leggo!" Goofy jerked his arm away.

Hannah screamed as she hit the concrete.

"Stupid, bitch!" Goofy pointed his gun at her head.

"No," she said.

"No," Bob muttered. He was going to shoot. That was water clear. He was going to shoot this young woman down in cold blood.

"No!" Bob brought his briefcase up as cover as he dove between Hannah and the gunman.

Something smacked into the briefcase, slamming him toward the ground as a searing pain lashed across his left side.

"Gotcha!" Goofy said.

"Shit!" Bob hit the ground with a thud. The pain was wicked, the curse didn't take a bit of it away. He struggled to get up as Goofy turned the gun back toward Hannah. Then his world started to spin out of control.

CHAPTER
TWO

FOUR WEEKS EARLIER Bob Heggie waited on the platform as the morning train pulled into Monkseaton station, brakes screeching. Normally he'd be walking the dogs over at Debra's, where he used to live, but today he felt like a little independence. So instead of letting a wife, who he was separated from and who found him boring, take him for granted, he decided to come into the city early, maybe spend some time at Starbucks over an iced coffee or maybe look at some motorcycles.

He sighed. Motorcycles, yes, he'd do that. He'd financed Alan Hotspur's mortgage, one of the salesmen at Just Harleys, a couple months back, maybe he'd go there and look around.

A shiver ticked up his back, touched the base of his neck. It'd been twelve years since he'd sold his Triumph, a dozen years since he'd felt the wind on his face on a warm summer's day. But also a dozen years since he'd been pelted with cold rain, shivering on a rain slicked motorway in the middle of the night. When a motorcycle is your only mode of transportation, you have to take the good with the bad.

However, Debra hated the bike, wouldn't even stand for it as a second vehicle. She was afraid he might hurt himself. Besides, she'd said, a motorcycle didn't suit a banker.

So what? he'd thought. He took the train into the city, walked to work from the station. Nobody cared whether he rode a Triumph Bonneville or a Rolls Royce Silver Cloud on his days off.

Except Debra.

So he'd sold the bike, got himself a trusty, but very used, Volkswagen Bug. The car may have been created the day after God created Adam, but it ran well, never failed to start and always got him where he was going, though not in style.

He sighed again as he got on the train. Debra had her Volvo, he got the VW. And she cried like a bleating cow whenever he drove her precious. Maybe he did turn out to be a boring old sod, but he'd had help.

He got up from his seat three stops early to give his place to a very pregnant teenager, who didn't look much older than his little girl. What was the world coming to?

The Train braked as it approached Jesmond. One more station to go, but as the train slowed to a stop, he started toward the door. Motorcycles, he'd look at them.

The shop was only five minutes from Jesmond Station. Why Not? He had time.

He jumped from the train, feeling apprehensive as he left the station's shadowy surroundings. He took the stone steps leading to the street two at a time and, as he came into the sunlight, his pupils contracted, causing him a transient flash of blindness. He shielded his eyes and, as they became accustomed to the brightness, he couldn't help feeling what a great day it would be to own a bike.

He crossed the busy Jesmond Road, jumped the pedestrian barrier and that brought him onto Portland Terrace. He looked across to his right and marveled at the horseshoe shaped row of elegant Victorian houses. Once the residences of the top surgeons, doctors and barristers of the city, a convenient walk to their place of work, they were now the offices of successful law firms, accountants and software companies. The prosperous professionals now preferred to commute from the coast and Darras Hall, Ponteland or Morpeth.

A tingle crawled up his spine as he turned onto Warwick Street and spotted the Harley dealership. A gleaming Road King Classic roared from the forecourt as he strolled up to the main entrance. Across the way, flamboyant murals had been painted on the walls opposite the classic Harley Davidsons. A black and chrome Fat Boy pulled out from the workshop on the side street, the sound of its exhaust drowning out the murmur of the morning rush hour. The street was known as Thunder Alley. He wasn't sure who'd originally called it that or whether it even existed on official maps, but he figured it had been well named.

They were just opening as he got there. Alan and

another man were drinking coffee out front as a lorry pulled up. Bob stopped to watch as the lorry driver ground the gears, trying to fit the truck into a space that anybody could see was too small. He finally gave up and shut the truck down in the middle of the road. The driver got out, lowered a ramp, then he and Alan maneuvered a pallet to the street. Heavy by the looks of it. Too small to be a motorcycle. Parts, Bob thought, as Alan pulled the pallet jack around to the back, probably to a loading dock.

Bob had never been to the Harley dealership before, but had been curious ever since he'd made Alan the loan. He sighed for what seemed like the hundredth time that morning. He remembered the freedom and the feeling of the open road and he wanted to experience it again. He took his mobile from his pocket and called the bank. He mumbled on to Julie Hansen, one of the cashiers, about a doctor's appointment, said he wasn't coming in.

Julie promised to inform personnel and wished him well.

Bob pressed end.

"Bob Heggie?" Alan said, coming back, hand out stretched.

"Yeah." Bob shook his hand.

"What are you doing here? The bank's not foreclosing already, is it?" He laughed.

"No." Bob laughed too. "I just got an urge to look at motorcycles."

"Then you've come to the right place, come inside."

The dealership was an Aladdin's cave of polished chrome treasure. Bob had no idea a motorcycle could look so elegant, within seconds the hypnotic sight before him hooked him in.

"From that look of rapture on your face, I'd say I've already made a sale today."

"I don't know about that." Bob laughed again.

"You got a license, you know, with motorcycle permission?"

"Yeah." Bob reached for his wallet, took out the license. "I used to ride a Triumph Bonneville."

"So, what do you like the look of?" Alan studied Bob's license. "You can take anything you want for a test drive."

"It's been about a dozen years since I've been on a bike." Bob gazed at the motorcycles and at the high price cards sitting astride the handlebars. "I'd be a little nervous about riding one of these."

"You could start with a Sportster, not that much different than a Bonny, except the shifter and the front brake are reversed."

Bob closed his eyes for a second, tried to imagine the difference. He flexed the muscles in his right foot.

"Yeah, you'd be braking with that one." Alan had noticed. "But don't worry, you'll catch on fast."

"Maybe you weren't listening when I said it's been about a dozen years. That's two more than ten, you know, a decade."

"Don't worry. I'll take you through everything, just like you took me through that loan. It'll all come back to you." Alan laughed. "Besides, we're insured."

"Thanks, mate," Bob said, "that makes me feel a whole lot better."

They sat at Alan's desk and he took Bob through the gearshift and braking system of the Harley range and Bob smiled as it all did come flooding back.

* * *

Hannah had been lying awake, listening to Jeff sleep the sleep of the wicked for the last hour or so. She was confused, hurt, angry and afraid. Last night he'd hit her, raped her, then hit her again. That had never happened before, though she had seen the warning signs. She just had not wanted to believe them.

She had to leave, had to do it now, before he woke.

She was so afraid.

She had to think, couldn't think through the haze of confusion and fear. How do you walk out on a controlling maniac when you have nowhere to go?

He knew that, Jeff did. Her parents had been killed in New York while they were away on vacation on that horrible September day, sending her into a spiral of grief so stark she thought she'd never be able to climb out of it.

Jeff had helped her, held out his hand and pulled her from the dark, brought her back into the light. He'd been kind and caring, understanding and nurturing. He was the big brother she'd never had and somehow he'd turned into the lover of her dreams. Her first and, she'd thought, destined to be her only.

He talked her into going back to school and now she was just about ready for her banking exams. She had a career ahead of her, thanks to him. He taught her how to appreciate fine wine, black and white movies, classical music and the Rolling Stones.

For almost four years she'd lived a dream life. Jeff introduced her to his parents and they'd accepted her as if she were their own daughter. Sir Howard Teasdale, Jeff's famous father, had invited her along with himself and Lady Teasdale to several of those social functions Jeff hated so much.

"Go," he'd say, "make Mum and Dad happy. And make an excuse for me."

She'd danced with Mick Jagger, had brunch with John Major, been kissed on the cheek by Tony Blair and had been complemented by writers and artists galore on her fashion sense. Well, when Lady Teasdale draped you with some of her most exquisite creations, gowns that had yet to see a model's runway, you were bound to get compliments.

The Teasdales had become her family and it hurt that she would probably never see them again. They loved their son more than anything, so there was no doubt in Hannah's mind, in leaving Jeff, she was leaving them as well.

But she couldn't stay. Not now. Not after what he'd done last night.

She closed her eyes and shuddered.

And she listened to the rhythmic sound of his breathing. He was deep asleep. Now was the time. Waiting till after he'd gone to work made more sense, but she didn't want to be around when he woke.

She never wanted to speak to him again.

A quick look at the clock across the room told her is was 8:30. She'd learned from experience that when Jeff drank as much as he did yesterday, that he'd probably sleep till noon. She wanted to be long gone by then.

She eased out of bed, rubbed her cheek.

It hurt.

She hoped it wasn't black and blue.

Careful not to wake Jeff, she went to the closet, took out her flight bag. She didn't know why, but since the

Christmas holidays things had started going down hill. At first she couldn't figure out what had gone wrong and she blamed herself for the tension in their relationship. She wasn't a coward, wasn't a quitter and she didn't want to quit on Jeff. But after last night she had no choice.

"No choice," she whispered as she stuffed a few changes of clothes into the flight bag. Next she put in her iBook and the power supply, making sure they were wrapped and protected by the clothes. For as long as she could remember, she'd been meaning to buy a computer bag, but had never gotten around to it.

There was very little else she cared about other than her iPod, which was loaded with everything from Billie Holiday to the Beatles; her well worn hardback copy of the Horse Whisperer, signed by Nicholas Evans; her photo album, which contained the only surviving photos of her parents and her cell phone. With her bag loaded, she was ready to go.

Her textbooks she didn't need anymore. Toiletries she could get new, the rest of her clothes, she could live without. Most of them were expensive creations designed by Jeff's mother anyway and it wouldn't be right to take those.

Just had to get dressed and she was gone.

"Where do you think you're going?"

"Jeff," she gasped, "I thought you were asleep."

"So, where you going?" He was framed in the bedroom doorway, wearing boxer shorts and a loose fitting tee shirt, both white enough to blind in bright sunlight. Until recently he'd sported briefs and a muscle shirt as underwear, but they went away when he started to notice the bit of flab on his stomach. If he couldn't have the perfect body, he wasn't going to show it off, even in his own bedroom.

She stared into his steely eyes, doing her best to act unafraid, but sweat was trickling under her arms. Her heart was racing. She wasn't going to make the clean getaway she'd hoped for. Should've waited till he'd gone to work, then she could've packed and gone at her leisure. Stupid.

"Did you hear me?"

"I heard you."

"So?"

"I'm leaving."

"I said I was sorry about last night." He smiled, showed those perfect teeth, whiter than any toothpaste ad, but his hypnotic eyes were cold. If the eyes were a window to the soul, she was seeing a place she didn't want to go.

She held her flight bag to her breasts, curled her toes in an effort to control her fear. He was a big man, but he didn't work out. He looked tough and she knew that had gotten him out of several scrapes without having to fight. In fact, until last night, she'd thought he was all bluff, that he'd never raise a hand to another. She'd found out the hard way that despite what she'd thought, he could cause hurt. She'd felt just a taste of the pain he could inflict. She didn't want to sample any more.

"You hit me."

"I said I was sorry. I had a little too much to drink. It won't happen again, I promise."

"I can't take the chance. I think we need some time apart to think things through."

"You're not leaving. How do you think it would look to Mum and Dad, to all our friends?"

"You should have thought about that before you did what you did."

"How many times do I have to tell you, I was drunk, it wasn't my fault."

"You raped me."

"Come on, I'd hardly call it rape. We've had sex hundreds of times and you've never complained before." His smile changed, now he looked like a snake.

"You held me, clamped your hand over my mouth, ripped my clothes of. That's not sex, it's violence."

"You're not leaving." He started toward her. "I think you should unpack that bag."

"No." She barely got the word out, knew how weak she'd sounded and all of a sudden she knew she'd made a mistake. She should've been tough, fought, kicked, screamed, because now she realized he had enjoyed her fear.

"Unpack the bag!"

"Or what, you're gonna hit me again?" She should have dressed first. She felt so vulnerable with only the old tee shirt she slept in. She balled a fist into the fabric of it. God, she didn't even remember putting it on. Her mind must have really shut down after what had happened. Well it was wide awake now and she was afraid.

"Come on, Hannah, it doesn't have to be like this. Just unpack the bag." He hovered over her, picked up the bag, dropped it on the floor. "Empty it out!" He fisted a hand in her hair, forced her to her knees. "Do it now!" He dropped to his knees as well, faced her with a look so terrifying that she was afraid for her life. How could she have misread him so?

"You can't do this, you shouldn't." She tried not to

whimper as she unzipped the bag, reached in.

"You can do it, babe." His face was inches away, she saw only violence on it. He was going to hurt her again.

She slipped her fingers into the bag, found her iPod, took it out.

"There, that wasn't so bad, now your iBook."

"I wrapped it in my clothes." Could that be her voice? It sounded like a frightened child's.

"Stop stalling!"

"I'm not." Still on her knees, she tried to face him down, couldn't. She turned away from his glare, went back to her bag, pulled out the tee shirts she'd wrapped around her computer.

"See it's not so hard."

She glanced over his shoulder, widened her eyes, as if she'd just seen something unexpected.

"What?" He turned to follow her gaze.

She pulled her iBook from the bag, seven pounds of tough white plastic, grabbed it with both hands as if it were a board, put everything she had into the swing, hit him full in the face as he turned back.

His head snapped to the right. Blood shot out of his shattered nose. He went down with a thud.

And Hannah went into overdrive. She stuffed her things back into her bag. Got up with hurricane speed, threw on jeans, pulled on a pair of Nikes, headed for the door.

He moaned.

She stopped.

She hadn't considered for a second whether or not she'd killed him, she'd been so frightened. Now she realized she might have seriously hurt him. He could be swallowing blood. He could suffocate.

She dropped her bag by the open door, went back to check on him.

"Bitch." He opened his eyes, was struggling to his feet.

She turned without a word, dashed to the door, grabbed her bag and in an instant was out in the street.

"You'll be sorry!" he shouted after her.

She looked back, saw him on his feet, blood all over his underwear as he stood in the doorway. Then she turned away and ran toward the tube station.

* * *

"So what do you think, Bob? Are you ready to take a ride?"

"Oh, I don't know, I don't really see a motorcycle in my future." He looked over at the gleaming bikes. He'd never imagined himself on a Harley. Truth be told, he'd always had a soft spot for British bikes, Triumphs, the old BSAs. However, now that he was actually in the motorcycle shop, he was picturing himself as sort of a motorcycle outlaw. Peter Fonda in Easy Rider, or maybe a Hell's Angel, not so boring Bob Heggie anymore.

"That gleam in your eyes tells me maybe you do."

"We can't always get what we want." He got up from the chair in front of Alan's desk, went over to a row of motorcycles, looked at the price card on a Fat Boy. "Besides, even if I did want a bike, there is no way I could afford this."

"We could work something out."

"Hey, what's that?" Bob pointed to a bike that looked like a the 2025 edition of the Triumph Bonneville. The Triumph of tomorrow, today.

"V-Rod. It'll handle a lot like that Bonneville you remember, but it'll go a lot faster, so you have to watch it."

Bob went over to the bike, stroked the seat, felt an electronic tingle zip from his palm straight to his heart. The bike was calling to him.

"Why don't you take it for a test ride, then we'll talk." Alan wheeled the bike out the side door, got on, keyed the ignition and Bob shook with excitement when the bike rumbled to a start.

"Beautiful," Bob muttered.

"There is nothing in the world that sounds like a Harley. This is the real deal, Bob." He got off the bike. "Take it for a ride."

"I'm not so sure." Bob hesitated. "Maybe this isn't such a good idea."

"It's a great idea and you know you want to. I'll go get you a helmet and gloves."

Bob couldn't wait to kick the bike into first gear.

"Open face, Bob, you have to look the part," Alan said, coming back with the helmet.

"Open face," Bob repeated as he held out a hand, took it and pulled it on.

"And you'll need these," Alan spoke loud enough to be heard about the rumble of the bike.

Bob nodded and took the sunglasses from Alan and also the black leather gloves.

"It's now or never," Alan said.

"I guess it's now." Bob swung his leg over the seat.

"Take it easy and watch out for the boys in blue."

Bob feigned a smile and found first. He eased out the clutch and the bike lurched forward. He dragged his feet along the side of it as he rode from the forecourt and approached Warwick Street. So much traffic, he thought as he waited for a break in the line. A red Corsa passed him and he saw the gap he had been waiting for. He released the clutch again, twisted the throttle, his feet instinctively found the foot pegs, then he moved on up through the gears, second, third, fourth, it was all so familiar. Bob couldn't help grinning as passersby took notice of the middle-aged man on his noisy toy.

He pulled a left at the top of Warwick Street and down Heaton Park Road. He cursed the speed bumps that restricted him and turned left onto Heaton Road. He powered through the gears again, this time with more confidence. The light up ahead was green as he approached and he shifted his weight to the right as he leaned into the bend. The bike gripped the road like a cougar and as he straightened he opened it up. The burst of acceleration threw him back into the seat and he hung onto the handle bars, the wind pressure pulling at his shoulder sockets. As he hit top gear he was conscious of his cheeks altering shape and stole a quick look in the mirror. He laughed at his peculiar profile and was grateful for the shades Alan had loaned him.

He was in harmony with the machine. It was as if he had been riding it forever. He angled the bike onto an approaching slip road and made for the signs to the city. The traffic got heavier as he roared into Haymarket and down through the busy streets toward the bank. It was another little protest against his employers.

He pulled up outside, twisted the throttle. The noise made several staff look up, but as Bob suspected they didn't recognize him. Why should they? Bob Heggie astride a Harley Davidson, dressed like they had never seen him before. He looked through the glass doors of the branch and saw Julie Hansen sitting at the customer service desk looking at him. Bob waived, found first gear, looked over his shoulder and powered away from the bank with a grin etched across his face.

Back at Just Harleys he got off the bike feeling ten years younger.

"So did you enjoy the ride?" Alan asked.

"Loved it." Bob handed him the helmet, gloves and glasses. "But there is no way I can afford that. Besides, it might be a bit to much bike for me."

"How much can you come up with?"

"Didn't you hear me? Too much bike, cannot afford."

"I heard. Look over there." Alan pointed to a Sportster with a bright yellow tank and fenders. "She's two years old. A gorgeous bike."

Bob went over, got on it.

"What do you think?" Alan said.

"This is more like it."

"How much can you come up with?"

"I can maybe get two thousand from my building society account, but I'd have to arrange a loan with the bank for the rest and I don't think I could do that."

"Why not?"

"Two reasons, I'm going through a separation that may turn into a divorce and if that isn't bad enough, I've got a boss who loves to make my life miserable. If there is any way possible, he'll fix it so I don't get the loan. He's the type of bastard who likes to work behind the scenes to make one's life miserable."

"You know what my mortgage payments are, could you afford that two thousand quid down and payments like

I'm making for maybe six months or so?"

"Yeah, I could maybe just about swing that." Bob looked at the bike again, saw there was no price card on it. "But that seems kind of low for something like this."

"It's yours if you want it, you know, if you can come up with that two thousand and make those payments. Just say the word and you can drive this baby out of here. I'll do all the paperwork and bring it by the bank tomorrow or the next day. You can give me the down payment then."

"I don't understand."

"Karma, Bob. It's all about karma and yours is real big."

"You wanna explain that?"

"I came to you with horrible credit, was turned down by several lenders, yet you got me a mortgage, got me and my family into our first home. You believed in me when no one else did. Now I'm going to return the favor. I bought a new Fat Boy last week. This," he stroked the handlebars of the Sportster, "is my old bike. You'd be buying it from me, not the shop."

Bob started to imagine himself actually owning the bike.

"I still don't think I can get the loan, even if I do come up with the down payment."

"No loan, Bob. Give me the down payment when I come in with the paperwork and make my mortgage payments for the next six months and the bike is yours. I'll sell it to you the old fashioned way, cash and a handshake." He held out his hand.

Bob shook it.

CHAPTER THREE

BOB WOKE TO THE BEATLES' YESTERDAY, an old tune. He'd spent all day Sunday on the Sportster and was paying for in now in the form of aches and pains on parts of his body he hadn't even known existed. How had he gotten into the shape he was in, or rather out of shape? Six days with the motorcycle and he was a wreck.

He stayed still, moving only his eyelids, as the song played. He fluttered a few fingers while he listened to the disc jockey's chitchat and gags. He blocked out the dreary news on the hour, but paid attention when the weather woman said it was going to be a filthy, muggy day, with more of the same for the rest of the week.

Muggy or not, he didn't care, because despite his aches

and pains he felt pretty good. What a good idea buying the motorcycle was. It had given him a new kind of confidence. He felt like he could do anything. Well, he felt that way yesterday, when he was on the bike. Now he just ached. And to make matters just a bit worse, he'd celebrated his new found confidence with a few too many glasses of wine last night.

He started to push himself up, dropped back to the pillow. Headache, not a hangover, never a hangover, he wouldn't admit to that.

If only he could sleep in.

Just once.

But he couldn't.

So he groaned, got out of bed, pulled on his sweats, stumbled down the stairs, forced himself out the door and started jogging. At a good pace he could reach his old home from his flat in Cauldwell Gardens in about ten minutes. When he got there he let himself in with the key Debra kept in the flower pot by the back door. Careful not to wake her or the children, he called the dogs out for their morning run.

Hamish was an old boxer dog with a star like blaze between his eyes and Cassius was a droopy beagle whose ears hung close to the ground when he walked, but flew behind him like Superman's cape when he ran. He'd inherited these old dogs when he'd married Debra. He'd never liked them and he felt the feeling was mutual.

However, he'd been pretending a master's love and affection for the duration of his marriage and now he was using that pretend love as an excuse to come by every morning and maybe have a few minutes with his children if they were up after he was done walking them. And today he knew Elisa would be, because she had to be at school an hour early, as she was trying out for the part of Annie in the school play.

Outside he followed the dogs as they shot down the lane, dashed through the thicket to the fields where they loved to roam. They seemed happy to see him, probably because even though they didn't like each other, without Bob they'd never get out of the house. But then Bob had to admit, without them he'd have no foothold in the old homestead, no excuse for coming around, no chance to win Debra back. Yes, thanks to the dogs, and the new Harley, things would return to normal, starting tonight.

And he could hardly wait. He hated that he had to run home after he dropped off the animals. It wasn't right. By the time he got back to the flat he'd be lucky if he got ten minutes to make and eat breakfast, before a fast shower and a quick walk to the train. And after he got to the station, all he had to look forward to was yesterday's paper, then after he arrived at his destination, another lousy day in the confines of a small office in the bank he had worked in for the last twenty years. A bank controled from regional offices by faceless men in grey suits, taking instructions from still other faceless men.

"Who said it was a dog's life?" he muttered as he fingered the control wheel on his iPod, while the dogs raced round the field, trying to raise the odd rabbit. These animals had no worries beyond breakfast. No heavy mortgage, no rent on a separate flat weighing them down, no monthly bills to choke on. After their morning meal, they'd doze the day away, not a care in the world.

Bob looked out over the field as the dogs broke into a run. He smiled as he found his song. He inhaled the night air, closed his eyes and all of a sudden he was not there. He was in a western town somewhere in America, the leader of a gang who had come to town to rob the bank. He was the Jack of Hearts. With eyes still closed, he fingered the control wheel again, turned up the volume and sang along.

Then, with Mr. Dylan's western ballad still raging in his ears, Bob Heggie drifted into heaven. His imagination floated him two thousand feet above a small market town, where he was walking on a mountain ridge. The imaginary view was spectacular as he negotiated the pleasant terrain above the low, patchy cloud level. Then he was at a rough ascent called Sharp Edge. He took account, then started to plan the climb, imagining each step, each handhold, as he pulled himself onward and upward.

Sharp Edge was a dangerous route to the top. But since he was doing it in his head, why not take it? He started up and imagined the mountain periphery falling away as he got higher, leaving an exposed path no more than a foot wide, with a two hundred foot drop on each side. The adrenaline kicked in, any step could be his last. He clutched his ice axe. The climb got steeper, he was really getting into it now. He looked ahead, his imagination had run wild, the route ahead was almost vertical, impossible.

Hamish barked, brought Bob back. Something had to be up for the dog to bark loud enough for Bob to hear him over the music. He looked around, pulled off the ear buds, saw a flash of white.

Rabbit.

Now both dogs were barking to beat the band. Then they were off.

"Go, Boys!"

The petrified rabbit sprang into survival mode. One false move or loss of footing would be her last. For some reason she'd allowed the dogs to get close, but now she was off and running, zigzagging across the field, the dogs following in her wake.

And they seemed to be catching up again, Hamish in the lead, but the frightened rabbit increased her pace as a boost of adrenaline kicked in. The dogs were still hopeful. The rabbit lurched left, smelling her lair and disappeared into the long grass as if she'd just been teasing her pursuers. The dogs found the entrance, a hole no wider than the beagle's nose. Now the yelping dogs were acting like puppies, pushing each other out of the way, sniffing and yapping at the hole.

"Come on, boys, she's not coming out."

More barking, nudging, pushing.

"Now!" Bob shouted and in an instant the dogs were at his side. "That's more like it, now let's get you lads home."

As they headed back, the morning sun rose between a gap in the cloud cover. The temperature rose too and for a few moments Bob pushed the drudgery of the day ahead out of his mind. But then it came back, as it always did after only a few minutes.

The job got Bob down. He hated it, but he had bills and he liked to eat, so like it or not, he forced himself into the weekly routine. On Mondays he would be in a severe depression and as the week progressed his mood would change. He started every week longing for Friday. On Friday night he started to come alive. Well, alive for Bob Heggie. He'd work late, making sure his desk was clear for

Monday morning and take home a takeaway meal and a couple bottles of claret. He looked forward to Saturday mornings when Debra dropped the children off.

With the week over, Bob felt like a different man. Fridays seemed almost like a sort of celebration as he planned his weekend, while he drank maybe a little too much wine.

The children always arrived with their own ideas about what they wanted to do, where they wanted to go and, without fail, Bob would tell them there was no way they could do everything they wanted, then they would wind up in an argument.

Cameron was five and in his first year at school. Elisa was eight, going on eighteen. She was at the stage when she frowned at her father just like her mother did. She'd learned from Debra and had the part down pat.

Back at the house Bob saw straightaway everybody was up. He went in the back with the dogs, caught Debra in her robe.

"Bob, I'm not dressed!"

"So?"

"We're not together anymore, are we?" She gave him a glare that would chill a polar bear.

"I'll just pop up and see the kids then." He started past her.

"Come on, Bob." She grabbed his arm. "You'll make us all late."

For a second Bob thought she didn't want him going upstairs because Stephen had slept over, but he pushed the thought out of his mind. She wouldn't do that, have him sleep over with the kids in the house. She wasn't that kind of woman.

"Mum, where's my yellow blouse?" Elisa sounded excited as she bounded down the stairs, blonde ponytail swishing like a palomino's mane. "Hey, Dad, I didn't know you were here." She turned, faced up the stairway. "Hey, Cameron, Dad's here!"

"Dad!" In an instant the lad was down the stairs and running into Bob's open arms.

"Wow! Are you ever getting heavy." Bob lifted the boy up and Cameron slapped the ceiling. It was an old game, one they both loved.

"Your father was just leaving," Debra said.

"Aw, Mum, can't he stay for breakfast?" Cameron said and all of a sudden Bob felt like there were three dogs in the family. His child was pleading for him to stay, how sad was that?

"No, he has to get to work."

"Yeah." He dropped Cameron into a chair at the kitchen table, waved to Elisa, then he was out the door, jogging toward Cauldwell Gardens.

Thirty minutes later he boarded the train, showered, shaved and ready for work. He kept his head down, just in case Hannah was aboard. She was working at the bank next door and the last thing he wanted was to listen to her mutter on about how well things were going with the job.

He frowned to himself. Hannah had been his baby sister's best friend. Bob used to tease them to no end, but the girls always came back for more. Many of his Friday and Saturday nights had been ruined, because he'd been stuck having to watch them while their parents, Hannah's and his, would go out to dinner or a movie. Their parents were best friends as well.

True, she'd grown into a beautiful young woman, but

she wanted to be a banker, thought it was a high calling. The way she bubbled on about the profession was mind numbing, made him want to scream. If he had his way he'd never ride the same train, but her stop was two before his, so it was out of his control.

He sighed and buried his head in yesterday's news.

* * *

Hannah Hart saw Bob Heggie get on the train and she slipped behind a fat man in a Saville Row three piece suit. Heggie was such a downer. She hated it when they wound up in the same carriage, but there was nothing she could do about it, she couldn't forecast what carriage he was going to get on, after all.

She'd made the mistake a couple of times of sitting next to him, only to wind up listening to his gloomy complaints about the people he worked with. Losers he called them, well if they were losers, then he was the chief of the bunch. The man had no ambition. Whatever get up and go he once had was long gone. Now he was like a caricature of the very people he complained about, a family man buried under his credit cards and mortgage. Somehow he'd managed to turn a terrific career into a dead end job.

In a few weeks she wouldn't be able to ignore him anymore, because he was going to be her boss once she started work at Martin's. Fortunately he didn't know it yet. She was going to be working under Bob Heggie and that was surely one of life's little ironies.

And it was probably the reason why she should go and sit next to him and make small talk. She'd prefer hiding behind the fat man and the way Bob Heggie had his face in that paper, chances are he'd never notice, but he was going to be her boss, so prudence dictated she make an effort at being nice, even though he'd treated her like an unwanted nuisance when she was growing up.

So she stepped around the well-dressed man, made her way to the vacant seat next to her future boss.

"Hello, Mr. Heggie, mind if I sit here?"

"What? Oh, Hannah, sure, have a seat." He set his paper in his lap. "And you don't have to call me Mister, you know that."

"But I do, you see I start work at your branch as soon as I finish my exams. You're going to be my new boss."

"What? You don't say?" He seemed flustered. "Just like Mackenzie."

"I don't understand." Hannah looked into his dark eyes, saw the anger start to build.

"The bastard!" He clenched a fist. For a second she thought he was angry with her, then he quelled her fears. "Not you, Mackenzie, the branch manager. I'm supposed to pick the people who work under me and I'd told him I was bringing in someone from head office. It would be a promotion for him, plus he's earned the position. Mackenzie agreed, but apparently he is going to stick it to me again, by surprising me with you."

"That hardly makes me feel comfortable, you know, coming to work for you when you were planning on someone else." Great, this was all she needed. Not only was she going to work for the man who'd taunted her when she was a child, but now he really had a reason for resenting her.

"You don't have to worry on that score, I'd never take it out on you. Besides, this isn't the first time Mackenzie has done something like this to me. Truth be told, I shouldn't be surprised."

"So I guess it'd be a fair assumption on my part if I came out and said it doesn't sound like you get along with him very well."

"Oh, we get along, just as long as I do my job, his job and anything else he feels like throwing my way."

"It's like that, huh?"

"Yeah, it's like that."

"So is he just a horrible guy to work for, or did you do something to get on his shit list." She bit her lip, she hadn't meant to say it like that. And she really didn't want to get involved in a petty workplace feud before she started working there.

"No, it's nothing I did. Two years ago the grey suit brigade decided to cut back on the amount of personnel at the regional office, so all the directors were sent out to actually work at the various banks in the region, along with eighty or so additional pen pushers. The result, one hundred unhappy people relocated into already overcrowded banks. Existing managers, like me, were moved to smaller offices within the branch to accommodate the higher ranked officials and the existing staff lost their valuable workspace because of the reorganization."

"So, that explains why you don't like him, but not why he doesn't like you."

"Yes it does," he sighed, folded his paper and she braced herself for a long lecture, which was that last thing she wanted, boy had she stepped into it. If only she could think of a graceful way to get up and go back to her safe hiding spot behind that classy looking fat man.

"I don't see it." Damn, why couldn't she just keep her mouth shut. She was just encouraging him.

"Well, the blue-eyed brigade, that's what we call the regional office people, were used to better conditions. Their office allowance had been generous, to say the least, and needless to say, that allowance disappeared with the move, which made them even more unhappy, as if that were possible, and Mackenzie was more unhappy than most, because to listen to him tell it, his suite had been the best in the regional office, 'Enjoying a stunning view over the River Tyne.'" Bob imitated Mackenzie's upper crust accent.

"That's funny." Hannah laughed. Bob had made a joke of sorts. She didn't think he'd had in him.

"Really?" Bob laughed too, then he went on in Mackenzie's voice and accent, "The river has seen a lot of change. Did you know decades ago the Quayside used to be an unsavory and dangerous place, full of rough sailors, dockers and stagers-"

"Dockers!" Hannah burst into his monologue with real laughter. "I thought Dockers were a pair of pants made by the Levi's people. I can see that quayside with pants all over the place. That's funny, Mr. Heggie."

"Oh, no, it's nothing to laugh about young lady," he said, sounding more and more posh. He really did have his boss down pat, "The Quayside was an area to avoid, especially after the pimps and gangsters moved in as the prosperity of the Tyne grew."

"Pimps and gangsters? Really Mr. Mackenzie?" Now she was joining in the fun, calling Bob Mr. Mackenzie.

"Oh yes, pimps to supply the girls for the sailors and the Levi's, I mean dockers. And gangster's to steal the pants, I mean the Dockers off the sailors."

"Stop, I'm laughing too hard."

"But it's different today," Bob went on, without breaking stride. "Now they've fixed it all up. Regeneration they call it and for once the town planners and councilors got it right. The Quayside warehouses are gone, as are the dry docks and the smelly old fish factories. It has been transformed into a modern cosmopolitan conurbation, famed across the world for its culture and night life." He sighed, still imitating Mackenzie. "And it used to be right outside my window."

Another sigh, deeper, almost mournful.

* * *

Bob couldn't believe it, he was actually making Hannah laugh. She was enjoying herself. It had been a long time since he'd made someone laugh and he'd never had a young girl laughing herself silly at something he'd said. In fact Debra kicked him out, because she'd said he was so boring. Maybe he ought to try a little of his Mackenzie imitation on her tonight.

"I hate to break the mood, but since you're going to be working under him, perhaps I should give you the low-down."

"What do you mean?" she said as he looked into her sparkling, sea green eyes.

"Well, he's bitter. The only person he seems to dislike more than the people who work under him is our customers. Lord help the man who actually needs a loan."

"He can't be that bad."

"He is. He's a bully, pure and simple. He seems to thrive on his power over others and he makes sure they know it. And, believe it or not, he seems to take particular pleasure in reducing younger female members of the staff to tears for little or no reason. He seems to enjoy abusing others. Nearly always the younger girls and no one ever accuses him of anything."

"What about sexual harassment?"

"Nope, he gets away with it."

"Let him try it with me, after I knee him in the balls, I'll bring him up on charges."

Bob sighed, easy for her to say. He'd boasted in the past that he wouldn't take any of the man's shit too, but he was the guy who took most of Mackenzie's apparent pent up anxiety. The man's favorite form of abuse was to ostracize Bob in front of the staff for petty reasons, a few minutes late for a meeting or forgetting to date a letter. It was predictable and Bob had come to expect it, learned to live with it. But last week the man had taken his persecution of Bob to a higher level. He'd made a bad loan, an error in the paperwork, something he should have noticed and it cost the bank several thousand pounds. He'd shifted the blame onto Bob, even issuing Bob a written warning about his incompetence.

A written warning was bad news.

Three such warnings meant dismissal and although Bob could appeal, everybody knew it would be a waste of effort. They were never overturned. Promotion was now on hold for five years and Bob could no longer apply for a position outside the region.

"Well, I have to say, I'd like to see that, you, or anybody else for that matter, putting Mackenzie in his place." He put on a smile, looked right into those eyes, tried not to melt. "You don't have to worry about me, I'll not hold the fact that you weren't my choice for the job against you."

"So, if you're doing his job, does that mean I'll be doing yours?" She smiled back and the sincerity of it sent a pleasant chill up Bob's spine.

"No, I'm not the lazy type. I keep my house in order."

"Mackenzie's lazy?"

"I'll say, yesterday he had one appointment, I had five. He made it a lunchtime appointment at the rooftop restaurant at the Baltic. He came back after three hours, smelling of alcohol and asking for his calls to be held, which means I take them. Then just before 5:00 I troubled him, like I do every day, to sign the letters to be posted out and as always he glanced at the first two or three, then put his scribble to them all without reading a word of the rest. These were major life changing communications for some of our customers, calling in overdrafts and account terminations and Mackenzie couldn't even be bothered to see what he was signing."

"But you care."

"Yeah, I care."

* * *

Ten hours later Mackenzie was a distant memory as Bob boarded the train toward home. He looked around, checking to see if Hannah was aboard, but they seldom met on the ride back. He took a seat, sighed and closed his eyes. He'd enjoyed his talk with her on the way into work, thought he'd enjoy working with her too.

Then he thought about Debra and all of a sudden it hit him. His grand plan of telling her how he was going to change, of promising more affection, promising to help her more with the children, promising her anything really, if she'd just take him back, was really all just a fool's dream. She'd left him because he was boring. Words weren't going to change anything. If he wanted her back, he was going to have to convince her with action. And what could he do, become a race car driver, a pilot or a writer? He had to face the facts, bank robbers were the only interesting people in the banking business and there was no way he was going to rob a bank just to get his wife back.

He opened his eyes, sighed again and looked out at the dark rain clouds as the train sped on. The weather woman had been right. It had turned out to be a filthy, muggy day.

CHAPTER FOUR

THE FOLLOWING TUESDAY Hannah was seated next to Bob on the train into the city and as usual she was babbling on about how ducky the banking business was. She was so looking forward to working with Bob, couldn't wait to help out people who needed money for their first home, a small business or maybe a new car. Did she think she was becoming a social worker or something?

Bob tried not to listen, but he couldn't very well stare into yesterday's paper with her talking to him like that. He wanted to go over again how the ponies had done. He enjoyed sussing out the horses on his ride to work, imagining he was at the races in person, had seen the horses giving their all as he checked and rechecked the stats. It was part of his routine and he didn't like change.

He tried to shut her out by mentally going over the last week. He'd taken the Sportster out every night for a short spin. He was getting it down, this motorcycle riding business. He had a long way to go before he'd be as comfortable on the new machine as he was on his Triumph all those years ago, but he looked forward to the effort, the challenge.

"So, my gladrags, Mr. Heggie, what do you think of them?"

A question. Bob had to answer. It was Gladrags Day at the National next door. They did it a couple times a year. The staff there could wear whatever they wanted to work, but to do so they had to give a contribution to the Newcastle Children's Trust. The tradition had become, the more outlandish the costume, the larger the contribution. A Darth Vader in full regalia could be expected to donate a hundred pounds or more. From the looks of her costume, Bob figured she owed the Trust about ten thousand quid.

She had some kind of orange dye in her hair, was wearing what looked like a century's old sweatshirt with cut off and frayed sleeves, cut off Levi's that exposed too much leg for a banker, old fashioned Converse basketball sneakers with no socks and she had freckles painted on her face.

He started with the freckles, worked down, stalling for time, trying to think of something good to say about her hideous get up.

"I don't know, pretty revealing, I guess. In the leg department, I mean. What are you trying to be?"

"An American hillbilly."

"Well, it looks to me like you've succeeded, that's exactly what you look like."

"Thank you, Mr. Heggie."

Bob turned away, looked out the window. Did she think it was a compliment? The girl couldn't be that naïve. He turned back to her, smiled.

"And that old leather coat in your lap, what's that for, you're not having Gladrags day at Martin's are you?"

"No." He set the paper aside, picked up the coat, held it out for Hannah to see. He'd loved that coat, was going to miss it, but Tom needed a coat and though they weren't close, he was the closest thing Bob had to a friend. "I don't wear it anymore, so I thought I'd give it to Tom, the paper-seller at the station."

"Can I see it?"

"Sure." He handed it to her.

"You know, just because it's old doesn't mean you have to give it away. This beauty really has character."

"I don't wear it anymore." He didn't want to tell her why he was giving it to Tom. In fact, he was a bit worried the man might be offended, but Bob hated to see him shivering on cold mornings in that thread bare thing he wore. Tom needed a real coat.

"Hey look, there's ten quid in the pocket here." She started to hand it to Bob.

"No, leave it."

"Ah, yes, I see." She put the money back. "You're afraid if you handed him the money outright, he'd be embarrassed and might not take it."

"Something like that."

"I bet he gives it back."

"Maybe he won't find it for awhile," he said. "Maybe

he'll think it's his and he forgot about it."

"Maybe," she said.

"I'm hoping anyway."

"Well, it's a nice thing you're doing."

"I don't know, it seems like interfering, but the poor man is always there, everyday selling those papers. He can't make very much money."

"It sure seems like a hard life," she said.

"Still, you have to kind of admire his independence." Bob didn't ever feel independent. He supposed that's why he'd bought the bike, so he'd feel a bit free, but it wasn't working, not really.

Tom was sixty-five if he was a day, but with his unkempt appearance and thinning, paper white hair, he sometimes looked ninety, however when he smiled and looked at you with that twinkle in his eye, Bob thought he was seeing the soul of a child. Ah, freedom, Tom had it. Maybe at times he smelled of yesterday's drink and maybe his hand-rolled cigarettes never left his bottom lip, but by God he was cheerful. And he was free.

"He's not, you know, independent."

"Sure he is," Bob said.

"No, he lives in the Salvation Army hostel close to the city center and he spends most of the money he earns at the Grapes, the pub opposite the station, with a pair of window cleaners named Peter and Jackie."

"How do you know this?"

"Jackie does some work for my uncle. I've known him forever."

"Really?"

"Yes, really." She clenched her hands in the coat, almost as if she were angry. "Those guys think they have life sussed. They only clean enough windows to earn their beer money. They can't even get out of bed in the morning without a drink."

"Still, they are independent."

"No they're not. They and your pal Tom meet up every day in the Grapes and drink away all their hard earned money. Then they stagger to the Salvation Army. That's not freedom, they're slaves to the bottle."

"Maybe." But Bob couldn't help himself, in a strange kind of way, he admired them. And he didn't want to listen to her talk about them this way anymore. "I really need to read the paper before we get to the station."

"Sure, that's okay, I've got the new Jack Priest book in my backpack."

"Debra likes that guy." Bob picked up the paper.

"So, is that good or bad, me and your ex liking the same writer?"

"Just making a statement." He started on the paper, saw her get the book out of her backpack from the corner of his eye.

They got off at Haymarket station and, as had become their custom when they wound up together on the train, they started off together toward their respective banks, to a job she loved and one he loathed.

Bob spied Tom, tossed yesterday's news in a bin.

"Morning, Tom."

"Been seeing you more and more with that pretty lady." Tom nodded toward Hannah, then winked as he handed over the morning paper.

"Look, Tom, I don't know if you want this, but I'm just about to hand it into a charity shop." Bob handed over the jacket.

"Wow!" The look in Tom's eyes told Bob he was pleased. "This is fantastic!" He pulled off his old coat in favor of his new treasure, turned and tossed the old one in the same bin Bob had used. He looked happy.

"So, do you like it, Tom?"

"Oh yes, Bob. Thank you so much, it's a belter." He grinned and smoothed down the jacket, seeming to enjoy the touch of the leather.

"I'm glad you like it." Bob walked away with Hannah, as Tom had another customer, then glanced back over his shoulder. Tom looked pleased as a king as he waited on an elderly woman, who was paying him for a couple magazines, when out of nowhere a black clad youth snatched the purse from the woman.

"Hey, you!" Hannah shouted and like a shot she was after the purse snatcher, who had taken off at a dead run, heading north up Haymarket.

* * *

"Out of the way." Hannah hit a beefy man in the chest, with the palm of her hand, pushing him aside.

"What? Young lady-" But Hannah heard no more of Mr. Portly's complaint, as she was out of earshot, weaving between a pair of college girls, who with the exception of the orange hair, looked like they'd been outfitted by the same person Who'd designed her gladrags get up.

The street was crowded, but the kid dressed in black was weaving through the foot traffic as if he'd grown up dodging pursuit. But Hannah was a runner, never missing a day without her five eight minute miles. She was gaining, even though she seemed to be knocking into many more people than the purse snatcher.

Running along the short street called Barras Bridge he seemed exposed. The crowd seemed to sense what he was and what she was about, as they parted, making way for both pursued and pursuer. Now her daily workouts were paying off, she was closing the gap, gaining.

The snatcher stopped at John Reid's bronze statue of St. George and the Dragon at the west end of St. Thomas's Church, turned, lowered his head and charged toward Hannah. She hadn't expected that, hadn't given a thought as to what she'd do if she caught up with the man. She tried to get out of the way, but he clipped her with his shoulder, slammed her toward the pavement.

She threw her hands out in front of herself, to try and break her fall, skinned her palms, felt instant hurt, pushed it aside and pushed herself up with a bloody hand and started back after the purse snatcher.

"Move!" She dodged a young couple who were holding hands. Couldn't they see what was happening? Everybody else seemed to get it.

* * *

Never had Bob felt so useless, so empty. He'd just witnessed a crime, a young man had stolen a woman's purse in plain daylight and he'd done nothing. But not Hannah, what a girl, she took off after the thief as if she were a cop. That slip of a girl giving chase like that, that was really something. Bob wondered what she'd do if she actually caught the man.

Not much chance of that though. However, she'd probably be the talk of her bank. All the coffee gossip would be about how she'd chased a mugger, giving it her all, but the crook had been too quick. Still, Hannah would be a hero of sorts, after all, she was the only one in the vast crowd to do anything, even if it was futile.

Bob felt like smacking himself. Why couldn't he have taken off after the guy? What a great story it would have been for the kids. It would have impressed Debra too, shown her that maybe he wasn't the boring Bob Heggie she thought he was.

As he moved out of the station, he looked up the street in the direction the purse snatcher and Hannah had gone. They were out of sight. He started toward the Grapes, a bit early for a drink, especially on a work day, but dammit, he'd blown the chance to look like a hero to Debra and the kids, stood by while Hannah took off after the black clad crook.

He heard the unmistakable rumble of a Harley Davidson, turned and saw what the Harley ads called, "The hot blooded, liquid cooled branch of the family tree." A V-Rod, a hundred and twenty horsepower, coal black, jaw dropping machine capable of doing a quarter mile in under seven seconds. The twin of the bike he'd done his test ride on just a few weeks ago. The rider looked like he was no more than seventeen, a bit young to be riding a machine that costs more than many men made in a year.

The kid pulled up in front of the Grapes, right in front of Bob. He toed down into neutral, gave it some gas. Bob loved that sound. He loved his Sportster, loved riding it, even though he still didn't think of himself as a real motorcycle rider. He had the bike, knew how to ride, but it still scared the bloody hell out of him every time he started it up. He still hadn't had the beast anywhere near the speed limit.

Long hair splashed out of the kid's helmet. He looked about as hard as a kid too young to grow a beard could get. Bob bet he rode that Harley as fast as he could. A kid like that wouldn't slow down just because his elders had seen fit to make screaming down the street at twice the speed of light illegal.

"Stop that man!"

Bob looked up the street, the mugger flew on by, running like that rabbit Debra's dogs had been after the other day. Then Hannah came charging past, still giving it her all. And she looked like she'd barely broken a sweat, she just might catch the man, after all.

She'd be in trouble then. Didn't she see it?

And again he'd had a chance to join the chase and again he stood by and did nothing. Lord he really was a loser. He deserved his lot in life. He looked after them, Hannah and the black clad thief, and clenched his fists.

He heard the Harley shutdown, turned, saw the kid get off the bike and all of a sudden he knew he'd been given a third chance to join in the chase, because he knew from his own bike that modern Harleys are factory fitted with an alarm that primes automatically after forty seconds. That means the driver does not have to lock or disable the bike and he can start the bike up again within that forty seconds without a key.

The kid was walking away from the motorcycle.

Bob ran, gave it everything he had, jumped on the bike the way those American cowboys jumped on their horses when they wanted to get out of town after they'd just robbed the bank. The panther looking V-Rod was quick and easy to handle. He could catch them on this.

He started the bike with seconds to spare.

"Hey!" the kid shouted, but he wasn't fast enough. Bob had the bike in gear and was off, leaving the kid breathing his own exhaust.

Bob saw the mugger in black turn right on St. Thomas, saw Hannah close behind. He gave it the gas and the bike took off like the thoroughbred it was. The front wheel shot off the ground. Bob had never done a wheelie before, but he instinctively leaned forward, let off a bit on the gas and the front wheel slammed back to the pavement.

By the time he got control of the bike the runners were out of sight. Bob gunned it, leaned forward, dodged an oncoming car and zoomed after them.

* * *

Pumping her arms to force her legs to move faster, Hannah was gaining on the purse snatcher. He pushed between a pair of businessmen with briefcases.

"Look out!" she shouted as one of the men brought his briefcase up to protect himself, or maybe as a weapon, she didn't know. Then she was past them and still gaining on the thief, who turned right on St. Thomas.

She pumped her arms, piston like, in an effort to get her legs to match the rhythm and she was gaining. She was breathing hard, a mixture of adrenaline and fear. She wanted to get that purse back.

The thief turned left on Queen Victoria, was running flat out toward the park. People were sparse here this early, giving him plenty of room to run. She was in shape, she was a runner, but apparently he was too and now he was pulling away.

* * *

Bob forgot for a second that not only was he gripping the handle bars with his hands, but that his right hand was wrapped around the throttle as well, and in a desperate attempted to keep from getting thrown from the V-Rod Panther, he accidentally gave it gas as he leaned forward, fighting the monster he was riding.

"Whoa!" he screamed, but the black dragon was not a bank robber's horse, it didn't answer to spoken commands.

He grabbed the clutch with his left hand, without letting off the gas with his right, and the engine screamed.

"Oh fuck!" Instinctively Bob knew if he let go of the clutch, before throttling down, he'd be a dead man. The bike had so much power that it'd spin right around, cracking his head open on the pavement, easily as he cracked the eggs for his breakfast.

Fighting his rising panic, he let go his right fist, the RPM dropped, he stuck his left foot under the shifter, pulled it up into second, then aimed the black missile he was riding up the street, threading it between the early morning traffic on the right and parked cars on the left.

He saw a flash of Hannah's long legs ahead as she went around the corner on St. Thomas. He gave it a little gas, careful not to overdo it this time. He wanted to arrive alive, still he was flying by the moving cars as if they were going backward. The bike just had too much power for a mere mortal.

Somehow, someway he corralled the bike around the corner, without skidding to disaster. He clutched, pulled it up into third, added gas and rode the rocket up St. Thomas, the wind whipping his hair, threatening to pull the skin right off his face. In less than an instant he was in uncontrolled flight, racing down the road, a passenger on a demon machine hell bent on his destruction. They zipped by the long legged Hannah, man and machine united on an idiotic mission that made no sense. He was going to die for an old woman's purse. Stupid. But he couldn't quit. The goddamn bike just wouldn't let him.

He whipped past the purse snatcher, downshifted into first, stomped on the rear brake and the bike skidded around as if he were a stunt driver and knew what he was about.

"Oh shit," the mugger shouted, skidding to a stop. Confronted with the sight of Bob on the monster looking machine, he panicked, threw the purse at Bob, then took off at a dead run into the park.

"Hey, Stop!" Bob wasn't sure who he was shouting at, the thief or Hannah who was right on his heels, but it was Hannah who stopped.

"Bob?" She was obviously surprised to see Bob on the bike.

"He dropped the purse, let him go!"

"Yeah, okay," she said. Then, "Where did you get the bike?" She was panting. "I didn't know you could ride."

"Can't everybody?" He smiled.

"Yeah, right." She laughed, picked up the purse, climbed up behind, looped her arms around his waist. "Okay, let's go."

And Bob thought he was going to burst with pride. He was master of a devil machine with an angel's arms around him. It didn't get any better than this. It didn't. He pulled in the clutch, toed it into first and was off, feeling just about as good as it was possible to feel, despite the distant wail of sirens.

After returning the bike and the purse, Bob realized he'd lost his paper. He sought out Tom to get another.

"On the house," Tom said as he handed one over.

"Thanks, mate," Bob said. By now the station was awash with police looking for a purse snatcher and a lunatic on a motorcycle.

"You see that copper over there?" Tom said, changing the subject. "Nosey bastard wanted to know me last name. I haven't had one of those in years and I sure don't give it out."

"Probably wanted it in case the police need a statement about the purse snatcher."

"I gave him his statement. I told him I'm no snitch. But he still wanted me name."

"I see." And Bob did see. A man like Tom wouldn't rat out a rat, much less a purse snatcher.

"I told him no way was I gonna turn my name over to a government servant, badge or no badge." He smacked his hand on a stack of papers. "I don't trust the government, never relied on 'em, never will. I would rather sell newspapers in a cold and windy station." He laughed, more of a cackle.

"So, I guess you didn't tell him your name then?"

"Oh, I did, I told him me first name was Old and me last name was Tom."

"Come on, Mr. Heggie, we can still get to work on time if we put a little hustle in our bustles," Hannah said, interrupting.

"You going in to work then?" Tom said. "I sort of thought I'd stand you to a pint at the Grapes."

"Of course we're going to work," Hannah said.

Bob shook his head. Didn't the girl realize Tom wasn't

speaking to her? And couldn't she figure out that he'd been thinking of taking the day off?

"What?" she said.

"Nothing," Bob said.

"Oh, and could we sort of keep our little adventure kind of quiet? I wouldn't want anyone at work to think I was a nut case, you know, taking off after that thief like that."

"I don't understand, it was brave thing you did."

"You too," she said, "but I'd still like it to be our secret. I have my reasons."

"Well, I can't imagine what they are, but if that's what you want, mum's the word."

"Thank you. I know it's a lot to ask, but it means a lot me that we keep this quiet, at least for now."

"Keep what quiet?"

"Oh, Mr. Heggie, you are a card. I'll owe you for this, big time, and I always pay my debts."

* * *

The clock read a minute before nine as he entered the oak paneled door, taking him to the secure area. A strict drill code was observed before anyone could enter. This was the area where the cashiers sat, completing their daily transactions with the public.

The directors' offices were also behind there, stopping the public from gaining direct access to them. It stopped desperate businessmen from carrying out acts of vandalism or violence on the unsuspecting directors, as had happened on odd occasions in the past. Shame, Bob thought.

He smiled to himself as he remembered a local farmer who had a long-standing dispute with the bank and claimed they owed him money. Eventually, after not getting anywhere, he took his revenge by spraying a trailer load of cow shit at the premises.

It went everywhere, through open windows, doors and mailboxes. It just about covered the whole of the building. Needless to say, the cleanup operation closed Martin's and the National next door for several days, attracting huge publicity and the attention of the local police.

Bob went straight to Mackenzie's office. The director acknowledged him and they began to discuss the day's appointments.

Mackenzie explained, as usual, the rationale surrounding the allocated appointments. He looked serious, as if he actually believed the stuff he was spouting. Why didn't he simply say, "You take the shit, I'll take the rest."? Why didn't he just say that?

The result would be the same and they'd both save an hour every morning. These meetings were a foregone conclusion, a waste of time. Bob kept his mouth shut and, as always, agreed with everything Mackenzie said. After all, he already had that written warning. So, as usual, he stayed silent, feeling trapped.

"Good news for you, Bob." Mackenzie peered at Bob over his glasses.

Bob was wary, puzzled, a feeling of dread passed over him. Mackenzie never delivered good news.

"Regional Office has decided to open our branch on Saturday mornings."

Bob groaned, he knew what was coming next.

"You've been chosen to be the manager in charge of the branch."

"What does that mean exactly, sir?"

"Four hours Saturday overtime each week." Mackenzie pulled his glasses from his face. "You should be pleased."

Bob was thinking of the additional three hours traveling time and his ruined weekends. He was thinking of the activities he'd miss, the activities that made his life bearable. He would miss the ten pin bowling and the football with Cameron, taking in a movie and a pizza after.

"I don't want to work Saturdays, sir. Can't another manager do it? One of the younger lads, a little extra money for someone else. I don't need it." Bob felt like a whipped dog. He hoped the man would reconsider. But Mackenzie never reconsidered. It would be a sign of weakness.

"I've made the decision, you don't have an option, Bob. You're the man I want in on Saturday. You're my most senior manager, the man I want at the helm. Aren't you pleased?"

"Yes, sir." Bob forced a smile.

"If you don't want the overtime, we can arrange for time off in lieu, but I can tell you, Bob, this will be a good career move for you, and you have me to thank for it. It was me that put your name forward."

It was supposed to be Mackenzie's idea of a compliment, but he had forgotten about Bob's written warning. The written warning he had instigated. He had forgotten that Bob's career was on ice. He hadn't selected a man to further his prospects, he had chosen the man who would be most upset at coming in on Saturdays.

Mackenzie turned away and Bob knew it was pointless arguing, the grey suits had made the decision on opening on Saturdays and the grey man had carried their instructions through. Mackenzie lowered his head. It was a well-recognized sign that Bob was being dismissed and he went to his office to get to work.

The monotonous and repetitive day drifted on and Bob spent the afternoon negotiating Sharp Edge in his mind, when he wasn't silently singing along with Bob Dylan about that bank robbery. After the final ascent he took in the view. The huge lake looked like a small mill pond from two thousand feet and the boats and leisure craft appeared like small toys. Someday, he told himself, he'd ride out of town on his new Sportster with a fistful of money, just like the Jack of Hearts. Someday.

As always, the Walter Mitty in Bob got him through to the final task of the day. He gathered up the letters for Mackenzie's signature. It was a joke. Bob downloaded the e-mailed attachments from various regional departments. He checked the contents and made any necessary amendments. He checked the addresses. The bottom line stated, "Should you wish to discuss the contents of this letter, please contact Mr. Robert Heggie, Customer Services Manager, on his direct line noted above."

Bob took them through to Mackenzie and, without even reading the contents, the man signed them. Just for effect he passed a comment on the third or forth letter. Generally it was a sarcastic or nasty remark. Today's third letter was advising a client that after banking with the bank for twenty-two years, the bank was withdrawing his £10,000 overdraft facility.

In truth, Bob understood the decision as the customer was going through a bit of a sticky patch. But he couldn't help feeling that a bit of support and backing from the bank, perhaps even an increase to the limit, would pull him through. He was a real fighter and Bob felt sure he would come good.

Not now, thanks to the bank. His checks will bounce and his credit rating will be worthless. No possible chance of a loan elsewhere, not even the possibility of opening a bank account elsewhere. They stick together—the banks—any late payments, bounced checks or loan defaults and the customer's goose was cooked. Credit files were stored on a database the banks could tap into. Suppliers would stop supplying, creditors would start chasing.

The bank had sounded the death knell for this poor bloke.

Definition of this branch under Mackenzie, "An organization that will lend you money if you can prove you don't need it."

* * *

That evening, when he went over to Debra's to walk the dogs, he worried about how he was going to break the news.

"Dad!" Cameron came running toward him the second he went in the kitchen. "The tickets have come."

"Yeah, the tickets," Bob said, all of a sudden remembering. He had applied for cup tickets for the football last weekend. The game would be a sell out and the tickets were like gold dust. He never expected to get them and, if the truth be told, he was probably more excited than Cameron.

"You don't look well," Debra said.

"I'm fine."

"There's something wrong," she said. "I can tell."

"Nothing, in fact I've been given a raise." This was as

good a time as any to tell her, he supposed.

"Really? That sounds like good news, so why the long face?"

"Well, there's a slight hitch, to get it I have to work Saturday mornings." Her face dropped. "Perhaps I can have them another night through the week? Two nights together perhaps?"

"Yes, Mummy two nights with Daddy." Cameron hugged Bob's leg.

"I don't think that's a good idea, you know the middle of the week and all. It'll play havoc with their school." She sighed, gave him that look he hated. "You can pick them up when you finish on Saturdays."

"Damned inconvenient, Bob," Steve said, coming into the kitchen. Bob didn't even know the man was there, but he supposed he shouldn't have been surprised.

"Yeah, Steve, damned inconvenient," Bob said. He felt so useless. Why couldn't he do anything?

CHAPTER FIVE

ANOTHER MONDAY MORNING. Bob stumbled into his sweats, jogged over to Debra's, he no longer thought of it as his home. That was progress, he supposed. When he got there, Debra, to his surprise, was up and dressed.

"I've got some news." She handed him a cup of tea. "Earl Grey, dunked five times, splash of milk, just the way you like it." She favored him with the kind of smile he hadn't seen from her in a long time.

"What's going on?" He took a seat at the kitchen table, took a sip of the tea. It was good.

"How would you like to move back into the house?"

"What?" He choked on the tea, fought to keep from spitting it out. This was the last thing he expected to hear.

"Not the way you think." She was still wearing that smile.

"I don't understand."

"Steve and I want to get married." The smile was still there, but now she looked radiant as well. And it felt like a punch in the gut.

"But—"

"I know, I'm already married. I need a divorce."

"So, it's really over?" He looked into his tea.

"You knew that."

"Yeah, I guess I did."

"But it's not all bad news for you." She was speaking fast, as she did when she wanted to make a point before he could object. "Steve doesn't want to give up his home in the city and I wouldn't expect him to, so we'll be moving in with him."

"The kids too?"

"Of course, but I'll make sure they get to spend plenty of time here with you. I'll bring them over right after you get off work on Saturdays"

"Here?"

"Haven't you been listening? Of course here. I don't want the house. You can have it, but there are a couple catches."

"And they are?"

"Well, you have to take the dogs, Steve's allergic, but you love them so much anyway, that shouldn't bother you."

"It doesn't," he said, thinking of the irony.

"And, since I won't be asking you for any support or anything like that, I'd like you to put aside a couple hundred quid each month for the children, so there won't be any worries when it's time for them to go to university, you know, in an educational account."

"I'll do that." He was already doing that, another little irony.

"Then that's about it. We'll be moving out tomorrow, should be done by Thursday. So, by the weekend you can have the place to yourself."

"Kind of fast, isn't it?"

"Best for everybody if we get this over with as soon as possible."

"I suppose you're right."

"Now we just have that small problem with Cameron this weekend. Are you going to tell him or do you want me to do it?" she said.

"Tell him what?"

"You haven't worked it out yet, have you?"

"How many days till the football, Dad?" Cameron bounded down the stairs, grinning wide and all of a sudden it hit him, this Saturday's big game was his first scheduled Saturday in the bank.

He groaned.

"Now you get it."

"Get what?" Cameron said.

"Nothing," Bob said. Then to Debra, "Can you take him?"

"Elisa is horse riding."

"What about your father?"

"Weekend in Prague."

"How many days, Dad?"

"Five." Bob couldn't tell him, couldn't break his heart.

"Bob!"

"I'll take him. I'll work something out."

"Work what out, Dad?"

"Stop delaying the obvious, Bob, you'll only make matters worse."

"I'll work something out."

Back home, showered and shaved, he found himself hoping he'd run into Hannah on the train, but he'd missed her and since it was Monday, he had no yesterday's news to pour over, so he closed his eyes and let the steady rhythm of the train lull him to sleep.

Forty minutes later he was wide awake and feeling bitter about the job. It wasn't fair a man like Mackenzie could screw around with his life. But there wasn't a bloody thing he could do about it.

At work he gathered up the morning correspondence, took it into Mackenzie's office and found the man's wife there instead.

"Morning, Bob," Vicky Mackenzie said.

"What a pleasant surprise. Nice to see you, Vicky." Unlike Mackenzie, his wife was interesting, often humorous, a good conversationalist and she was pretty as well. All and all, not a bad combination. "What are you doing in the city so early?"

"Shopping, what else?"

"Ah." Bob couldn't understand the attraction she saw in Mackenzie. She was at least ten years younger and took pride in her appearance, visiting the gym several times a week. She watched her diet and never wore anything that didn't have a designer label on it.

"How's your life been?" she asked. "I heard about the separation, I'm sorry."

He wanted to tell her his life had taken a bad left turn to a place he didn't want to go, thanks to her husband, but instead he said, "Fine, yourself?"

"You sure you're fine? I mean, how are you holding up?"

"I'm doing okay, really. It's probably for the best."

"For the best? Are you serious?"

"It's like we were peas from a different pod. I guess we just weren't meant for each other."

"But what about Cameron and Elisa?"

"We're doing our best to make it easy on them." Bob was surprised she knew their names.

"Oh, hello, Bob," Mackenzie said, coming into the office. "I just popped out to get Vicky a coffee."

He had two cups and Bob took that as his cue to leave.

"Thank you, darling." Vicky took both cups from her husband, handed one over to Bob.

"Ah, thanks." Bob took a sip. Any other time and he would have set the cup down and beat a hasty retreat. But this wasn't any other time. Mackenzie had just ruined his weekends with his children and if standing in his office made the man a bit uncomfortable, Bob was going to enjoy it.

"So what have you been up to lately, Bob," she said.

"I bought a bike, Vicky."

"Going to get a little exercise, work on the heart?"

"It'll get my heart working all right, Vicky, but not in the way you think."

"I don't understand."

"I got a motorcycle, Vicky, a Harley Davidson."

He knew it bothered Mackenzie when he called his wife by her first name, but she'd insisted, not just to him, but to everyone, almost as if she were ashamed of Mackenzie's name, so he made a point of repeating her name as often as possible and he found he was enjoying himself, as she was sort of berating her husband in a not too serious way.

"You know, honey, you'd look good on a Harley," she said to Mackenzie.

"Oh, I don't know," Mackenzie said.

"It's a man's thing, you know, macho. Bob understands, don't you, Bob."

"I do, Vicky."

"See, dear. If you got a Harley, you could go riding with Bob, really enjoy yourself."

However, Mackenzie's disapproving frown, which turned to a glare, told Bob the man was not enjoying himself now and he sure as Hell was never going to enjoy himself on a motorcycle, much less a Harley Davidson. Bob knew it was time to make his exit, even though Vicky seemed to be having such a good time at her husband's expense.

Vicky came back to the branch several times during the day, each time off loading carrier bags into Mackenzie's office. During one return she popped her head round Bob's door and told him he was working too hard.

She lingered awhile and he felt a slight dampness beneath his collar and she seemed to grow in confidence at his demeanor. She was in no hurry to get back to her husband. She walked over to his desk, leaned on it, giving him perhaps a bit too much of a view.

"Sandwiches, Bob?" She picked up the plastic box on his desk. "You need a nice long lunch, so you can chill out some. You're working too hard." Was she suggesting something more than a lunch? She smiled. She looked good.

"I'd love to, but I have too much work to do."

"Hey, Bob." Mackenzie walked into his office without knocking. "Oh, Vicky, what are you doing here?" He seemed surprised to find his wife with his under manager and Vicky played on his embarrassment.

"Oh, John, you always spoil things. Bob and I were getting along so well together." She stood up, ready to leave. Mackenzie forced a laugh as she glided out of the room, then he scurried after her.

What a strange marriage, Bob thought. Then he realized that maybe his marriage might have seemed just as strange to someone else. Maybe all marriages were strange. He shook his head, put Mackenzie, Vicky and Debra out of his mind, but somehow Hannah crept into the space left behind and even though he kept his head down for the rest of the day and did his job, he couldn't get her out and she was still there when he bought his evening paper, still their as he made his way through the station.

* * *

Hannah saw Bob Heggie board the train, quickened her step, caught up to him just as he took his seat.

"I'm glad I ran into you." She scooted past him, took the window seat. "You're probably wondering why I didn't want anyone to know about what happened the other morning."

"I was, but then I figured it was your business. Something to do with the possible publicity, I guessed. You didn't want it."

"Exactly." She bit her lip. She wanted to tell him,

wanted to tell someone, but it was so embarrassing.

"You don't have to say anything. You don't owe me, or anyone else, a reason for wanting to protect your privacy."

"No, I want to tell you." She felt so awful, so inadequate. "I lived with this guy while I was at university. He was abusive." She felt so small. "Well, not during the whole relationship, just toward the end. He hit me and I left."

"Sounds like you did the right thing," he said.

"Yeah, but it wasn't easy. I was afraid if he heard about me, you know, like read about it in the paper or something, he might start calling me again. It was a bad relationship and him being reminded of me, maybe coming around, well that's the last thing I want."

"It sure sounds like a relationship you're well out of." He sighed.

"I know, you don't understand how something like that could happen to someone like me." Truth be told, she didn't understand it herself. She turned away from him, looked out the window as the train started to move, felt like she was about to cry. "I was in love with him."

"Sometimes we don't think straight when we're in love," he said. "I know."

"You do?" She turned back to face him, saw pain in his eyes. "Tell me about it."

And he did. He told her how much he'd been in love with his wife Debra, how he loved his kids, loved everything about his life, except the awful job. Then one day out of the blue, his wife told him she'd been having an affair. He'd never suspected, was devastated when she told him she wanted him to move out.

"And the worst part is," he said after he told her about

how she was moving in with her boyfriend and giving him the house back, "is that she thinks I'm boring." He sighed. "Ah well, at least on Thursday I'll be out of that tiny flat. Lord I hate moving, but at least I'll be going back to my own house."

"Boring, she thinks that? How could anyone think a guy who'd steal a motorcycle right out from under its rider to go chasing after a purse snatcher boring. She's nuts." And all of a sudden she realized she meant what she was saying. Bob Heggie was kind, funny and very brave. His wife was letting a fine man slip away.

"No, she's got me pegged about right. I'm a pretty boring guy. And looking back, I can see that the love I'd thought we'd had, had been evaporating over a very long time."

"I have a confession to make," Hannah said. "I never liked you when we were kids."

"Why am I not surprised? I wasn't exactly the ideal playmate."

"No, you were not." She laughed. "But obnoxious as you were, you weren't boring then and you're not boring now."

"I'm glad somebody thinks so." He seemed so down. Hannah didn't know what to do.

Then she got an idea.

"Hey, I could help you move back into your house."

"No, that's all right."

"No, it's not all right. After all you've done for me, I owe you. And this is a chance to start paying you back. I insist. Plus, I'm thinking your wife needs to see you with a younger woman. Not that you're old. Oh, you know what I mean."

"Not exactly, no." He had the deepest brown eyes she'd ever seen. They reminded her of home.

"I'll pretend like we're a couple. It'll give her something to think about."

"I don't know."

"Oh yes you do, it'll be fun. Just wait, you'll see."

* * *

The next three days flew by for Bob. Even though Mackenzie did his best to make his life miserable, the man's machinations rolled off his shoulders. All Bob could think about was Hannah and how her being with him was going to go over when they showed up with his stuff. Would Debra hand over the key without comment, or would she take offence because he showed up with another woman?

He almost hoped it would tick her off.

But it didn't.

He met Hannah after work, rented a van, loaded his things into it, but when they arrived, Debra greeted Hannah as if they were old friends, as if she were happy Bob had found someone.

"Don't forget the game Saturday," she said as she was getting into her car.

"Yeah, I won't." He waved, wondering if she'd ever loved him the way she apparently loved Stephen.

"What game?" Hannah asked.

"The United game this Saturday. I'm taking my son."

"I'm going too, with friends, maybe we can get together afterward and have a drink."

"Any other time and you couldn't keep me away, but after the game my daughter's coming over. It's my day with the kids."

"Okay," she smiled, "a rain check then."

* * *

And Hannah found she was looking forward to him picking up that check, though she doubted it would ever happen. It was strange how life worked out. Bob Heggie was the last man on earth she'd ever thought she'd be interested in. Plus, he was loaded down with baggage. He couldn't get over a wife who'd left him, hated his job, which was an occupation Hannah loved, and his outlook on life just plain sucked. She couldn't think of a better word for it.

Still, there was something about Bob Heggie. She couldn't stop thinking about him. He was too old for her. He obviously wasn't the least bit interested in her and probably never would be. It was stupid, her asking him out after the game and she hadn't been surprised when he begged off, using his children as an excuse.

"Knock it off, Hannah," she mumbled to herself. "He's not the one for you." She was probably only interested in him because he was the first man who'd paid her any attention since she'd fled her relationship with Jeff. "That's it," she said under her breath, "I'm a girl on the rebound." She shook her head. "I've gotta put him out of my mind."

But she was still thinking about him two days later as she got ready to go to the game.

* * *

On Saturday morning Bob picked up the phone, punched in the numbers for the bank. No one was there, of course.

He knew that. The answer machine kicked in. He left a message, saying he wouldn't be in due to a stomach bug of some kind.

He hung up and looked forward to the game, but not to Monday morning.

Then he went to Stephen's, well Stephen's and Debra's now, to pick up Cameron for their special day together. When he got there he found everybody up. They were just leaving, Debra, Stephen and Elisa, for the horseback riding. Bob sighed. He wished he could spend a day with the horses himself, not the kind you ride, but the kind you bet on.

"Like to stay and chat, old man," Stephen said, "but we're running late. Cameron's getting ready upstairs. You can make yourself at home. There is some leftover pizza in the fridge."

"Thanks," Bob wanted to not like the man, but it was hard, because Stephen seemed about as genuine as they come.

He kissed his daughter, watched them leave, then he went to Cameron's new room, found him sitting on the bed. He was wearing a club tee-shirt, staring at an oversized poster of St. James' Park Stadium that he'd taped to the wall.

"You know what day it is?" Bob said.

"You bet I do!" He smiled and it was radiant. "It's match day!" Cameron loved the big games. He was only five, yet he had already been to half a dozen. He loved everything about them.

"Yeah, it's match day. Are we gonna have fun or are we gonna have fun?"

"We're gonna have fun!" Cameron said, and he

couldn't stop talking about how much fun he was going to have right up till they got to the train station. Cameron loved the train journey with his fellow supporters, asking over and over again. "When are we gonna be there, Dad?"

He soaked up the atmosphere during the short walk to the grounds and he loved the hustle and bustle as people pushed to get in. The singing and chanting fascinated him.

Cameron glued his eyes to the field and kept them there throughout the match. They were playing Sunderland, the local rivals, and the rivalry that existed between the fans rivaled hatred. Even though the cities were only fifteen miles apart, football had turned the residents into bitter enemies.

The first fifteen minutes of the game seemed to be the usual game of chess with the teams sounding each other out, but no matter, Cameron was enthralled. After a few meaty tackles, the central defender from Sunderland and the Newcastle center forward were shown yellow cards for an off the ball altercation.

Sunderland took the lead seconds before half time with a disputed penalty. The Newcastle crowd stayed quiet during the interval with the Sunderland fans taunting them throughout the break. However, they shut up five minutes after the restart, when Newcastle pulled level. Cameron jump up with a scream when his favorite player kicked the ball into the back of the net.

The rest of the half seemed to be a constant onslaught from Newcastle and Cameron was ecstatic, hoping for another Newcastle score, but it seemed as if luck was riding with Sunderland.

"Dad, we have to score, we have to!" Cameron said.

"We will, son," Bob said, feeling sure he was telling his

boy the truth.

"But it's almost over."

"But it's not over yet, have faith."

The Sunderland fans found their voice again and they were screaming, a din so loud it felt as if the stadium was vibrating.

"They think Sunderland's gonna score, Dad," Cameron said.

"They won't, son."

Then, deep into injury time, Newcastle's French winger gained a free kick thirty yards from the goal. He started his run-up ten yards from the ball, kicked it hard, the sound coming to Bob's ears a split second after the Frenchman connected.

A hush filled the ground as fifty-two thousand fans watched the ball in mid-flight. Bob screamed as the ball struck the back of the net. Cameron, along with every man, woman and child in the Newcastle crowd, went wild. The winger peeled away, running toward the crowd as his team mates mobbed him, knowing it was too late for the visitors to reply. The noise from the crowd was deafening. Everybody was on their feet. Bob looked down upon his son and couldn't remember the last time he'd felt so good. This was worth whatever was going to happen to him on Monday morning.

* * *

Hannah couldn't believe the coincidence, thousands of people in the stands and she and her friends were sitting just a few rows above Bob Heggie and his son. She half wanted to go down and say hello, but she remembered the way he'd said it was his day with his children. She'd thought it was an excuse, so that he wouldn't have to be with her, but seeing him with his son, seeing how much he loved him. She knew he was sincere. She wanted to get up and say hello, but she was afraid to intrude.

And she also wished she understood a little about the game unfolding in front of her, so she could talk to him about it the next time she ran into him on the train. She felt so stupid. She'd only come because her uncle's bank had purchased four seats to every game and they gave them out as perks to the employees. Three girls were going this week and they'd invited her. She didn't want to come, but she wanted to make friends, so here she was.

What if Bob asked her about the game? What if he wanted to talk about it? She didn't want to admit she knew nothing about the sport so many of her countrymen loved so much.

Oh, the heck with it, she thought. She should just go down there, say hello and tell him why she was here and claim total ignorance. Yes, that's what she'd do. She stood up.

No, she shouldn't. She sat back down. It was his day with his son, she should respect that. Still, it would have been nice.

* * *

Bob recognized Mackenzie's car parked in front of the house as he piloted the VW up the drive. Mackenzie was sitting behind the wheel and from the look Bob had seen on his face as he passed him on his way up the drive, the man was furious.

"Feeling better, Bob?" Mackenzie asked when Bob and Cameron got out of the car.

"Go inside, son." Bob handed Cameron the key. "I need to talk to Mr. Mackenzie for a few minutes.

"Well, are you feeling better?" Mackenzie said again after Cameron was out of earshot.

"A lot better, thanks. Did you have a good day?"

"Me?" Mackenzie's grin vanished. "Of course not! It was ruined. We had a weekend up at the lakes planned. It's been booked for sometime. We were due to celebrate the old anniversary, Bob."

Bob felt his stomach knot and an acid bile lined his throat.

Mackenzie went on to explain that his weekend away had been cancelled, Bob felt for Vicky. Mackenzie walked right round behind Bob, slowly and deliberately.

Bob couldn't face him. It reminded him of his visits to the headmaster's office at comprehensive school. He was awaiting his fate, waiting to find out which punishment the principal would dish out. The wait was always worse than the punishment and the principal dragged it out. The strap was the worst. Well at least he didn't have to worry about that. Mackenzie could fire him, if he wanted, but that's all he could do.

"Enjoy the match?" Mackenzie said.

The game had been televised and either Mackenzie had seen Bob on the tele or he was taking an educated guess. Either way Bob couldn't deny it. He muttered that he had actually felt a lot better by the kick off.

"You know the rules, Bob, if you're sick from work, you stay home. Sick from work, sick socially. Too ill to work, too ill to play." Mackenzie had Bob in a corner. He stared at Bob for an eternity, waiting for a denial Bob couldn't give.

"I have no option but to inform personnel you were at the game. They frown on this sort of thing and really, Bob, you should be setting an example for the other staff."

Bob hated him with a passion and yet strangely didn't regret the decision, even though he had been found out.

CHAPTER SIX

STILL ANOTHER MONDAY MORNING in a sea of Mondays. Bob got off the train, wondering if Mackenzie was going to make good on his threat of turning him in to personnel. He probably would. That would mean a second written warning. Yes, Mackenzie most likely was going to issue one.

Ten minutes from now and he'd be at work. Fifteen minutes from now he'd probably get called into Mackenzie's office. Just another day wasted away at the bank, but Bob suspected he was going to remember this one.

He sighed, took the escalator up to ground level, ignoring the other passengers. He made for the exit, where he found Old Tom, who had the morning Journal in his hand and a smile for Bob, even though he was waiting on another customer.

He hung back, waited till Tom was finished, then asked him if he'd pick up the Jack Priest horror novel for Debra. Then he started the five minute walk to the bank.

He stopped in front of Starbucks, but this morning, having spent his extra money on the book, he decided not to go in. He was about to continue his short trek, when he caught his reflection in the coffee shop window. Damn, he had food or something on his chin. What was that? Egg yolk from breakfast? He scrapped it off with a thumbnail, forced a smile at his window reflection, then continued on. Just a short way now and all of a sudden it started raining. Well, why should he be surprised? It was just one more thing gone wrong before he got to the bank. He felt like he should quicken his step, but it was only a drizzle and besides, he wasn't in a hurry.

The rain started to come harder, but still he moved along at his turtle's pace. He shook the wet mop of unruly hair out of his eyes. By the time he got to the bank it was coming down hard, had been for about a minute. Lightning flashed in the distance, thunder roared. It was going to be a stormy morning.

He looked up for an instant at the doorways to Martin's and the National next door. He took the first step. God he hated this job, his boss, his life. One step, two, three, he climbed, eyes on the wet concrete. At the top he started toward his bank when he heard an explosion.

"What—" his explanation was cut short as Mickey Mouse, with a pistol big as his ears, burst out of the

National.

Thunder roared off in the distance and if Bob hadn't seen the gun in the mouse's hand, he might have thought the explosion he'd heard a few seconds ago was thunder too. Then he saw the mouse's trembling hands. Had he just shot someone? Was he robbing the bank, this odd looking mouse in an expensive suit?

"Out of the way!" Mickey roared.

Bob jumped back, not about to argue with a mouse brandishing a gun.

Mickey turned, pointed the gun straight at Bob's heart and for a flash of a second, that seemed a lifetime, the two men stared at each other. Even through the rain, Bob registered the bluest eyes he'd ever seen behind that mask. Frightened blue eyes. Unforgettable. The man was terrified and all of a sudden Bob realized, he was not.

For an instant he almost wished the man would pull the trigger and put him out of his misery. Just put him down the way you did a dying dog, because that's what he felt like, a mortally wounded animal. Life had boarded the train and left Bob Heggie at the station without a ticket.

Mickey's hand started shaking. He was going to pull the trigger. Quicker than a wink of God's eye, it was all going to be over and Bob would learn the answer to life's ultimate question.

"Get it over with," Bob, beyond caring, spit the words out.

"You stupid mother—"

"Fuck, fuck, fuck," Donald Duck squawked as he shot out through the National's front door, colliding with Mickey, just as the mouse pulled the trigger and the bullet went wild.

Donald pushed the mouse away from Bob, toward the steps leading down to the street. "Get going!" He gave Mickey a shove, took off at a run.

"Arrrgh," Bob heard Mickey scream as he stumbled halfway down the steps, crashing to the ground. But his adrenaline must have been kicking into overdrive, because he was up in an instant, as the door burst open again. Goofy this time. He had a gun too. He also had his arm snaked around Hannah's neck, dragging her in his wake. Hostage or cover, was Bob's first thought as the Disney dog released her with a shove.

Hannah stumbled, fought to stay on her feet and grabbed onto Goofy's gun hand to keep from falling.

"Leggo!" Goofy jerked his arm away.

Hannah screamed as she hit the concrete.

"Stupid, bitch!" Goofy pointed his gun at Hannah's head.

"No," she said.

"No!" Bob brought his briefcase up as cover as he dove between Hannah and the gunman.

Something smacked into the briefcase, slamming him toward the ground as a searing pain lashed across his left side.

"Gotcha!" Mickey said.

"Shit!" Bob hit the ground with a thud. The pain was wicked, the curse didn't take a bit of it away. He struggled to get up as Mickey turned the gun back toward Hannah. Then his world started to spin out of control.

* * *

Hannah squinted her eyes against the expected shot.

She was going to die.

She was helpless.

"We gotta get out of here," Pluto screamed as he exploded out of the National with his bat, colliding with Goofy as the gun went off, the shot going wild.

Hannah dropped to the ground, hit the concrete next to Bob Heggie.

"You stupid-"

"Come on," Pluto who'd managed to stay on his feet, pulled Goofy up, dragged him toward the waiting black cab and the other members of the gang.

Hannah pushed herself to her knees, leaned over Bob, checked to see if he was breathing and was relieved to see he was.

"Bob, are you okay?"

He moaned. He seemed to be coming around.

* * *

The alarms at both banks were screaming when Bob opened his eyes.

"You all right?" The speaker was young. She barely looked old enough to drive.

"Hannah?" Bob said.

"Who?"

"You're not a doctor?" A stupid thing to say, but it was all he could think of.

"No, a paramedic. You've been shot. Just a graze, you're very lucky."

"The girl, Hannah, is she okay?"

"I'm fine."

Bob blinked against the sunlight, saw Hannah behind the paramedic. Thank God.

"You're going to be fine," Hannah said. Then, "You

saved my life."

"Can I sit up?" Bob was flat on his back, out on the concrete. The rain had stopped.

"You hit your head when you fell. How do you feel?"

"I'm fine."

"Do you know your name?" the paramedic asked.

"Sure, of course."

"And it is?"

"Bob Heggie."

"Good. Who's the prime minister of England?" she asked.

"Bob Dylan," Bob said.

"You're going to be fine," she laughed.

Hannah did too.

He pushed himself into a sitting position, looked at the graze on his left side. He felt cold. The paramedic had cut his away his jacket, cut his shirt too, to get a look at his wound.

"A few inches to the right and I'd have a new belly button." He sighed, there was just a tiny bit of blood. He had indeed been lucky. "You ruined a perfectly good suit." He laughed. "Well, maybe not a good one, but serviceable."

"Sorry, but we didn't know how bad the damage was. Fortunately you won't even need stitches."

"So, I guess the guy got off more than one shot. The first one, the one that knocked me down, must have hit the briefcase. The second one hit me." He closed his eyes again.

"Barely even a graze," she said. "But you could be in a state of shock. You got a nasty bump on your head when you fell."

"Fell?"

"When you were knocked down."

"I don't think I'm in shock."

"You could have a concussion," she said.

"Don't think so." He looked right, looked left. He'd been in an auto accident several years ago, had a concussion. The world seemed to spin out of control when he'd turned his head. It was steady now. "No, I don't think I'm concussed." He took a deep breath. "Actually, I feel pretty good, but I'm getting bloody cold. Do you think we could take this inside?"

He got up, despite the girl's protests, and made his way to his office, with Hannah and half the staff in his wake. He did feel a bit dizzy, but damned if he was going to let on, not in front of Hannah. Besides, the last thing he wanted was a trip to hospital. In fact, what he really wanted was the rest of the day off.

"I need a new shirt and jacket," he said.

"Not a problem." I have my husband's dry cleaning in the car. It's just outside."

"Vicky?" Bob looked up, saw Mackenzie's wife. What was she doing here so early?

"Yeah, I came by because John forgot some paperwork. Lucky I didn't unload the cleaning yesterday."

"Can you bandage this?" Bob pointed to the graze.

"Sure thing," the paramedic said.

"We've got some questions," a policewoman said. Where had she come from?

"I'm not going anywhere," Bob said. "Let the girl here finish patching me up and let me get into some dry clothes." He just realized his clothes were soaked.

Thirty minutes later he studied himself in the mirror

above the sink in the men's bathroom. He was surprised that Mackenzie's suit, much more expensive than anything he'd ever owned, fit. He always thought of his boss as portly and himself as on the thin side.

"Bloody embarrassing," he muttered to himself. Then he vowed to go on a strict exercise regime and to cut down on all of the wrong kinds of food. Healthy eating for him from now on. He couldn't stand the thought of having the same physique as his boss.

Still having a hard time imagining himself shaped as Mackenzie, Bob went to the staff room where several detectives were talking to the people he worked with. A policewoman handed out strong coffee from the machine and several girls were trying to calm down an elderly cleaner who had just been about to leave the branch as the men struck.

* * *

Hannah watched as Bob Heggie came out of the restroom. He looked like a million dollars, despite his disheveled hair. Amazing the a difference a good suit can make. The police started right in on him, asking him question upon question.

"I'm sorry," she heard Bob say, "But all I can tell you is that the man had blue eyes and was a lousy shot." He turned away from the detective inspector who had been questioning him. Started for the door, then turned back around. "Oh, yes, I almost forget, the one in the mouse suit dresses very well.

Again, Bob turned away from the police, started for the door.

"Mr. Heggie," one of the detectives said.

"Look," Bob said, "I appreciate the fact that you have a job to do, but I told you all I know. Now I intend to take the day off. I'm going home."

"We've got a full schedule today, Bob," Mr. Mackenzie said.

"Sorry, it'll have to wait. I won't be any good to the bank today."

Hannah wondered if he always stood up to his boss like that. If so, it might explain why he didn't like the banking business as much as she did.

All of a sudden she decided that she wanted the rest of the day off as well. She left Martin's, went back next door to the National, told her uncle she was going home and, of course, he said it was okay. It was her last day, after all, and with the assault on the bank, he was thinking of giving everybody the day off anyway.

She hurried outside, tried to catch Bob, but he was gone.

* * *

Bob made his way back to the station. He felt a bit unwell. As he passed the Grapes, he peered through the smoke stained window. He could see Tom at the bar. He hesitated for a moment, looked at his watch. It was just after noon and the train left on the hour, so he had time for a couple.

Tom spotted Bob as he entered the bar and before he could speak, he held up the Jack Priest book.

"I didn't forget you." He handed the book over to Bob.

"Thanks, I appreciate it."

"You look a fright." Tom eyed him up and down.

Then signaled the barman and ordered Bob a whisky.

Bob caught his reflection in the mirror behind the bar window. He looked pale.

"Thanks again," Bob said as the barman handed him his drink.

"You were involved in what happened up at the banks?" Tom said.

"Yeah." Bob wasn't surprised at Tom's question. The man knew where Bob worked, so it probably wasn't hard, putting two and two together.

Tom's friends Jackie and Peter were there too. Bob sighed, then told them it hadn't been his bank that had been raided. He didn't mention his part in what had happened.

"How come you're dressed so fancy?" Tom was no dummy. "These are not the clothes you went to work in. I saw you this morning, remember?"

"Ah, well, you got me there, Tom."

"So tell us what went down."

"Okay, you win." Bob told them what happened, leaving nothing out.

They listened in amazement. They had heard Chinese whispers of six shootings and four deaths, but Bob assured them this was not the case. As he reached the bottom of his glass, someone put another in front of him and only then did he begin to realize how close he had come to being killed.

Halfway through the second glass he began to relax. He started noticing the decor and the clientele. They were both shabby. Looking around the bar, the first thing he noticed was how busy it actually was. Of the occasional wine bars Bob had frequented at lunchtime, none were as popular as this. The punters were serious drinkers and there were several tables like Tom's, noisy tables, full glasses and friendly faces, happy tables, tables you would want to sit at.

Bob listened in to the conversations at two or three tables around him and to his surprise everyone was talking about the big incident. Two o'clock came and went, as did the train. So did 3:00 and 4:00. Bob didn't notice and felt strangely relaxed and at home in the smoke filled bar.

He looked around and noticed he was the only client with a shirt and tie. The vast majority of the drinkers seemed happy and content and nobody seemed in a hurry to leave. These people were clearly not governed by the corporate lunch hour, nor did they have any kind of work schedule or commitment.

Much later, Bob walked along Monkseaton Drive and for once felt like a successful banker. He imagined the curtains twitching and the bored occupants within, wondering how and when his ship had come in. He liked his new suit and felt light headed. He approached his home and fumbled in his pocket for the key. No way was he going to turn into work tomorrow. He'd made his mind up to take the rest of the week off and his unofficial holiday started tonight.

Inside he was immediately assaulted by the dogs. They wanted an evening walk, but he was in no condition to go traipsing around the fields with them. However, he knew the animals well enough to know they wouldn't stop hounding him till they got their way. Not unless he treated them to a better alternative.

"How about an early meal, boys." Now they really were excited. As much as they liked the great outdoors, they liked to eat more. They never walked away from a dish that had food in it, had never met a table scrap they didn't like. Once fed, the dogs quieted, found their beds and in no time were asleep.

Bob went into the kitchen, looked at the table, where his children should be sitting, and started shaking. The tremors seemed to shoot through him. He buckled at the knees, sank to the floor.

"Delayed shock," he muttered as he pulled himself up, using the table as a handhold. He was familiar with it, but had never experienced it, not even after he'd been under fire in Iraq. He made his way to the cupboard, grabbed a glass. Then he started for a bottle of Blossom Hill Red, changed his mind, pushed it aside, reaching instead to the back of the shelf for the familiar square shape of the Jack Daniel's bottle.

He fingered the bottle, drew his thumb along the beveled signature of the founder of the oldest registered distillery in the United States. Not bothering to remove the black plastic seal, he twisted and it snapped in his grip.

He woke the next morning in the same chair. He cursed as he looked down at the elegant suit he had been given the day before. The trousers were creased and his borrowed jacket lay in a heap on the floor. He turned, saw the half empty bottle on the table. His head beat like crazy with the sudden movement. He turned away from the bottle, hoping that the gremlins hammering away inside his dehydrated brain would appreciate him not staring at the cause of what set them off. They didn't.

He made his way to the lounge with the intention of making for his bedroom. He didn't make it and instead crashed out onto the sofa. Several hours later he woke again and made his way into the kitchen, where he drank a carton of orange juice and smiled as he pulled the keys from the hook above the cooker. Then he got his helmet.

Outside he journeyed to the outbuilding that contained his pride and joy and levered the old wooden door open. It creaked as if not wishing to give up the treasure within.

He figured if he was sober enough to get up off the couch, he was sober enough to ride. And ride he did. He thundered in front of an old Vauxhall Astra, causing the elderly driver to brake suddenly. Bob raised a hand in an apologetic gesture, then slowed to almost a crawl as he made his way down Monkseaton Drive. He smiled as the rumble of the exhaust triggered a car alarm.

The glistening North Sea loomed before him as he approached The Links and he gave a quick glance to the right, before sweeping away northward, all too aware that his foot peg was very close to ground level. He was still leaning at dangerous angle, when he twisted hard on the throttle. The angled tire screamed out for more traction and the back wheel drifted toward the middle of the road. He guessed right away what was happening and his natural reaction was to brake. It was the worst thing he could have done. The back wheel found its grip and locked up with a puff of black smoke, the bike suddenly righted itself, lurching across to the left of the road and he found himself hanging onto the handlebars with his rear end searching for the seat.

Somehow he hung on and found it. He scrapped his foot on the tarmac and pain shot up through his calf and thigh, right into his groin. He winced, raised his feet onto the foot pegs as he eased the throttle right down. He brought the bike to a stop outside the Whitley Bay Cemetery, took off the helmet and wiped the sweat from his brow.

He looked up at the gathering clouds and figured It was time to head home.

CHAPTER SEVEN

WHEN BOB GOT TO WORK on the Monday following the bank raid, he went straight to his office. He'd been off a week and suspected nobody had done his job in his absence. There would be a mountain of work for him to do, probably more e-mail than his daughter got in a week and she got a lot.

He went to his computer, checked the messages and to his surprise someone had been covering for him. There was only one message. Bob didn't know if that was a good or bad sign. Did it mean they were thinking of replacing him? Or did it mean they'd recognized what a good job he'd been doing and wanted to keep him caught up? He suspected the former.

He opened the message. It was from Lord Joseph Harris, the chief executive, via the head office. The letter was addressed to every member of staff, including Mackenzie and Bob. It read:

I was very concerned and saddened to hear of the horrendous occurrence, which took place at the National Tuesday last.

I was further dismayed to hear about the fatality and the brutal violence used during this terrible occurrence. I wish it to be known that as a caring employer, we continually review all procedures and the safety of our staff is paramount at all times. We have requested a security report from the National and intend to fund a joint investigation to ascertain whether or not this unfortunate incident and subsequent death of an employee could have been avoided.

At the same time we are also carrying out our own internal inquiry, involving senior management, police and private security experts.

As soon as the results are known, we intend to cascade these down to branch level. We will then organize a series of meetings and staff training to implement any recommendations.

I would like to pass on my thanks personally to everyone concerned at the branch for the good conduct and professionalism shown during this unfortunate episode and can assure all employees we will take every precaution to ensure the safety of all branches and all staff at all times.

Please keep up the good work.

As Bob's requisite required, he printed copies of the message for all the staff members and took the copies in for signature by Mackenzie and, as usual, he signed them without looking at them. One of them, of course, was addressed to him and he still signed it. It tickled Bob as he had added to the bottom paragraph:

I would personally like to pass on my thanks to everyone concerned at the branch for the good conduct and professionalism shown during this unfortunate episode. That is except for that fat bastard Mackenzie who has never shown an ounce of professionalism in his entire life.

Bob had acted out of character and just about kept his laugh in as Mackenzie finished the last of his signatures. He questioned his actions, such a big risk for such a little laugh.

Back in his office, he balled up the message with the ending he'd falsified and tossed it in the bin just as Hannah came in.

"Bob, I mean, Mr. Heggie, Mr. Mackenzie asked me to give this to you." She handed him a brown envelope.

"You're working here now?"

"Yeah, as of last Wednesday, the day after the robbery. I've been sort of doing your job as I'm going to be your assistant."

"That explains why I'm not swamped today." So Mackenzie had the new girl, someone who hadn't even been with the bank a few days, do his job while he'd been away. Was the rat bastard sending him a message?

"Well, I've got stuff to do. If you need me, just call."

"Will do," he said as she left.

Then he opened the envelope. It was his second written warning. Mackenzie hadn't even had the courage to give it to him himself. Because it was his second warning, he was required to attend an interview with the head of personnel.

"What's wrong with those people," he muttered. He'd been shot, well, barely shot, but shot nevertheless, in defense of a bank employee. If anything, he reasoned, they should be giving him a medal, not a second written warning.

He sighed.

In retrospect, he had to admit he'd been shot protecting someone who worked for the competition. Maybe head office didn't know. Or maybe they knew and didn't care. In either case, he supposed it was their way of protecting themselves in the event of a claim for unfair dismissal. Two written warnings, an interview. A third written warning, the sack, an exit interview, nice and clean. Follow procedure, do not proceed to court. Shot or not, they didn't care.

The personnel department was located in the regional head office in a town center bank branch. It was an old fashioned, badly designed, impractical building with modern furnishings that looked out of place. It had many offices with lots of nooks and crannies and anyone having a bad day could go astray for several hours, dodging their responsibilities without being missed.

All of the letters from personnel for Bob's branch were sent to Bob by e-mail from this building. Letters that Mackenzie signed, changing peoples lives through promotion, relocation or in extreme circumstances, dismissal. And yet he never gave them as much as a second glance. How long before Bob would be asking him to sign his own dismissal letter? And, more importantly, would Mackenzie even read it?

Tracy Miller was the first person to see Bob. She had worked for him back at his branch before her transfer and they were old friends. She was full of chat and seemed glad to see him. However, she didn't tell him she knew the reason why he was there and the very fact that she didn't, made Bob suspect that she did.

He was early for his appointment, so he and Tracy caught up on old times over coffee. She told him how much she missed the old branch, then told him all about her turbulent love life and insisted they should have lunch together soon and catch up on everything. Bob agreed, thinking it probably wouldn't happen.

The interview time came round too quickly and Bob found himself sitting in front of another familiar face. Neil Stoves was one of Bob's deputy managers a few years back. He had applied for promotion at the old regional office and had worked himself into the lofty position as head of the personnel department. It was his job to read the riot act to Bob. No smiles, no small talk, just frighten the shit out of him, in the hope he would knuckle down and bow to the company line.

Bob was annoyed just looking at him sitting in his oversized chair behind his uncluttered desk. He wore a full three-piece suit, despite the closeness of the day. He acted the part, but acted it badly. Bob decided to take the piss. He'd been shot, after all. He'd earned the right.

"Hey, Neil!" He grabbed him by the hand. "Great to

see you again."

"Look, Bob," Stoves grimaced, "don't make this any harder than it has to be, you know why you're here."

"What do you mean? We go back a long way, good mates remember?" It was a lie. They were never mates. Neil had tried to impress because Bob had been above him in the bank's pecking order.

"Can't we just get this over with?" Stoves looked uncomfortable, like he didn't want to be doing this. He was the wrong man in the wrong job and it looked to Bob like deep down Stoves knew he was out of his depth. Bob had supervised him, trained him, treated him well and looked after him in the three years they'd worked together. Bob had covered for him several times because of his inability to do the job. When the head office job had come up, Stoves, a man who envisioned himself as a mover and a shaker, couldn't wait to apply. Bob had given him a glowing reference. He wanted rid of him.

"Just give me the paper and I'll sign it. I don't want any lectures."

"But it's company procedure to notify you of the consequences, should you fail to adhere to the—"

"Just pass the pen."

"All right." Stoves pushed a cheap pen across the desk.

Bob glanced over the letter and signed on the dotted line. That was it. Not too difficult, but Bob knew his career was finished. However, for reasons he couldn't understand, he felt relieved. He realized at that point that his life couldn't get much worse. The pressure was gone now, promotion was a non-event and although progression was impossible, as long as he wanted to keep his nose clean, the bank would find it difficult to get rid of him.

"I'm sorry it's come to this." Neil got up from his chair.

"You know, Neil," Bob said, getting up too, "I'd never really made my mind up about you, but today you've confirmed what I've always suspected, you really are a wanker, aren't you?"

"No need for that, Bob, I'm only doing my job." Stoves had a look of abject horror on his face as he stepped away from his desk, eager now to terminate the interview.

"Then do your job and sack me." Bob moved around the desk, cutting off his retreat, moved close to the man, close enough to smell his breath, slightly sour, too much coffee, too many cigarettes and too much small talk. "I've just called a senior manager a wanker."

"You aren't thinking straight, just go."

"Wanker," Bob said again, spoiling for a fight.

"Bob please, if you call me another name, I'll have no option. I'll have to give you a third warning, and you know where that will lead."

Heaven, Bob thought, that's where it will lead. No more written warnings, no bank, no politics, no losers, no wankers, no shit. Do it, he thought, just before remembering the mortgage and monthly commitments. But he couldn't help himself, he was beyond caring.

"What if I don't call you a name? What if I just think it?"

"Nothing I can do about that." Stoves put a hand to his chin. "You can think what you like."

"In that case, I think you're a twat."

Bob had pushed him to the limit. It was decision time for the head of personnel. Stoves stood in silence. A bead of perspiration on his top lip. He opened his mouth to say something, but no words came and Bob left to a deafening silence, sauntered down the long corridor, daydreaming of good things.

"Are you okay?" Tracy asked, bringing him to his senses.

"Couldn't be better." Bob smiled long and hard.

Tracy looked puzzled. Of course she knew why he was there. All the e-mails were sent through her computer. While she couldn't read every one, he knew she went over as many as she could.

"So," Tracy said, "when would you like to have that lunch?"

Bob was about to refuse, when all of a sudden he pictured the Jack of Hearts and bingo, right out of the blue he thought of a way to get even with Stoves, Mackenzie and the whole bunch.

"Sure, love," Bob answered back, "I'd love to." He stressed the word love, because it hit a chord in him that chilled up his spine, because in all the time he'd known her, from way back when she was a new hire working under him, love13 had been her password, and he bet it still was. "How about Friday?"

"That'd be good," Tracy said. "I'll look forward to it."

"Great, see you then," Bob said and all of a sudden he really was feeling great, because he'd just had an idea, probably a crazy idea, but something that might keep him amused for a few days. He'd think about it, plan it and imagine it taking place over and over in his head. And then, just when he was ready to take action, he'd laugh at how ridiculous an idea it had been and move on to his next fantasy.

* * *

When he got back to work the branch was full of inspectors and senior personnel from outside the region. Bob wondered if they'd been around every day last week or if they were just getting around to starting their investigation. He also wondered why they were here and not next door. Then he decided that he didn't care.

He put them out of his mind and went to his office.

The next couple of days were very strange, because as well as the police interviews and the counseling sessions, many senior managers also frequented the branch. One thing that came out of the internal inquiry next door was how ill prepared the staff were for a raid. Many mistakes had been made and many senior managers had been criticized for lack of putting procedures in place. Bob suggested that training should be given and mock-ups should be staged once a year with staff role-plays.

Most of the staff acted like they couldn't imagine acting out as victims of a bank raid. To be fair, none of the senior mangers had even mentioned this. However, the more Bob pushed the idea, the more they seemed to think it made sense. He even mentioned this to the detective inspector who had questioned him on Wednesday just before lunch.

"It certainly wouldn't do any harm," the detective said. "The bank staff should be prepared. There should be guidelines to follow." The detective went on to criticize the actions of Reggie Swaggart who'd tried to intervene. "What in the world was he playing at? A fifty-three-year-old, overweight pen pusher, trying to tackle four armed and dangerous criminals."

He was right. All Reggie had managed to achieve was to antagonize the gunmen even more. They were already pumped up with adrenaline and who knew what else. Why on earth didn't everyone stand back and let them take the money?

One thing's for sure, Bob thought, Gloria would have been spared her life.

The detective dragged out the interview. Bob had explained at the beginning that he had been the last one to arrive and witnessed next to nothing. Plus, he'd kind of had his hands full, getting shot and all. However the policeman insisted on Bob's exact movements, right from the moment he stepped from the train. He wanted to know what he saw and who he spoke to.

He even seemed interested in Old Tom. Then it dawned on Bob that the police were checking every detail, hoping someone would get caught in a lie or even give a story that didn't stack up. No doubt they would speak to Tom in the forlorn hope that he may even suggest Bob hadn't traveled by train that day. They were looking for nerves in the interview room and sweat on the brow.

The detective asked just about everything there was to ask and Bob answered without hesitation. The detective had exhausted every line of approach and Bob felt the interview coming to an end. What else could he ask?

Then the young detective annoyed Bob. He asked about his family and then his financial situation. Were there any financial worries? How was he handling his family life, his separation? The detective was clutching at straws and, while Bob knew this was probably only routine, it angered him.

"Come, come, Mr. Heggie, everyone knows you like a

bet on the horses."

"Sorry?" Bob said, almost insulted.

"Perhaps you haven't been doing well of late, perhaps got a bit behind with your bookie. Maybe he's even put a little pressure on you."

It was true, whenever a big race was taking place, Bob enjoyed a little flutter. Everyone in the branch knew. What annoyed him the most was that someone had actually primed this copper with the information.

Again Bob acted out of character. This time he would risk the copper's wrath.

"I don't know what you mean." Bob tried to sound as sincere as possible.

"Look, Mr. Heggie, don't lie to us," the detective said, changing his approach, "we know."

"Okay, its true," Bob said. "I like a bet, no harm in that."

"No harm, Bob, you're right, as long as you win occasionally, keep it under control," the detective said.

They looked at each other in silence, daring not to be the first one to speak. It was a mind game, who speaks first loses. Bob stared at the clock over his opponent's right shoulder. He waited until twenty seconds had passed.

"I even keep a book on how much I've lost," Bob said, surprising the detective.

"Don't worry, Mr. Heggie, I understand." The detective smiled, trying to look sympathetic. "It's a disease, but we can get you help. Please continue."

"I've lost a fortune this year. I keep getting seconds." Bob sniffed and tried to imagine tears in his eyes. "Every time I look at the running total in my book I want to kill myself."

"There, there, Mr. Heggie." The detective stood, put a hand on Bob's shoulder, "we can help. Just how much have you lost this year?" Bob could well imagine what must be going through the policeman's head. He was most likely patting himself on the back about how his sharp interviewing technique had cracked the case.

"It's so sad." Bob looked up.

"How much, Bob?"

"Well," Bob took a deep breath, looked up and stared into the man's eyes, seemingly pleading for clemency, "just a wee bit over thirty-six pounds."

The detective looked at Bob and the penny dropped.

"You piss taking bastard." He grabbed his coat, stormed out of Bob's office. Bob hadn't felt this good in a long time.

Mackenzie, Bob thought. He must be the one. They must have asked him who he thought might be having financial problems. He was the boss, the one who should know.

Bob went straight to his office.

"Afternoon, sir. Nice lunch."

"Yes, thanks, Bob. Had the interview with the old constabulary?"

"Yes, sir, just finished." Here was his chance.

"Any problems?"

"No, sir, nothing to it, over in two minutes. I just explained that I arrived after it all happened, got shot trying to stop it and that was it. Nothing much to interview me about really."

"Good stuff, Bob." Mackenzie looked up, frowned, the man had to know Bob was on to him. "Back to your office then, you must have lots to do."

Bob walked along the corridor and left his office door open a few millimeters. He took up a position on the back wall, so he could see Mackenzie's office door. He waited until Mackenzie left. Bob knew where he was heading. He gave him a few minutes start, picked up a handful of letters and made his way to the makeshift police incident office.

He waited in the corridor. The door was closed. He prayed nobody would pass and wonder why he was loitering in the passageway. Just then he heard someone behind him and he pretended to be studying the letters, taking slow steps toward the room where he was convinced Mackenzie would be questioning the young detective about his interview.

"Interesting, Bob?" It was Jim Moody, one of the under managers.

"What do you think? Inspiring."

Bob had no choice but to walk with him, away from the incident room, down the stairs behind the counter. Bollocks, he thought to himself, I'll never make a Sherlock Holmes. He spent a few minutes chatting with the staff about how smoothly the counter operation was running, until he saw Hannah walking by carrying a cup of tea. It was Mackenzie's cup, fine bone china in a matching saucer, trailing the unmistakable aroma of strong Earl Grey.

Bob stepped in front of her.

"Here, Hannah, is that Mackenzie's? I'll take it up, I'm on my way upstairs anyway."

"Good on you, Bob," she whispered so the others couldn't hear. "You were right about him, He makes my skin crawl."

"Told you." He took the tea from her grateful fingers.

Seconds later he walked into the incident room as if he belonged there.

"Your cup of tea, sir."

"Ah, thanks, Bob." Mackenzie had the look of a sly little schoolboy caught with his stubby fingers in the biscuit tin.

"You're welcome, sir." Bob about turned and even though he allowed himself a momentary feeling of triumph at his success, he was enraged.

But he would get even.

* * *

The next morning Bob picked up the routine he used to have, back when he lived in the house with Debra and the children. He got up to walk the dogs.

And they seemed to be enjoying themselves as he thought about his lunch date with Tracy. They returned home after a good five miles across the fields, without any rabbits to brighten up their walk. The dogs were filthy and Bob hosed them down outside the back door. They hated it, but it had to be done.

He had them cornered between two brick walls leading to the neighbor's gate. It was so comical watching them push each other to the front, trying to escape the water. After a few minutes he got a towel and they charged him, each attempting to be the first one dried.

The dogs settled on their beds for the long sleep ahead and Bob envied them for a moment. He showered, changed and jumped into the car, for the short ride to the station. The one thing he did like about that horrid flat he'd been living in, was the fact that he could walk to the station. Battered and bruised as his old VW was, he still didn't like leaving it there all day long.

He left the branch at 11:30 instead of his usual 12:00, because of his lunch date with Tracy. He jumped off the train a few stops early, giving himself a fifteen minute walk down to the regional office on the Quayside. The brightness of the day hit him as he climbed the stairs of the gloomy underground station. He looked up at the imposing monument of the second Earl Grey, towering forty-one meters above. The Father of Newcastle some would say. Bob wondered if the young people today knew that Earl Grey had been elected to parliament at the age of twenty-two and that he was the youngest person to ever hold the office of Prime Minister. How many of them knew the famous Earl Grey tea, enjoyed by so many, had been named after him? Not many, Bob thought.

He went down Grey Street, marveling at the graceful architecture and atmosphere of this wonderful street. For big business's this was the street to be on. Your company or organization had arrived if it were able to rent office space on Grey Street. The Theatre Royal was housed here, as well. So too were many of the select wine bars and restaurants that served the more wealthy workers of the city. Above all it was the home of the major banks and financial institutions. Bob passed them one after the other, sometimes three and four in a row. He counted them and couldn't understand the logic of dozens of banks in one street. He would never understand. The long elegant sweeping curve of Grey Street took him down to Dean Street, where he crossed the road, showing up at the head office at 12:15, fifteen minutes early.

"Just a few last minute things to do before I can go," Tracy said and she ran around several offices, before disappearing into the toilet just prior to lunch hour, leaving Bob alone with her computer.

CHAPTER EIGHT

ANOTHER MANIC MONDAY and Hannah was on the train into Newcastle alone. She got off the train, nodded to Old Tom when she passed, was about to start the short walk to the bank, when she spied Bob Heggie up ahead. He must have been on a different carriage. She quickened her pace to catch up, was closing the gap when he turned and started toward the park.

What was he doing? Where was he going? He was going to be late. Didn't he care? Well she cared, so she turned away, headed toward the bank and work, but her curiosity got the better of her. He was headed away from the bank and she wanted to know why.

* * *

After today Bob would be towing the line at work, but right now he needed some time to think, to get his head together, before he set upon his great adventure. He tightened his hand around the handle of his briefcase, feeling the blood rush from his fingers, he'd never really set upon an adventure before, in fact the most daring thing he'd done since he'd come home from Iraq over a decade ago was buying the motorcycle.

Debra had been right to leave him, he was, or rather had been, boring. Just plain old boring Bob Heggie. Well, not much longer. He was about to put Boring Bob to rest, bury him deep. No more Walter Mitty moments. No more negotiating Sharp Edge in his mind. No more imaginary bank robberies.

From this moment on he had to be focused.

And from this moment on he was through taking anybody's shit. He'd play along with Mackenzie at work for the next few weeks, because it was necessary for his plan, but other than that, no more kowtowing.

"No more," he muttered to himself as he took a seat.

He had a plan in mind and he'd outlined it all on his PowerBook and now, first thing Monday morning, he was on his way to the bank with his plan on his laptop. The chances were astronomical that anybody would access his computer, get by his password and see them, but it wasn't a very bright thing to do, walking into the bank with enough evidence to hang himself in his briefcase.

Pretty stupid actually, he thought. So best to come here and erase the info before he went into work. He could've, should've done it at home, but he didn't think about it till he was on the train and he didn't want anybody else looking over his shoulder, while he checked over his plans one last time before he deleted them.

"What are you doing?" It was Hannah.

"I was about to open my briefcase and check the racing form," Bob lied.

"You'll be late for work."

"I am sometimes. I don't think they'll fire me."

"But they might fire me, so I guess I'll get out of here."

"Wait," Bob said as she turned to go.

"What?"

"You followed me, why?"

"Just curious, you know how women are."

"Not really," he said, getting up from the bench. "I'll walk with you. The racing form will wait till this evening." He laughed. "Or maybe I'll sneak a peak when I get into my office."

"Okay," she said, "let's go to work."

To work he thought. Not much longer, not if he was successful. He thought about his computer and the information on it. He'd delete it during lunch. When they got to the stone steps leading up to the bank, Bob couldn't help but reflect on how normal everything looked now. Not so long ago he'd been laid out on that concrete. He thought about Gloria, imagined her tortured face and the twisted shape of her body as she'd hit the ground. Everyone had forgotten her. No one cared anymore. As long as they were able to withdraw and deposit their funds that was all that mattered. And yet, did he expect anything else from a society governed by regulations, time schedules and money? The answer, no, but not much longer for Bob Heggie, not if he was successful.

When he got to his office, he went to his computer, booted it up and checked his e-mail. Fifty-six messages, boring, uninteresting memos from head office, regional office, personnel and various directors. Boring, boring, boring, except one. He clicked on the e-mail sent from Lord Harris via regional office. However, Lord Harris hadn't sent the e-mail, it was Bob's creation.

Further to my latest memo with reference to the recent bank raid, I am pleased to advise that we are now in possession of the various recommendations to be implemented by our recently formed liaison committee.

Details will be forwarded in forthcoming months, regarding various training sessions and group discussions to be put into practice. It is the intention of senior management to be prepared for any eventuality relating to any incident likely to happen within a banking branch, including any major serious criminal activities.

Needless to say any details to follow are strictly confidential and sensitive and must not, repeat not, be discussed with any member of the public and that includes your families. Disciplinary action will be taken against any member of staff discussing any matters of security with any person connected or otherwise with the bank. In extreme breaches of confidence, an employee will be instantly dismissed.

The first action to be executed will be a mock bank robbery to take place on Wednesday 24th May at approximately 9:15. While this may sound rather extreme, the entire security team, including the police, feel a group role play will be invaluable.

There is absolutely nothing to be concerned about. Should any members of staff feel strongly about taking part in such an exercise, we will listen to them sympathetically. However, we will be able to put into place real situations in which employees are thrown into a dramatic situation and forced to think on their feet. Mistakes will no doubt be made, but they will be evaluated and further exercises of a similar nature will take place at a later date. The raid will be carried out by professional actors, making the exercise as realistic as possible.

I would further add that once you have digested the contents of this letter, it must not be discussed again until a debriefing has taken place following the exercise and it must also be destroyed immediately by shredding.

All employees will be asked to carry on as normal when the branch reopens at ten o'clock and await further instructions. It is absolutely crucial that customers are unaware this exercise has taken place.

As mentioned in my previous letter, we intend to keep all staff informed, regarding all aspects of security both now and in the future. We must never ever put ourselves in the dangerous situation that sadly occurred several weeks ago at the National that resulted in loss of life.

Management's singular aim is to provide a working environment that feels as safe and comfortable as possible for all members of staff.

Once again I thank you for your cooperation.

Bob added the names of all members of staff, checked the grammar and spelling, then printed thirty letters. His hands were shaking a bit as he printed the first, but he regained his composure as he progressed with the task. It seemed strange, printing a letter for himself, but these letters were for every employee, including Mackenzie.

In actual fact Mackenzie would have two. The first would be the one he would read with paragraphs four through seven omitted and the second would be the same as the others for his circular file. It was a requirement that senior management had a chronological filing system of all internal memos and circulars. Mackenzie had quite naturally delegated the task to Bob.

It was crucial Mackenzie read the first letter fully, otherwise he might get curious as he continued with his signatures. Bob couldn't take the chance on him reading about the raid. He was confident all of the other staff would do as the letter said and keep quiet, but if Mackenzie knew about it he would more than likely be on the blower to his pals in high places.

Bob printed out the envelopes and marked them "Private & Confidential." He laughed as he thought about writing TOP SECRET on them, but decided against such a ridiculous action.

For a second or so, he thought about not going through with it, but then he pictured the Jack of Hearts and shelved those thoughts. No more Walter Mitty, he'd promised himself. He was a man of action now.

After all, he'd planned everything with military

precision. All the details were locked in his mind, and on his laptop, but he'd erase that at lunch. Naturally it could all go wrong, but he'd planned it so that he could abort the operation at certain stages without any comeback linking himself to the events that happened along the way. His adrenaline was pumping. He felt sharp.

He printed the other memos and circulars from that day as well as a few left over from the Friday before. He would present Mackenzie with a grand stack for signature today.

Mackenzie had his head buried deep into a report as Bob walked into his office. As usual he didn't look up straightaway and as usual Bob didn't interrupt him. Mackenzie was a control freak and needed to be in command of the situation. Bob let him have his power surge and after a couple minutes he looked up and Bob sat to discuss the day's letters as Mackenzie looked at the unusually large pile.

"Bloody hell, Bob, what's all this?"

"Just the usual, sir, plus another individual staff memo, it shouldn't take too long."

"What's the staff memo about?"

"I'll get to them in a second, sir."

Bob was stalling, but it was part of his scheme. He took Mackenzie through several boring letters, drawing his attention to insignificant point after insignificant point. He made him wait until he had double-checked them and he started a discussion relating to one of the clients.

"Come on, Bob, we haven't got all day!"

It was working. Bob could see him getting annoyed. He couldn't wait to get back to his precious report on figures, statistics and his beloved targets.

"Just this last one, sir, then we are nearly through."

Bob dragged the last letter out as long as he could and Mackenzie signed the bottom without checking a thing. He came to the memo and held it out in front of him.

"I really think you should read this, sir."

Mackenzie seemed to take Bob's instruction literally. He took forever reading it, but as Bob watched his eyes carefully study the wording, he began to notice him speed-read the bottom of the document. He was so predictable.

"Much ado about nothing Bob, if you ask me." He signed his own letter for filing. Of course, it wouldn't be filed. It would be destroyed.

The letter to be filed included paragraphs four through seven and had been inserted within the pile. He wouldn't even notice his name at the top as his attention span had been spent.

Mackenzie waded through the thirty or so letters for signature, making his mark and occasionally pretending to notice and be interested in the staff they were going to. As he finished, he paused. Bob froze as he held out the last letter.

"You're, slipping, Bob."

Bob glanced at the letter, horrified. His heart took off like a jackhammer, however he was ready with his reply as planned. He was ready to terminate the operation. Mackenzie would no doubt call the staff together for a briefing, then contact head of security who would know nothing about the letter or the raid.

An internal enquiry would take place and Bob would simply state that he had downloaded and prepared the e-mail as his normal morning routine required. Nevertheless shit would hit the fan and no doubt certain procedures would be criticized and changed, but Bob was comfortable he would be above suspicion.

"Problem, sir?" Bob was shaking inside, but outside he remained composed.

"I'll say. June Mitchell's letter, have you seen it?"

"No." Bob shook his head.

"She's addressed as June Dixon."

Bob couldn't speak, he had nothing to say. He was unprepared. What was Mackenzie talking about?

"She was married four weeks ago, Bob. Personnel must still have her registered under Dixon. I thought you would have picked that up."

It suddenly registered and Bob couldn't help his sigh. He'd forgotten about June getting married. At the same time he was furious with himself. The stupid mistake could have drawn attention to the contents of the letter.

"She won't mind, sir, I'm sure. Well spotted though."

"You'll have to be more careful in the future." He signed the letter and sat back, looking smug.

Bob allowed the man his little triumph, content that stage one had been successfully concluded. He went back to his office and put the signed letters into the pre-named envelopes. He took a deep breath and went out into the secure area to begin distribution.

This was also a carefully orchestrated exercise.

Bob began handing the letters out and watched the first few envelopes being ripped open. The first staff began reading and Bob slowly and deliberately began looking through the stack he held, looking for the names of the department he was in.

He didn't have to long to wait.

Coincidentally, it was June who made the mistake.

"Flippin' heck, girls we're gonna have a bank raid!"

Bob sprang into his uncharacteristic, pre-planned mode.

"Can't you bloody read, June," he shouted. "Did you know you could be fired for what you just said?"

Her colleagues looked shocked. They had never seen good old, salt of the earth, mellow Bobby Heggie off on a rant like that.

He turned to the rest of the section and continued loudly. He informed them that if he heard anyone else even breathe a word about the exercise, he would not hesitate to start formal proceedings of disciplinary action.

He also pointed out that June had been mouthing off while customers were actually in the bank and if word of this leaked to the public, the whole exercise would have to be called off.

His little tirade left them in no doubt as to the seriousness of the situation. The staff were no different than Bob. They needed their jobs. They needed their salaries. Caught in a financial trap. They were mere puppets, with the bank hierarchy pulling the strings. Do this, do that or else. Or else no holidays, no cars, no meals, no house, no mortgage. We are in control, understand?

Do what we say, not what we do.

Bob knew there would be whispering in the toilets and behind closed office doors, but he was confident their little secret operation would remain in branch.

If it didn't and Bob heard any rumors, then the raid would simply not take place.

He was sure he had covered every angle. He left and made his way upstairs, hoping his outburst would reach most of the staff, but hopefully not Mackenzie.

CHAPTER NINE

BOB WOKE AROUND 6:00 on Sunday after a poor night's sleep, which he blamed on having to go in on Saturdays. He'd kicked the duvet onto the floor and at some point during the night he'd pulled off his sweatshirt. He got up and wandered down the hall to Cameron's room. A knife plunged through his heart when he looked at the empty bed. His kids should be here with him, it was the weekend, after all. But Stephen's mother was up from London and Debra wanted to introduce the children to her. Bob could hardly say no.

He went downstairs.

The dogs heard him coming and fussed around him as he entered the kitchen. He went to the fridge and took out the bacon sandwiches he'd made last night. Then he clicked on the kettle, before heading into the garage for his rucksack. Back in the house he loaded the sandwiches into the rucksack, filled a thermos with tea and loaded it into the rucksack as well.

The dogs were excited. Cassius came through with his lead in his mouth and Hamish sat with an expectant look, waiting for the signal.

The lakes and mountains were only eighty minutes away on a quiet Sunday morning and Bob could tackle the mountain and, with luck, still be back in time for lunch. The dogs sat patient and hopeful. Their ears ready, anticipating three little words.

"What, lads?" Bob said, "what do you want?"

Their heads tilted from side to side, waiting, hoping.

"In the car."

They bolted toward the gap in the door, almost knocking him over. Bob laughed and followed. In the car he turned on the radio. The weather-woman predicted a clear day and Bob was glad of it. He needed to get out and clear his head. He needed to put Walter Mitty to rest.

He had arranged to meet Debra and the kids for Sunday lunch. Something they thought would be good for the children. Bob wondered if it had anything to do with Stephen playing rugby each Sunday afternoon. Then a few beers with his team mates, of course. Yes, a nice Sunday lunch was sort of convenient for Debra.

Bob would confirm it from the top of the mountain, if he made it up. He shivered, because soon he would be Walter Mitty no more. Now he was going mountain climbing for real.

He drove for just over an hour and the mountains

came into view, but the top of the hill he was going to climb was hidden by a swirling mist. He watched the shadows changing the shape of the mountain as the sunlight peaked through the broken clouds.

The dogs were getting restless. He didn't know how they knew they were getting close, but somehow they did. They started whining and pacing the back of the car. The last ten minutes of the drive were very strange, because as they got nearer the mountain, the dogs got louder and more anxious. By the time he parked, they were barking and pleading to be let loose. He opened the back of the car and they shot out and charged toward a thick bush at the foot of the hill. The dog's public conveniences, their first toilet spot. After a few minutes they bounded back to the car.

Bob finished lacing his boots and looked up in anticipation. The mist was beginning to clear and he prayed for a good day. He could just make out the snow-topped peak three thousand feet above as the clouds dispersed slightly. The dogs ran ahead, leading the way. He hoped the climb would clear his head and he could continue with his plan. And he hoped he'd make the top.

Twenty minutes into his trek and he started to feel the perspiration on his back. The rucksack prevented his pores from breathing, but he didn't ease up on the pace. He felt good.

The dogs kept up, yipping and barking, happy just to be out. He stopped at the first crest, drank some water and looked back on how much ground he had covered. Then he started up again.

Cassius found the dog's first watering hole, a fast flowing stream. He lapped at the water and alerted

Hamish, who joined him and they drank long and hard. Once refreshed they continued with their antics. It fascinated Bob how much ground the animals covered. The way they ran about, it seemed that for every mile he covered, the dogs ran several more.

They would disappear into a wood or dart back down the mountain after a rabbit or even just a smell. It seemed they had no concept of walking in a straight line.

As he climbed higher, Bob felt the temperature beginning to drop, but his quick pace was keeping him warm. By the time he reached the height where the rocky ground started to freeze, the dog's pace had slowed up quite a bit. He stopped and turned back toward the car park. Several cars had parked up and he could just about make out the shape of other climbers and walkers beginning their ascent.

He set off again, mind focusing on his plan and how it would allow him to leave the bank forever. Several stages of the operation had been completed successfully, the next phase was the actual raid. It was by far and away the most dangerous part of the scam. That's what it was, a scam. Bob loved the word. Scam. It wasn't a raid or a robbery, it was a swindle, a con, a trick. A scam.

He wouldn't hurt anyone. He would simply walk into the bank, almost invited. Everyone would or should stand back and let him walk out a few hundred thousand pounds richer. No one would be financially affected. No one that is, except a bank, which seemed to live for screwing as much money as possible out of anyone and anything. He would simply give them a taste of their own medicine.

He allowed himself the luxury of thinking about the future. So sure was he of each detail of the plan, he was beginning to plan his life afterward. He had always wanted to move to a warmer climate. While touring on his Triumph in his early twenties, he had discovered an area of Spain southwest of Seville. It was unspoiled, undiscovered and property was cheap. He had fantasized about selling up and buying a small farm or maybe even opening a restaurant that he could supply with fresh vegetables that he'd grown himself.

It would be small, compact, friendly and fun. He would keep the prices affordable and enjoy what he was doing. He would dine with the customers occasionally and, of course, share an odd bottle of wine with them. The wine would be local. He had sampled many wines of the region at only a few euros per bottle and had liked them all. But he would have to be careful that he didn't share too many bottles.

He would work just enough hours to cover the bills and enjoy the rest of his time, integrating into the Spanish way of life. He had done the sums, worked everything out, but was unfortunately a couple hundred thousand short. A problem he hoped to rectify very soon.

His calf muscles started to ache, but the summit was in sight and he kept going, determined to make the top and he was huffing when he finally did. But as out of breath as he was, he felt like shouting. He'd done it, climbed a mountain. Well, hill really, but it was a first step and he was on his way. Walter Mitty was well and truly dead.

The dogs were out of breath and looked at him with pleading eyes. He took his final few steps to the summit, wondering what it must feel like to conquer Everest or K2 after months of planning and effort when he felt so good after only a two hour climb. He saw a stone cairn and sheltered behind the pile of stones. He pulled his rucksack off and positioned it for extra protection. He pulled up the hood on his waterproof to cut out the sound of the wind. He was cozy and secure.

He opened the plastic container, pulled out a cold bacon sandwich. It smelled good and tasted even better.

Hamish barked.

"Sorry, boys, forgot." He took out a couple sandwiches and tossed them to the dogs. After they finished he gave them some dog biscuits, then washed his sandwich down with a flask of hot tea. Nothing tasted better. He wondered how he might simulate the taste in his little Spanish eatery.

He looked at his watch, 9:30. He took out his cell phone and called Debra. Elisa answered.

"Where are you?" she wanted to know.

"Paradise."

"You must have left early."

"I did," he said. "Are we still going to the pub?"

"Oh yes, Daddy, yes please. Do you want me to get Mummy?"

"No, that's okay, darling. Just tell her I'll be home in plenty of time."

"Daddy," she said, "where's Paradise?"

"Right now it's on the top of a mountain."

"Really?"

"Yes and you should see the view." He spent the next ten minutes telling her about everything in sight, describing it all. He'd never felt so close to his daughter and he hated to end the conversation.

Afterward he lingered on the summit for a bit, savoring what he'd done, but the temperature was hovering just above freezing, the wind turned fierce and the dogs were huddling behind a rock, seeking what shelter they could. It was time to start back, so he packed everything away, swung the pack onto his back and set off down the hill with the dogs right behind.

The ride home was a little busier and Bob regretted leaving the mountains behind. He viewed them in the rearview mirror every few minutes until he couldn't see them anymore. The dogs were sleeping in the back, one of them snoring. The countryside and greenery gradually disappeared as the dreary landscape of the city came into view.

As he neared the ring-road he headed east on the bypass toward home. The landscape once again began to change and after twenty minutes he turned into the small farm track leading toward the house. He got out of the car and straightaway felt the tightness at the back of his legs. He stretched, walked round to the back of the car to let the dogs out.

"Come on, lads, bath time."

No response.

They were shattered and had no intention of leaving their comfortable lair. They looked up at him, begging to be left alone. Cassius closed his eyes and let out a pleading sigh. They wouldn't leave the car willingly now that they had heard the dreaded "bath" word. Bob didn't fancy the idea of a fight with them, so he decided to leave them and enjoy a bath of his own. The dogs could wait a bit.

Each step up the stairs pulled on the back of his legs. He made the top and moved toward the bathroom. He turned on the tap and wandered into the bedroom and stripped off. He selected something suitable for the CD player and turned it up. He chose, of course, the song he'd been playing in his head ever since he'd decided to separate the bank from some of its money. "Lily, Rosemary and the Jack of Hearts."

He lowered himself into the hot tub and sighed. He sang along with Mr. Dylan. He sank deeper into the water and stopped as it reached his chin. He groaned with pleasure. Heaven, he thought. He felt sleep coming on, that familiar feeling of drifting to another world, not caring about time, his mind empty of thought. He awoke with a start at the sound of the back door slamming.

"Daddy, where are you?" Cameron shouted.

"He'll be in the bath," Bob heard Elisa work out.

He heard them running up the stairs.

"Are you in there?" Cameron shouted.

"I'll be right out." Bob got out of the tub, dried off, changed quickly and went downstairs. Debra was outside.

"How have you been?" she said.

"All right, you?"

"I've been better, too much champagne last night. Stephen and I took the kids to the new tapas bar on the Quayside, they absolutely adored it."

Bob couldn't help it, Stephen may be one of the nicest guy in the world, but it annoyed him that his children got on so well with him.

"Come on, Bob, let's go," she said, "I'm getting hungry."

"Gotta let the dogs in first." He went to the car. "Come on, boys, no bath today." They bounded out, went straight to their beds. Happy animals, they.

"Okay, let's go," Debra said.

"I'm coming." Bob said and he led them to the public

bridleway and across the fields as they made their way to the Ridley Arms. The Ridley was a wonderful old country inn serving home cooked food in large portions. Bob opened the final gate that led to the village and Cameron and Elisa raced across the village green before disappearing through the door.

"What's it to be today, Bob?" Debra asked when they were standing at the bar.

"Whale and chips," Bob said, referring to the very large portion of fish served in the Ridley. The mountain had built his appetite and, for once, he felt like he could clear his plate. His Sunday couldn't get much better.

"Guinness, Bob?" the landlord asked.

Normally Bob would have nodded, but not today, not after completing his first trip up the mountain. All of a sudden he felt healthy and it was a good feeling.

"No thanks, Gary, just a pint of fresh orange juice."

Gary and Debra looked at Bob in disbelief. Gary had already started pulling the Guinness.

"You're kidding, right?" Gary laughed.

"No, I'm going to lay off a bit."

Gary hadn't stopped pulling the pint. He smiled at Bob as the beautiful black liquid settled. He lifted the glass and put it in front of him.

"That's on the house, Bob." He laughed again. "Now tell me you don't want it?" By this time Gary's wife joined the scene, realizing the game Gary was playing.

The Guinness had settled and seemed to be staring at Bob and he could taste it. He was tempted. He gripped the glass. It was cold and enticing, but he thought about the mountain and pushed it away.

"Thanks, Gary, but I really do just want orange juice."

Gary stopped smiling and Bob felt bad refusing his generosity. Debra ordered a Diet Coke, probably feeling the effect of too much indulgence the night before. Then they made their way to what was once their favorite table and Bob sank into the soft furnishing. Cameron and Elisa followed, but as soon as they had settled they spied some friends on the other side of the room and drifted over.

Bob and Debra sat in silence for a moment, taking in the friendly atmosphere of the room and for a short while Bob had forgotten they were about to be divorced.

"So what have you been up to, Bob?"

"Oh, a little of this, a little of that." He thought about how he'd bought a motorcycle, how he and Hannah had chased that purse snatcher and how he'd finally put Walter Mitty to rest and climbed that mountain. He sighed.

"Just a little of this and a little of that, nothing more?" she said.

"Nope, nothing more. I lead a pretty simple life. I'm just plain old, boring Bob Heggie, remember?

CHAPTER TEN

ANOTHER WEEK, ANOTHER MONDAY and the day that would make or break Bob's life was just ten days away. He was in the gym by 7:00 for his first day. It was an important part of his plan and he'd want the people there to remember him when the time came, so he made a point of being just a little slow when Gwen, the girl who was introducing him to all the machines, explained how he was supposed to use them. She wouldn't forget him. Not today, not next week either. After the session, he took a hot shower, then left the gym and walked through the park to the bank.

The park was beginning to come to life. It was spring and the bulbs were beginning to flower, bringing much needed color to the surroundings. The grass was looking greener and in need of the first cut of the year. The council gardeners stood in groups of two or three, poking and prodding the soil. They had already pulled the early weeds and placed new bedding plants in strategically arranged patterns. More workers rested than worked, with the smokers among them seeming to enjoy longer breaks.

He walked out of the park and into the street, turned the corner and his mood deepened as he saw the dreary building ahead. The bank never changed, not even for spring. His mood picked up some as he remembered his days there were numbered.

By the time he got to work he felt fit and focused, but unable to stop perspiring. On the plus side, he was brimming with energy and enthusiasm. He somehow wished he could direct some of that enthusiasm into his career, but he couldn't, he wouldn't. It was all too late.

He wished Hannah were here, but she'd called in sick. He thought that a bit unusual for someone as gung ho as she, especially since she'd only been on the job for such a short while, but if you're sick, you're sick. Best not to pass it on to your co-workers.

He put Hannah out of his mind and studied the staff for most of the morning, looking for signs and signals, little clues that would tell him all was not well. He watched the juniors, he watched the managers and he paid particular attention to Mackenzie, flitting in and out of his office all day. He seemed nervous, on edge.

The staff seemed different, nervous too, and excited. There was a buzz of anticipation, no one would be late on Thursday next week, that was assured. They seemed to be looking forward to the drama that was about to unfold.

Bob knew exactly how they would perform. Some would act the parts they were supposed to play, others would grin like idiots and some may try to be heroes to impress their colleagues. Their work would suffer this week and slow to a crawl next Monday. They were buzzing, yet nobody uttered a word.

As he studied the staff his mind was full of details and timing, but every now and then he would daydream of Spain and the small fishing village he loved so much. He couldn't help himself. The climate of Spain and the laid back attitude appealed to him. He imagined a life without the bank, without the strict 9:00 routine, told when to arrive, when to leave, when to take holidays, what to wear, shirt and tie please, double cuffs too.

Ah, well, best to quit dreaming and get back to work. The rest of the day he worked normally, making sure everything ticked along as usual. It was important not to neglect any of his duties, so as not to arouse suspicion. He remembered the crime thrillers on television. The detectives were always looking for unusual activity or different work patterns. He knew they would point the finger of suspicion at him. It was inevitable. But they would find nothing.

After work Bob went straight to the station, but his train was twenty minutes late. He grabbed two coffees on the platform and made his way over to Old Tom, who handed Bob the evening paper as Bob gave him his coffee. They talked the minutes away and Bob was glad of the company, happy to concentrate on conversation as opposed to the other details crowding his mind.

Tom was a bright man and Bob never tired of his tales, stories and his philosophy on life. Bob wondered about his past. He never talked about it, Bob never asked, preferring to imagine him as a former smuggler or perhaps a jewel thief.

He'd have hit the bottle after losing everything in a high stakes poker game. He would have been happily married with a large family and that fell by the wayside, doesn't see them any more, no family get togethers, no birthdays, no Merry Christmases for Tom.

Tom was a great people watcher and as he handed the evening paper to several punters, he told Bob all about them. Bob didn't know if he made them up or if the tales were genuine.

"Do you notice anything, Bob, about the people in the good positions, the high flyers, those with the good salaries?"

Bob watched as another well-dressed, attractive, thirty-something woman approached Tom. He raised his eyebrows, quizzing him, waiting for his synopsis. Bob was curious. Tom handed her a paper and smiled. She didn't smile back, she didn't look at him. For her, Tom didn't exist.

"They're all good looking, Bob."

"Sorry, Tom?"

"The pretty people, they get all the best jobs, not the ugly bastards like me."

"Don't be daft." Bob laughed and for the first time detected bitterness in the old man.

"You think about it on the way home. Think about your fellow commuters. Look at the punters in the business suits and expensive leather coats, then look at the ones in the overalls and shop assistant uniforms, the cleaners and the factory workers. Just take a look, Bob."

The PA system drowned out Tom's voice as it announced his train and Bob bid Tom goodbye. The train lurched from the station and Bob prepared for yet another uneventful journey home. He couldn't help thinking about Tom's latest philosophy and took a look around the train.

A middle-aged man sat opposite Bob in work clothes and a donkey jacket. His nose was misshapen and he had stained teeth, strong tea and nicotine. One of the man's front teeth was missing too. He was not pleasant to look at.

Bob looked a little farther a field and saw a slim girl in her early thirties or so. She was talking a little too loud on a mobile phone about deals and contracts. She wore too much makeup, but was without a doubt from the pretty people school. Her clothes were expensive and tasteful, all color coordinated. The young businessman on the far side of the carriage, lightly tanned from a weekend in Barcelona or maybe the south of France, slicked back, wet look, gelled hair. Italian designer suit, successful and handsome.

The council refuge collector next to him, bloated with excess drink and a poor diet, his face reddened and wind scorched from the years on the bin wagon. He had a pair of scars on his face and a nose broken and flattened from one argument too many. He was squashed next to the window, careful not to sit too close, careful not to mark the designer suit with dust and grime from the honest working day, knowing his place.

Bob shivered with the thought of what Old Tom had said. Could he have been right? Pretty people got the good jobs? He didn't want to believe that, didn't want to think about it. In fact, he didn't want to think about anything at all. He opened the paper, something he hadn't done since he'd conceived the idea of his bank scam, and tried to lose himself in the news. As usual, none of it was good.

The train slowed as it neared Bob's station. He got up and reached for his briefcase. At home, he changed and went out with the dogs. It was a pleasant evening, still warm out. Bob imagined how hot the sun would be in Spain and dreamt of a new life. On holidays, sometimes on an odd weekend, he'd fly the kids across.

The food on the barbecue would just be about cooked and he would call them from the pool. No need for long baths out there, a quick poolside shower would be okay.

Cameron would pull on some dry shorts and Elisa would wrap a towel around herself, she would moan about changing before tea. A warm breeze would blow around the pool and the dogs would be seeking shade under the table.

Grilled meat, salads and vegetables, healthy eating. The kids would thrive there. Elisa would lose the puppy fat she'd managed to store up in England. Wouldn't it be nice if they could stay with him forever? No dark winter evenings spent at a computer or television screen. The after school activities would be swimming and tennis. No worries, no pattern to life, no clock watching, no bank, no pressure.

The sun had gone now and Bob cooled down quickly. He called the dogs back from the far side of the field, saw their breath visible in the cool evening air. It was almost dark by the time he got home. He had wandered further than he should have. He opened the door into the kitchen and the dogs dashed to their beds.

* * *

Hannah hesitated as the brakes on the train began to bite against the wheels. Several passengers began to collect their goods and others made their way to the doors. Hannah sat tight. What on earth could she say to Bob if she just turned up unannounced? "I was just passing by?" "The train broke down?" No, that would look stupid. Yet she really wanted to talk to him tonight. There was something wrong with her and there was no way she was ever going to get to sleep until she figured out what it was.

One thing she did know was that she couldn't work with Bob Heggie. She was too attracted to him and that was just plain nuts. But she couldn't help herself. At least she thought she couldn't. Fortunately, she could go on calling in sick forever if she wanted, because she didn't need the job, not really. The money from her parent's estate, plus their life insurance, was a tidy sum. And in addition to that, all the families of those who were killed in the 911 tragedy got a very healthy settlement and even though she thought it had been unfair, she let the money sit in her bank account, had used it to finance her way through school.

So here she was, a rich girl, who couldn't get her mind off a middle-aged banker who loathed his profession. What was that all about? Should she make up some excuse and drop in on him? Test the waters, see if the attraction was real or all in her head? Or should she just forget the whole thing?

She was lost in her thoughts when the doors opened and the commuters started to make their way to the exits. She hadn't quite figured out what she wanted to do when the sharp shrill on the guard's whistle made her mind up. She jumped from her seat and ran to the door. It slammed in her face and the train jolted forward. The guard put his hand up and shouted something barely audible through the thick double skinned glass. The distance increased between the guard and the door as the train picked up speed. Hannah opened the door a split second before the automatic locking system kicked in. She jumped onto the platform, running in the direction of the train. It was all she could do to keep from falling onto the grime ridden platform.

"You're not allowed to do that!" The guard bellowed.

"But I just did."

"Don't get smart with me or I'll call the station police."

"You're right, I'm sorry. I won't do it again."

She turned from him, walked away.

She worried about what to say to him on the cab ride to his house. When she got there he answered her knock straightaway, his dogs behind him, probably curious about the visitor.

"I was wondering if we could talk a bit about my career," she said. How lame did that sound?

"Now?"

"Sure, as long as you've got nothing planned."

"No, I don't have anything planned. Come in, let me take your coat."

"Thanks." Hannah shook of her coat and handed it over, trying not to look as awkward as she felt. Bob beckoned her through to the lounge, then he went into the kitchen and came back carrying a half empty wine bottle and two glasses.

"You'll join me?" He asked.

Hannah nodded and wondered if this was part of his nightly ritual. He handed her a glass and she took a sip.

For once Bob wasn't dressed in his grey corporate attire. He wore a pair of faded Levi's and a white tee shirt.

"So, are you having second thoughts about the world of corporate banking and finance?"

"Sorry?" Hannah swallowed, regretting her decision as the wine caught the back of her throat.

"Your career, you wanted to talk about it."

"Oh yeah," Hannah tried to composed herself. "I just wanted to try and get down to the politics of the job, you know, how to get on, how to get promoted, how to keep in with the right people, you know what I mean, and most of all, who are the right people?"

"The million dollar question," Bob said as he got up and started pacing, "is not who are the right people, but what do you want out of life."

"Yes, I can see that." She felt a bit uncomfortable as she gazed up at him.

"I hope you don't want what you think I've achieved, because my working life hasn't exactly been all that rewarding, at least not to me."

"Surely not, you've—"

He held up a hand to quiet her.

"I was just like you twenty years ago, embarking on a career. I was so excited. I had dreams and aspirations and a vision of big salaries and a top office with staff at my beck and call." He dropped to the sofa beside her and sipped at his wine. She moved just a bit closer. She couldn't help herself.

* * *

Bob looked deep into her sea green eyes and at her enlarged pupils. Her shadowy black hair hung in soft ringlets, partly covering her face and he absorbed her crimson lips as she smiled. What did the smile mean? What was the real reason for her coming here?

"Bob," she said. "If I asked you for your definition of Utopia, what would you say?"

"Spain," he answered without hesitation. "I dream of living there." And he went on about how he wanted to buy some property, open a restaurant, maybe have his kids down there. He couldn't stop himself. He'd never told anybody before and dammit now he couldn't stop. He felt foolish. He felt out of his depth with her, but most of all, he felt good that he was sharing his dream with someone, even if it was only for tonight. When he finished, he said, "That would be Utopia for me, Spain."

"I think that's nice." She got up. "Now I have to go. Thanks for the advice."

Bob wanted to ask her to stay. All of a sudden he was aware just how much she meant to him. He got up too. He wanted to kiss her, but as he moved toward her, he saw a picture of her in his mind as the little girl that used to tag along behind him. She'd been so innocent, still was.

She got her coat and he followed her to the door, where she surprised him by giving him a quick kiss on the lips.

"See you tomorrow then?"

"No doubt." He couldn't believe what had just happened.

"Your wife, Bob," Hannah fastened her coat against the cool evening air, "she is crazy." She gave him another quick kiss, then she was out the door and gone.

* * *

Bob got to bed later than usual that evening, pushing thoughts of Hannah from his mind as he entered the bedroom, but she came right back after he crawled under the covers and she was right there as he drifted off to sleep.

He woke the next morning, ready to call off the whole operation. His mind was in turmoil, he couldn't concentrate.

The pressure was building. He needed to escape. Fuck Mackenzie, fuck the bank, he decided to call in sick. For a second he worried about that third written warning, but it wouldn't happen, because he wouldn't be going anywhere where he was likely to run into Mackenzie, or anyone else from the bank for that matter. And there darn sure were no TV cameras where he was going.

He picked up the rucksack and packed it, then he and the dogs piled into the VW and drove to the mountain. No people, no distractions, just a clear day with the dogs. He watched as they ran through the trees at the foot of the mountain. He watched as they climbed higher and higher, leaving the forest far behind. He had exactly one week to go and that made this his D-Day. Decision Day. He'd come up here to clear his head, to go over the plans one more time. Back down there, he'd be too tense, too wound up to think. This was where he was going to make the final decision.

He reached the summit and looked out over a vast lake at the foot of the mountain. It was a calm day. Small yachts tacked across the water, searching for a light breeze to guide them on their way. The more sensible boatmen engaged their engines, making their way leisurely, round the islands in the middle of the lake.

The sun warmed him and yet it was a strange cold sun. The dogs didn't seem to mind as they stretched out on the mountain top.

Cassius knew something was worrying Bob and he sat at his feet, looking up with his doggie brown eyes. Bob stroked him and reassured him everything was okay. On his way down the mountain, he made his decision.

He had nothing to lose. He had a lousy job and a shit of a manager he wanted to strangle. Staying in the bank would only lead him into trouble. Sooner or later, he was going to go for Mackenzie and then they'd sack him.

He needed to escape. He needed to escape far, far away. The only way out of this mess was to leave the bank forever and there was only one way to do that.

He tortured himself on the way home. He kept thinking of the worst possible scenario. Jobless, excommunicated from his children. More than likely he would end up an alcoholic. Just like Old Tom. He kidded himself that sitting in the Grapes all day wouldn't be such a bad thing. He imagined himself like Tom. Happy-go-lucky, a little dirty perhaps, who would care? He imagined himself aging rather quickly and blending in better with the likes of Peter and Jackie. It couldn't be any worse than his life in the bank.

The house was quiet and the dogs went straight to their bed as soon as he opened the door.

He looked for something to do, something to occupy his mind.

He made another cup of tea and packed the new gym

bag.

The sports holdall had different items in it today.

Items Bob had kept hidden for many weeks, a children's clown mask, a plastic replica gun, and a thin sports tracksuit, two sizes too big.

There were also two shoe inserts, which would increase his height by at least two inches. The CCTV cameras would capture his every move.

The experts would analyze the footing, complete their calculations and establish the suspect to be six-foot in height. The tracksuit on top of the full business suit would also give the appearance of a far larger man, all designed to throw them off track.

Bob had even practiced trying to walk in a different style. A short stepped bounce with a slight swagger, his head floating like a long distance runner or a dog's head in the back of an old battered estate car. It had taken many weeks, but he had perfected a complete new style of walking and he was able to turn it on at will.

He sat in the kitchen for well over an hour. Thinking, planning, worrying.

Eventually Hamish wandered through. A bit later Cassius followed and as daybreak arrived, they set off across the fields.

He walked at a fast pace and soon left the house far behind. It was mild morning, a thick blanket of fog hung over the valley, the air was damp and it was quiet.

The dogs were quiet too. Cassius unnerved Bob, as he would not leave his side. Had he sensed something different in his manner?

Bob persevered with the walk and eventually Cassius ran off with Hamish and left him alone with his thoughts, occasionally looking back to make sure Bob was still there. Searching, checking, making sure he hadn't disappeared.

By the time they got back home the fog had lifted, the sun had broken through and it was hot and muggy. Bob was soaking with sweat and the dogs were panting hard.

He took a cold shower and gathered his thoughts. He dressed, then wandered from room to room. He imagined the children fast asleep. He opened a window upstairs, allowing a pleasant breeze into the house.

He'd made his decision back at the mountain, so why was he having second thoughts? He closed his eyes, clenched his fists, pushed the worries from his mind. He was going ahead.

CHAPTER
ELEVEN

ON THE FOLLOWING THURSDAY, the day Bob was
going to put his plan into action, he woke well before the
alarm. The twin problems of Hannah and what he was
about to do ate at him. First, he'd had hardly a word with
Hannah since that kiss. It was almost as if she were
avoiding him. Had he done something? Said something to
turn her away? He didn't think so. Maybe he should have
paid her some attention, but he'd been lost in his
thoughts, worrying about this second problem and
whether or not he was going to wind up with the money
he needed to finance his move to Spain or if he was going
to spend a lot of years behind bars.

He went downstairs and clicked on the kettle. The hot

tea cleansed his mouth as he sat in the dark. Strangely enough he wasn't nervous. He felt calm, he knew everything had been planned. He did worry about the weather a bit though, because it was supposed to be hot, too hot for a suit and he imagined sweating like a pig with a tracksuit on top. However, it would only be for a few minutes and, in any case, the staff were used to seeing him sweat.

Before he left for the train, he visited the children's rooms. He kissed their pillows. He prayed he would be seeing them next Saturday. This week may be different. Perhaps he wouldn't. Perhaps he would end up languishing in a police station, undergoing questioning. He tried not to think of the consequences of failure.

The platform was quiet, with only a few people waiting for the early train as it groaned into the station. With a deep sigh, but with an air of optimism, Bob climbed aboard, thankful that Hannah wouldn't be going in this early. He wanted to see her, wanted to talk, but not this morning. He really didn't want to face her before the day's events.

During the journey into the city he accounted for every minute of the day ahead. Timing was critical and the key to success or failure.

The train pulled into the station and he sort of shuffled to the side of the crowd. He waited until Tom was busy with a customer, supplying the man with his daily take on the world, then, when Tom was looking the other way, Bob headed straight for the exit. He made his way to the gym through the park and arrived to a locked door. However in a few minutes the owner turned up, looking sleepy and bit surprised.

"Christ, Bob, you get earlier and earlier," he said and that was true. Bob had been coming in early every day for the last week, establishing his new routine.

In the gym he went through the motions, building up a sweat, but not as enthusiastic as his sessions of late. Within a few minutes some people began to join him and Bob made sure he talked to as many of them as possible. He wanted to be noticed, today more than ever.

After he finished his workout, he showered, changed and made his way to the bank, carrying the sports bag. He lingered in the banking hall, pretending to study the latest advertising on the wall. He loitered for a while. Three or four members of staff came in after him and he passed the time of day.

At 8:20 he took the backstairs to his office and made a point of calling in on Mackenzie. They exchanged morning pleasantries.

He went into his office, sat at the desk and opened the gym bag. The clown mask peered at him from within. He zipped the bag back up, then made his way back to the banking hall. He tidied a few leaflets and went into the secure area. Everyone was on time and at his or her workstation.

No one was late, no one was absent and nobody wanted to miss the drama that was about to unfold.

Bob called into the offices of all the managers, wishing them good morning and asking them if everything was all right. It was a clear reference to the false bank raid they had all been waiting for.

The last person Bob called in on was Jim Moody. Jim was one of the under managers and their association went back a long way. In recent years they had gone to the races together and he had even joined Bob a couple times at the Cheltenham Race Festival. This year Bob hadn't asked him.

Jim loved a bet and studied the form back to front every day. As usual the Racing Post was the first thing Jim read and the morning edition was sitting in the middle of his desk.

"Fancy anything today, Jim?"

"No, not really." He pawed at his bushy moustache. "Just keeping in touch, you know."

Bob allowed himself a short conversation with the man, then returned to his office where he picked up the gym bag. Then he hurried along the back stairwell to the gent's toilet.

He went into a cubicle, unzipped the bag for the second time that morning and took out the mask and a bright ginger wig. He took out the plastic pistol, then the oversized tracksuit, which he pulled over the top of his suit. Immediately he began to heat up, but he couldn't worry about that. He took off his shoes and pulled on the cheap new trainers with the artificial heels inside. He pulled out the second, larger, flimsy holdall and put the sports bag inside it, covered by a newspaper to hide it from view. The sports bag took up little room. He had packed it lightly the night before. No sweatshirt, no over-trousers or socks, just a thin vest, trainers and shorts.

He pulled on the bright wig and mask and looked at himself in the mirror. He rigged up the voice disguise.

He'd bought it last month at a Dr. Who stall at a science fiction event. He spoke quietly into the sound system and heard the unmistakable sound of a Dalek.

Lastly, he pulled on the clear polyurethane surgeon's

gloves.

It was a strange sight, Bob didn't recognize himself and he didn't think anybody else would either, nor would the CCTV cameras be able to accurately guess the profile of this cunning criminal.

He walked a few times up-and-down the length of the toilet, making sure he had his new gate down. When he was confident he had it mastered, he left the toilet and went out into the corridor. Halfway down the stairs he paused, listening.

He heard the normal sounds of a bank. The sounds of money being counted, printers printing, the general hubbub and morning conversation of the staff. But there was a different sound. It was quieter than usual. They were waiting for something different.

Bob bided his time, waiting for the secure door to open. At this time of the morning the staff continually went in and out, carrying out routine tasks and visiting the toilet. He waited. Nothing happened. He looked at his watch, it was 8:41.

He had to be within the secure area by 8:45, leaving sufficient time to raid the safe and carry out the remaining tasks.

Still he waited, sweating.

What if nobody came out today?

Maybe they were all afraid they'd miss the action?

He hadn't thought of that. He wondered if he could make it back to the toilet without being seen.

Still he waited.

At 8:44 Bob heard the familiar sound of the secure door clicking open. He rushed from the stairwell, covering the short distance of the banking hall in an instant.

June Mitchel froze in horror as she watched Bob rushing toward her. The door was wide open and Bob screamed at her to get back inside. The rest of the counter staff looked up in surprise, realizing that this was it.

Some of them were smiling, trying to look cool.

June made a half-hearted attempt to close the door, but Bob grabbed it and push her back inside. His first challenge had been completed.

He was now behind the secure area of the bank and had access to the safe. He looked around at the curious members of staff. Some of them he had talked to only a few minutes earlier. He bellowed at them in the strange voice. Some looked worried, others laughed a bit, but they all did as they were told.

"Where is the safe?" he asked Clare Williams, one of the more nervous tellers. She balked at telling him. He looked over at Hannah, and for a second he thought about grabbing her as his pretend hostage, but he shelved the thought straightaway, she'd been held hostage during a real robbery, the last thing he wanted to do was to traumatize her.

"I mean it, lady," he pointed the gun at Clare's head.

"Over there," she pointed. Of course he knew where it was, but he had to be careful during every stage of the operation. The police would suspect an inside job, but he didn't need to help them with their investigation.

"That's better, show me." Bob gave her a push and she made her way through the door toward the open safe.

He followed her inside, closed the entrance door, then went back out into the banking hall and made an announcement.

"I now have a hostage and I will be pointing a gun at

her head. If I hear any talking or any alarm, I will kill her!"

Bob studied their reaction.

They seemed a bit shocked. No one was smiling now. Everyone was quiet and Hannah seemed to be looking right through him. Bob turned and re-entered the walk in safe. He faced the startled girl, pretended to look around and located the high denomination currency. He wasn't interested in small change. He would load the bag with twenties and fifties. He would leave out the hundreds, as they were a little more difficult to get rid of.

He filled the bag, then closed the zip. Clare was getting a little agitated. She was probably wondering why the actor was actually taking the money. Bob took no chances. He left her within the confines of the huge safe and closed the heavy door, glad that it couldn't be opened from the inside.

He had no idea how much he was carrying as he walked back into the main secure area. The rest of the staff were still standing around, unsure of what to do. He moved toward the secure door and ordered one of the tellers to release the escape lock. Gordon Westhaven, who was in his mid-twenties and hadn't been in the bank long, apparently wanted to make an impression in front of the girls.

"No, I won't." He looked to his colleagues for some moral support. He got none. Their smiles had gone, replaced by worried looks. Bob hadn't planned for this. He didn't know what to do. He had to think on his feet. He raised the gun and pointed it toward him.

"Open the fucking door!" he shouted in his menacing alien voice and Gordon's smile evaporated as Bob moved toward him. He thrust the gun into his temple and repeated his command. A trickle of blood appeared below his hairline and the sight upset Bob a bit. No violence, no shooting, no death.

Before Bob had a chance to threaten him again, he heard the unmistakable voice of Mackenzie.

"What the hell is going on here?"

This too was unplanned. It was going wrong. He hesitated for a moment. The seconds seemed like minutes. He could do nothing.

Get a grip, get a grip, he said to himself. Thoughts of the children flashed through his mind.

He looked at Mackenzie. His face had turned pasty white. Gordon noticed it too and the color began to drain from his face as well.

Bob pointed the plastic gun at Mackenzie's heart.

"Open the door!" he commanded.

"Yes, right away," Mackenzie blubbered, "anything, but please don't shoot."

Gordon seemed relieved the responsibility had shifted to Mackenzie. However, he was clearly surprised at Mackenzie's reaction.

Bob looked round, everybody else seemed surprised as well. He needed to distract them before anything else went wrong. He needed to act fast.

"Open it now or you're a dead man." He lifted the gun to Mackenzie's face.

"No," Mackenzie whimpered, "please don't. I'll let you out." He rushed toward the release button beside the door and pressed it. The sound of the catch echoing through the enclosed area was music to Bob's ears, but he had to keep himself from laughing as Mackenzie lost control of his bladder, leaving a wet stain between his legs.

"Shit man, you just pissed yourself," Bob said, then he hurried toward the exit, ready to enact the craziest part of the operation. He had wondered long and hard about appearing in the street with a clown's mask. He had thought about removing it in the doorway but it was too risky. CCTV cameras would pick him up, someone in the street would recognize him. The mask and the orange wig would need to stay on a bit longer.

He reached into the zipper pocket, pulled out a handful of lollipops. He sauntered down the street and immediately people began to take notice. He walked up to the first pram and handed the small boy one of the lollies. His Mother smiled and asked if a circus was in town. Bob didn't answer.

He walked further up the street, looking for the next child.

A police car drove up the street toward him. Bob made out the shape of an overweight driver and as the car got closer, he noticed a young policewoman in the passenger seat. She looked over at him and the car slowed to a crawl.

Bob felt like he had lead in his legs and he forced himself to put one foot in front of the other.

He spied another child, a girl.

The policeman seemed to be frowning.

Bob bent down in front of the girl and her father. He waved at her and extended an arm of friendship, within it, a bright red lollipop. The child charged forward and took the prize.

There were no alarms, no hysterical staff rushing from the branch and no dead bodies lying on the pavement. The policewoman smiled at the clown, turned to her colleague and the car sped up and drove on by.

After befriending several children, Bob reached the top of the busy thoroughfare. He looked up at the last CCTV camera and turned the corner toward the park. He was now out of sight of prying electronic eyes and hurried toward the public toilets, resisting the urge to tear off the mask.

He edged around the door, to his profound relief they were empty. As he had expected, the general public tended not to use them during the day, when more pleasant facilities were on offer at the various pubs and shops on the high street.

The stench of ammonia took Bob's breath away as he pulled off the mask.

He entered the lone cubicle and pulled off the wig. Next he took off the tracksuit, gloves and oversized shoes. Then he pulled a paper bag out of the holdall and stuffed the mask, wig, gloves, tracksuit, plastic gun and those oversized shoes into it.

He pulled his gym bag out of the holdall, took his black brogues out of it, put them on and laced them up. He paused for a moment as he caught sight of the money inside. The enormity of his crime hit him as he began to make a rough calculation of his treasure. Each bundle held a hundred notes. The fifties would therefore contain five thousand and the twenties two thousand. There were over a hundred bundles packed tightly into the bag. He tried to count it up, but gave up, unable to concentrate.

He fell on to the toilet seat and couldn't move for what seemed like an eternity. He forced himself to get up. The lead was back in his legs.

He took six bundles of fifties out of the holdall and put them in the gym bag along with his workout clothes. He wouldn't touch the rest of the money for at least a year. He zipped up the bag and walked out into the sunshine as Bob Heggie, banker, suited up and ready for another dreary day at the office.

He checked his watch. It had taken him just over ten minutes to complete the raid and to change his appearance. Now he needed to make his way down to the station and be back in Mackenzie's office by 9:00. He went via the park avoiding the CCTV cameras.

As he neared the station he crossed the road to the building site, where they were refurbishing a large hotel. As always, at this time of the morning a large fire was burning, incinerating the rubbish from the previous day's toil. A few builders stood around, talking, laughing, some smoking, trying to prolong the start of the working day just a bit longer.

He dropped the carrier bag into the heart of the fire. The bag burst into flames, revealing the clothing and the gun. After a few seconds the nylon tracksuit was afire and right after the plastic cap gun began to lose its shape before igniting.

The temptation to hang around and watch the evidence disappear was great, but he didn't have time, so he hurried toward the station. The Victorian facade peered across the city, the grand clock accurate to the minute. He looked high above it to the lone camera covering the street. It was trained on the entrance.

He was in a hurry and the bag was getting heavy. But he waited until the camera turned away from the entrance, then he darted across the concourse to the left luggage enclosure. It was busy, yet designed for privacy. He moved through the narrow channels. A young girl was struggling with an over-sized rucksack, hardly able to lift it from the floor. On another day he would have helped her. Not today.

He made his way down the last alley and found a locker. He looked around, no one was watching, why should they? He pulled open the steel door, tried to cram the bag into the tight space. It was too big. Too much money, too heavy, too greedy, but he persevered, using the leverage of the door to push it in. He barely managed to turn the key and breathed a sigh as he eased it from the lock.

He turned and fell back against the locker and smiled.

He'd done it.

He allowed himself a few seconds of self-satisfaction. He must have looked a strange sight, grinning away for no apparent reason, but no one knew what he knew. The masses of travellers and commuters had no idea what had happened today. They knew nothing about the respectable bank manager turned criminal and what he had done. And they didn't know, couldn't know, what was behind the door of locker twenty-eight.

The town carried on as normal, preparing for the beginning of a new day. Shops and offices were beginning to open, the wheels of commerce beginning to turn. Everyone was going about his or her daily routine. They didn't know of the bank robbery that had taken place this morning.

Not yet anyway.

He concentrated on being calm, then went in search of Old Tom. He made a point of talking to him for a minute, telling him he had been to the gym, but forgotten to collect his usual morning paper. Then he left the station, making sure the camera caught him this time, minus a few hundred thousand pounds of course. He almost felt like giving the camera a little wave just for the hell of it.

It was 8:55. A quick walk would get him into Mackenzie's office just after nine.

He got to the bank as the first customers of the day walked in. He mingled with them, the CCTV camera moved around and focused on the counter staff, he seized the moment and hurried across the banking hall and ran up the back stairs to his office.

He grabbed a message pad from his desk and headed for Mackenzie's office. As usual he knocked and walked in. He gasped at the scene before him and for once he wasn't acting.

Mackenzie was sitting at his desk, sans trousers, his thin white legs shaking. He seemed to be in shock and two of the older female cashiers were fussing around him like mother hens.

"What's going on here." Bob asked.

"I thought I was dead, Bob." Mackenzie sniffed, apparently unconcerned at his current state of undignified undress. He picked up the letter Bob had filed for him several weeks earlier. "Didn't read it properly, Bob, just skipped over it as usual, thought the raid was for real, thought my number was up."

"But what happened, sir." Bob began to act once again. "It was just a training exercise, what went wrong?"

"A robbery, Bob, that's what went wrong, a bloody robbery didn't you see it?"

"No, sir, I didn't, must have been when I nipped out for my newspaper."

Jim Moody pulled Bob out of the room and told him

what had happened. Bob listened, gasping with pretend shock.

"Pissed himself with fright," Jim said.

"You're kidding." Bob tried not to laugh as he saw Jim's mouth curl into a grin.

"No, I'm not. Poor man is going to be the butt of a thousand jokes."

"I better get back in there," Bob said.

"Here, look at this." Mackenzie thrust his copy of the letter at Bob as soon as he walked back in the door. "You knew all about it, I suppose?" Mackenzie said.

"Why, of course, sir, and I assumed you did as well." He went on, "Don't you remember? I even handed it to you personally and suggested you read it carefully."

"Yes, yes, of course I do, but you know how it is when you're busy, you just skim over things." He looked like he was making a conscious effort to regain his dignity, difficult under the circumstances.

Bob stayed with him as the rest of the staff drifted away. Jim Moody was the last to leave.

"Mrs. Mackenzie is on her way with a clean suit," Jim said and he turned to leave the room. "She should be here soon." He left and Bob was alone with his boss.

"A meeting, Bob," Mackenzie said, "we need a meeting with the staff." He wiped his brow. "Today, as soon as possible. I don't want the bastards to leak any of this. I'll be a bloody laughing stock." The man had gained enough equanimity to be arrogant and selfish once again.

"Yes, sir, a meeting. That's a good idea," Bob said.

"I'm talking instant dismissal for gross misconduct, don't leave them under any illusions, Bob."

"No illusions, sir." Bob wondered whether Mackenzie

could face the staff again. He had to be embarrassed. This was probably the worst day of his life. It was bad enough the staff witnessing the bladder emptying occurrence, but they must also realize now that he had been negligent in not reading the head office circular. He was Mr. Efficient, Mr. Meticulous, Mr. Particular, the man at the top and apparently the only person in the branch to have screwed up. He'd disciplined and ostracized staff members for far less, how could he look at them again?

Vicky came in without knocking just as Bob was about to leave the room, breezing past him with a clean suit in hand.

"What happened?" she asked. "They wouldn't tell me on the phone, just said I had to bring a suit in."

"You tell her, Bob," Mackenzie said. "I can't talk about it yet."

Vicky looked over to Bob and he told her what had happened. He explained about the circular from head office and the mock bank raid. He went on to tell her about Mackenzie's embarrassment.

Vicky was speechless for once. Did Bob detect a wry smile? Was she as sympathetic as she appeared?

Mackenzie got up and made his way over to the stock room with the clean suit, closing the door behind him and Bob made his excuses and left the office. He needed to get out of the bank. He need some fresh air. He needed to walk and think. He made more excuses, said he was going for an early lunch. Then he headed for the park, where he wandered in a bit of a daze.

He reflected on the morning and his temporary career as a bank robber. He was pleased with his performance. The Jack of Hearts would be proud. He'd carried out his the plan, had acted cool when the job had gone wrong and resisted the urge to run down the street in a panic afterward. He was particularly pleased with his acting in Mackenzie's office and was surprised at how easy it had all been.

He'd done it.

He'd robbed the bank.

There was no turning back now.

He had the chance to start a new life, the chance to leave the bank forever. But he knew there was still much to be done. The money in his sports bag had to be hidden. The rest of the money had to be laundered and turned into clean money. He prepared to undergo hostile police interviews and a severe grilling from his employers. He was under no illusions, he knew a decent investigator would come up with the name Bob Heggie sooner or later, probably sooner.

He needed to keep calm. He had to keep up the act during these sessions and be on his guard not to give anything away. He was confident they would discover nothing. Every track had been covered. After he had survived the questioning, he would need to time his resignation, so as not too arouse further suspicion. Then after all that had been achieved, he could plan the rest of his new life in the sun.

He felt satisfied and confident as he made his way toward the Grapes. He felt like a drink, either as a calming influence or perhaps even celebratory. He walked in and looked over at Tom's usual table. He was laughing and joking with his pals. They were the picture of contentment and Bob walked over to them. Old Tom noticed him first, welcomed him and insisted on buying him a drink.

"A large whisky," Bob said.

Tom looked a little surprised, but made his way to the bar. Bob sat with Jackie and Peter and Tom joined them a few minutes later. They seemed pleased to have Bob in their company. He couldn't imagine too many bank managers joining them on their lunchtime soiree. They must have looked a strange sight to the other drinkers. Bob dressed in a business suit, his three companions one-step away from tramps.

The boys were on top form, especially Peter. Bob had never met anyone who laughed longer and harder at the slightest thing and his joviality was infectious. Bob's anxiety seemed to drift away and when he left the Grapes he felt he was ready to face the situation at the bank.

By the time he got back, Mackenzie had gathered some of his composure.

"I've called a meeting for 3:00. You can take it. You understand, I can't be there." He was still embarrassed and for a brief instant Bob pitied him. The moment passed as soon as Mackenzie opened his mouth again. "Leave them under no illusions, Bob. If any of this gets out, either to head office, their families or the general public, I'll have their guts for garters. They can kiss their careers goodbye and I'll make their lives hell, that's a promise."

The bitterness in the man had surfaced once again.

At 3:00 Bob made his way to the staff lunchroom and walked in on the assembled group. It was noisy and there was only one topic of conversation.

"Mr. Mackenzie won't be joining us," Bob started. "He's had a real fright and sends his apologies. I think he's in a temporary state of shock."

"What's up, Bob?" Gordon, the would-be hero said,

"away shopping for some incontinence knickers is he?" He burst out laughing along with a few of the staff. The more senior managers and elderly members of staff didn't join in.

"First of all, Gordon," Bob said, glaring at him, "since you have drawn attention to yourself, I want to see you in my office immediately after this meeting. By all accounts your actions during the exercise brought this all about. You were stupid and foolish. Had this exercise been the real thing you would have put everybody in danger.

"Secondly," Bob continued, "the point of this meeting is to inform you all of the consequences of bringing into disrepute the character of a senior director. Mr. Mackenzie has promised disciplinary action for anyone caught disclosing this incident to anyone. I also want to remind you of the contents of your letter received prior to the exercise. I cannot emphasize how serious this is."

"When will we get the money back?" Jenny MacPartland, the head cashier asked toward the end of the meeting.

"What do you mean?" Bob switched into drama mode once again.

"He took the money. About a half million quid, Claire reckons."

"Took the money?" Bob repeated, trying to look puzzled.

"A half million, we think," Hannah said and Bob had to resist smiling at her.

He looked around at the others in the room, acting out his astonishment. It was plain everyone in the room knew the money had been taken. Good old Gordon interrupted and remarked on exactly what Bob wanted to say.

"Probably just to make it a little more realistic, right Bob?"

"You're probably right, Gordon. I wouldn't worry too much about the money. I expect we should have it back by the end of the afternoon."

The meeting finished, the staff made their way to their various locations within the bank and Jenny seemed half convinced the missing funds would be replaced. Bob had a further word with her and suggested she make a note in the ledger book, just in case the funds didn't materialize immediately.

Bob went back to Mackenzie's office and told him what had come out during the meeting. He wandered through to his own office to deliver a bollicking to Gordon, who was waiting for him. He went over the top again, warning him about making his mouth go inside and outside of the bank. For the first time in his management career he swore at a member of staff junior to him. He reminded him again they were talking instant dismissal.

Gordon stood without a word, nodding his head like a schoolboy in front of the head master. Afterward he would go downstairs to his peers and over dramatize Bob's words. They would sympathize with him and hopefully keep quiet for a few days.

Jenny informed Bob at 5:00 that the money hadn't arrived. He told Mackenzie and not long after left for the evening.

He spent the train ride home mulling over the day, but toward the end of the journey he allowed himself the luxury of thinking ahead. He thought of Cheltenham, the horse racing and a little break. And, of course, he gave more than a thought or two to Spain.

The next day he continued with his performance. He telephoned downstairs several times to enquire whether the cash had arrived. Each time he made a point of visiting Mackenzie to tell him.

By now the branch staff were beginning to suspect that maybe it hadn't been a training exercise after all. He called another meeting after the branch closed.

He made them aware of the suspicions, but drew their attention to the head office circular. The circular that notified them to expect a debrief. They were puzzled and on edge, twitchy, uneasy, they asked Bob question after question and he answered them carefully, trying to look as confused as they were.

He went on to explain the debrief. He suggested it would be sooner rather than later, but possibly might not happen until next week.

Of course there would never be a debrief. No one would call. No one would arrive. No meetings, no evaluation, no money. The shit would hit the fan next week. Too bad Bob's vacation leave started Friday after work. No Saturday morning for him this week. No putting up with Mackenzie and his problems or the bank's problems either, because, just by coincidence, Bob was going to be far away in Cheltenham.

CHAPTER TWELVE

THE FOLLOWING DAY, Friday, the branch ran out of money.

A customer couldn't believe what he was hearing when the cashier told him the bank had no cash.

"But this is a bank for Christ's sake!" he exclaimed.

Bob intervened and took him to one side. He explained the cash van had unfortunately broken down and there was nothing the cashiers could do about it. A little later the cash machine outside ran out. The staff put notices on the door, informing customers that because of a technical problem the bank was unable to dispense cash. He kept all this from Mackenzie until the last possible minute. He dropped the bombshell just before 5:00.

"I think you should ring head office, sir."

"It's a bit late now. Everyone will have gone home."

Absolutely correct, Bob thought. Mackenzie didn't want to make the call and Bob felt sure he would hold it over till after the weekend. He helped him to make his decision.

"I suppose first thing Monday would be okay, sir. We can't do anything over the weekend anyway."

"What a fucking mess." It was the first time Bob had heard Mackenzie use the word and at that moment he knew the man suspected there was more to this than a training exercise gone wrong.

"It'll probably come out okay, I wouldn't worry," Bob lied.

"No, I don't think so. Something isn't right." Mackenzie's color drained from his face for the second time that day. He sighed and rose to his feet. "I need a drink."

"No harm in that, sir."

"And a shoulder to cry on, if you'll join me?"

"Yeah, I think I could use one." Bob, although surprised at Mackenzie's invite, had agreed because he knew it would delay that call to head office.

They were last to leave the branch and Bob led Mackenzie to the Grapes. Bob chose the venue, explaining that it was next to the station. He saw straightaway that his three friends weren't there. Probably just as well.

"Two whiskies," Mackenzie demanded of the barman, a little less politely than Bob would have liked.

The barman gave a look of disapproval, but nevertheless brought the order across to them. Bob sat with his colleague and waited for him to speak.

"Two years till I retire. Two years and now something like this has to happen."

"Something like what, sir?" Bob said.

"The money for God's sake." Mackenzie peered over his glasses, looked at Bob as if he were something scraped off his shoe. "The money, it's gone, disappeared, vanished."

Although Bob knew the words were coming, the sound of them took his breath away and he struggled momentarily for something to say.

"I think you're overreacting, sir. The money will probably be there first thing Monday morning."

Mackenzie looked long and hard at his whisky, then took a drink. He swallowed deep and it seemed to react painfully as the harsh blend hit his throat. He opened his mouth and Bob smelled the peaty fragrance as he spoke.

"You're missing the big picture, Bob. This wasn't a training exercise." His words shocked Bob once more. He had to give the man credit.

"You've lost me, sir."

"I've worked in the bank for nearly forty years." He took another drink. "Half a million pounds doesn't just disappear during a training exercise. We've been stitched up. I don't know how they've done it, but we've been stitched up good."

"Don't be daft." Bob laughed, doing the best he could to seem surprised. "You're talking bloody shit now. You need another drink." Bob got up before he had a chance to decline, went to the bar and ordered two large whiskies.

"It was that circular," Mackenzie said when Bob got back, "the one I didn't read. If I'd read it, I would have made tentative inquiries at head office. Then they would have been rumbled."

"They, who are they, sir?" Bob said. "It was just a training exercise."

"It was no training exercise." He looked at Bob as if he should know the truth of his words. "No training exercise."

"I still think you're wrong, Mr. Mackenzie. Everything will be okay on Monday. I'm sure of it." Bob worked hard on him, plying him with more whisky, trying to convince him he was wrong. After two more large ones and Bob's constant onslaught, he began to doubt his own theory, even though he was right.

"It's just too clever and too simple for anyone to think of." Mackenzie was slurring his words, "A dodgy circular and everyone stands back and lets them get on with it." He sighed and reached for his glass. "But maybe you're right. Maybe I am overreacting."

By the time Bob left him, Mackenzie had seemed almost convinced everything would be okay on Monday morning. But Bob would bet that he'd torture himself all weekend. When he sobered up and eventually made the call, his worst nightmare would be confirmed and he would look to his right hand man for support.

But Bob Heggie wouldn't be there.

* * *

Bob got home an hour later, collapsed into a kitchen chair with a sigh and mentally went over each stage of his operation, racking his brain, trying to think of something he may have been careless with, but he couldn't think of anything. He drifted off to bed well after midnight and fell straight to sleep.

He left the house just after 6:30 the next day. It was a brisk spring morning and the dogs were eager to go. He picked up his rucksack, containing several bacon sandwiches, a flask of tea and thirty thousand pounds in stolen money.

He made his way down the lane, across the common and within the hour was deep into the heart of the deserted moorland. The wind had increased, with little to break its path. It was unpleasant terrain, wild, uninhabited, bleak and marshy underfoot. Even the wildlife was scarce, no deer, no fox, no rabbit, just an occasional bird blown off course.

He had chosen the spot well. This wasn't a route favored by the hikers and hill walkers and especially not for the Sunday strolling brigade. The only creatures who enjoyed this harsh environment were dogs and an occasional sheep.

He went toward a small cluster of trees and the dogs followed close behind. He searched deep within for the tree he had earmarked on an earlier visit. The dogs looked on in bewilderment as he started to climb. Hamish began to bark after a minute or two and Bob shouted at him to be quiet. The dog obeyed. Up in among the branches he pulled the rucksack from behind his back, opened it and put the sealed plastic bag inside a natural crevice in the heart of the tree. He jumped down and made his way back across the desolate moor.

The money would only be there for a few days, but Bob felt more comfortable now that it was out of the house.

Later that evening he sat alone watching television. He was tuned into the football, but his mind focused on only one thing, the raid. The game was just not exciting enough to take his mind off it. As he began to go over his walk to the station the telephone rang. He sensed before he lifted the receiver that it was Hannah.

"Fancy a bite to eat? I've been stood up."

"Where are you?" Bob pictured Hannah sitting alone in a restaurant.

"The Ridley Arms, that's why I thought of you, it's only a ten minute walk from your house."

"Give me twenty and I'll be there." He could think of some very good reasons why he shouldn't spend the evening with Hannah, after all she would only want to talk about one thing. But the lure of a night with her was too great.

"Fantastic, see you when you get here."

Bob took a fast shower, then pulled on a pair of beige chinos and a loose fitting plain white shirt. He layered the usual styling wax through his hair, but instead of flattening it in the style of a middle aged banker, he ruffled it up a little and dispensed with the parting. He pulled deck shoes on, was about to start his walk to the Ridley, when he had a better idea. He beat a fast track back into the house, grabbed his black leather jacket and headed back out again. He would take the bike.

"Seventeen minutes, I'm very impressed." Hannah said as he approached her at the bar. "You must walk very fast."

"I didn't walk," he said.

"Then you must have a fast car," she said, eyeing the jacket.

"Motorcycle."

"Really?" She kissed him on the cheek. "A Harley, I

suppose."

"Actually, yes." He felt his face flush. She was beautiful and he couldn't take his eyes of her claret red lips.

"Sort of like the one you chased that purse snatcher with?"

"Sort of, but enough about that. I'm wondering what sort of crazy guy would stand you up?"

"Oh, I'm sorry," Hannah laughed, "you thought it was a date. No, it's just one of the girls stuck in the middle of traffic somewhere in Yorkshire."

"I did think it was date. I guess I'm glad it's not." He smiled and deep inside his heart fluttered as a waitress came and showed them to a table.

Hannah reached across the table, gave his hand a quick squeeze that seemed to set his body tingling. What the heck is happening to me? Be cool, he told himself. But he couldn't. He felt like a teenager on his first date.

"You look different tonight," she said.

"I was thinking the same about you, you look nice." Nice, was that all he could come up with? He felt like an idiot.

"Thanks." See seemed to be blushing, maybe nice had been the right thing to say, after all.

"That jacket makes you look sort of mysterious." Hannah leaned across the table and Bob smelled the sweet taste of her breath as she spoke.

"Oh, I forgot about it." He couldn't believe himself, he was wearing the jacket in the restaurant, at the table. He wasn't a kid trying to act defiant. What he was, was out of his depth with this girl. He pulled the jacket off.

During the meal the bank robbery came up several times. Bob kept guard and was careful not to seem too interested, but finally he had to put a stop to it.

"But the money's gone!" she said. "It's disappeared. Where do you think it is?"

"I'm sure it'll be back first thing Monday morning." He sighed, tried to make it look like he was bored with the whole thing. "Head office has their reasons for doing things the way they do. It's true that more often than not I can't figure them out and I think it's kind of dumb, this whole business with the fake robbery and all, but they don't consult me and I don't give them advice." He sighed again. "I'd just rather not talk about the bank. I don't like it when I'm there and when I'm not, I'd just as soon not think about it."

"Point taken." She nodded in understanding

"I'll get the bill. We can have coffee back at mine." He cringed as the words came out. He expected a reaction, a rebuff or an excuse.

"Sounds good." She gave him an appealing smile. He could almost swear her eyes were twinkling. "I could use a good cup of coffee."

But Bob didn't want coffee. His head was full of distant memories from a bygone age. He was the awkward eighteen year old, trying to make the first move on his girl. He felt so clumsy, so awkward.

* * *

Hannah smiled to herself as they made their way out of the restaurant. She hadn't been stood up by a friend stuck in traffic. She'd made it up. She felt a bit naughty, but she couldn't get Bob out of her mind, ever since that kiss at his place. He was all wrong for her, she knew that. But she couldn't help herself.

"Damn." She stopped suddenly as she walked into the car park. "I don't have a helmet."

Bob went to the bike. His helmet was hanging from the handle bars. He took it off, for a second she thought he was going to offer it to her, but instead he looked around, like a gangster making sure the coast was clear. Then with a great underhanded swing, he tossed it into the air. She watched as it arced up, backlit by the star filled sky, and she kept her eyes on it till it landed in a field adjacent to the car park.

"Now I don't have one either."

"We could get in trouble?"

"You didn't say that the last time you climbed on the back of a bike I was riding."

"I wasn't thinking back them. I'm thinking now. It's against the law." The last thing she wanted was to be cited by the police.

"Haven't you ever felt like breaking the law, just a little?"

"Not really, no."

"What are they gonna do, lock us up and throw away the key?"

"No." She thought for a second. This was a side of him she'd never seen. And for some reason it made him seem even more attractive. What was wrong with her? "But, I'm not dressed for this."

"You can wear my jacket."

"My skirt will be flying in the breeze."

"Are you wearing knickers?"

"Bob?" She laughed. "Of course."

"Then you won't be showing too much." Now he laughed. "Besides it's dark."

"Bob?" She laughed some more.

"You're repeating yourself." He offered her the jacket.

"Okay, you win." She took it and felt a delicious shiver shimmy up her legs as she thought about what she was going to do, wanted to do when she got to his house. Bob started the bike and she shivered even more at the rumbling noise. I'm gonna be frozen, deaf and dead before we ever get there. She hitched up her skirt, threw a leg over the back of the huge machine.

She moved her hands around his waist, pulled herself into his back. The closeness aroused her and the sound and smell of the engine heightened her excitement further.

Bob eased the bike out of the car park and immediately she felt the wind whip past her face. She smiled as she caught his gaze in the mirror. He winked and she nodded her approval. Bob navigated through the village, obeying the speed limit, but kicked through the gears as he hit the open road. The wind picked up, drowning out the noise of the exhausts. She tightened her grip around him, gripped his thighs with her own. She sneaked a wicked thought as her pubic bone made contact with the back of his belt. She resisted the urge to move any further. All of a sudden the bike lurched to the left and she thrust herself upward fighting the gravitational pull. Bob eased off the gas and turned around.

"Don't fight it. You won't fall off."

She knew what he meant and concentrated as he leaned into the next bend, watching in horror as the ground came nearer and nearer to her face, but to her relief the bike gripped the tarmac steadfast and he sped up as he straightened up onto a long open road. By the third or fourth corner her confidence increased and she rode pillion like she'd done it all her life.

She closed her eyes as the wind speed increased and imagined a long ride up into Scotland or across to the Lakes on a warm day. It would be hot and sweaty, with the smells of leather and dirt. Then a hotel room on the edge of a loch as they stand to face each other. A long lingering kiss as he eases her from her clothes. They fall where they lay and she makes no attempt to pick them up. Bob falls to his knees as he eases her panties to the floor. She puts a hand on his shoulder as she steps out of them. She is naked and vulnerable.

His head moves forward and she tingles all over as his lips brush her thighs. A long deliberate movement with his tongue and she grips the back of his head. He guides her backward and her legs buckle as she falls onto the bed. Her legs ease open voluntarily as she feels his hot breath. His tongue thrusts forward, locates her clitoris. He laps at her with deliberate movements as every nerve ending in her body begs release. Harder and quicker he continues bringing her to the point of no return. She grips the brass headrest as she feels the familiar journey beginning deep inside. He pushes her hips down into the bed, preventing further movement as she trembles. A low murmur escapes her lips, then a muffled scream as she begins her orgasmic voyage. He doesn't stop until her body stiffens then relaxes.

"You can open your eyes now, we're here."

She heard dogs barking.

* * *

The dogs were howling as he pulled up the drive and Bob was immediately on guard. They would normally sit silent behind the kitchen door awaiting his return. Not tonight.

"Something's wrong," he said

"How do you know?"

"The dogs, they're barking."

"Aren't they supposed to?"

Bob moved toward the back door. As he opened it the dogs ran out into the cold night air barking, howling, searching, their breath bellowing upward like steam trains on a wayward mission. Bob hurried on inside.

The kitchen seemed normal as he scanned the room. He hurried toward the door leading to the hallway, picking up a heavy cast iron pan enroute. He raised it level with his shoulder. Hannah stood in the outside doorway.

"What is it?" she said.

He held up a hand to quiet her. He looked at the door. The dogs had been at it, had scraped paint from it. The poor guys had been locked in the kitchen, but they'd done their best to try and get through the door, to get at somebody who had been in the house.

He opened the door, stood in horror unable to move. He was conscious of Hannah holding his hand in silence.

"The bastards," was all he could think to say. It was as if a mini tornado had raged through the house. He went through to the lounge as if reluctant to survey the damage. Every drawer and cupboard had been ransacked. The floor was covered in paper, books and items worthless to anyone else, but so personal to Bob. They were strewn everywhere. Every glass framed photograph Bob possessed was scattered over the floor, smashed and broken beyond repair.

He picked up the first school photograph of the children. A glass spider web distorted the image of their smiling faces and Bob felt a rage building. Upstairs had been trashed as well, but he couldn't pinpoint anything that had actually gone missing. Televisions, CD players, his PowerBook, all were where they'd been prior to his night out. He went from room to room and, as he came back downstairs, he saw Hannah punching 999.

"Police please, I'd like to report a burglary," he heard her say.

He looked on as she gave the details and directions to the house. The police arrived within minutes. They suspected kids, possibly seeking drug money, instant cash for an instant fix.

"Then they're out of luck," Bob explained to one of the policeman. "I don't keep any cash in the house."

"That's probably why they've trashed the place," the policeman said as his partner was carrying out the fingerprint exercise.

Bob turned to Hannah.

"I'll ring you a taxi, these guys might take a while."

"Perhaps another time?" Hannah shrugged her shoulders.

"Yeah, I'll call you."

The taxi arrived soon after and not long after that the police left and Bob was alone with his thoughts once again. He felt violated as he climbed the stairs to his bedroom, but on the bright side, he thought that stashing the cash in that tree out in the moor had turned out to have been a pretty good idea.

CHAPTER THIRTEEN

BOB GOT UP EARLY on Monday morning and cursed his luck when he heard the rain hammering against the windowpanes. It was relentless and before he reached the tree where he'd hidden the money he was soaked.

The dogs watched again as he climbed the tree to retrieved his ill gotten gains. Back home he climbed into the shower and turned up the hot water so that it was just about bearable. He groaned as his blood began to circulate again and his bones began to thaw. He would have liked a long shower, but he had a train to catch, so he got out, dried off, then went through the hall toward the bedroom.

He caught sight of the cracked spider's web picture of the children. He'd carried it up to his bedroom the night of the break in and kept it there since. He hated being a part time father.

He pushed the feelings from his head, picked up his suitcase, threw it on the bed. He selected his clothes, studying each item as he pulled it from the wardrobe. No jeans and running shoes this week.

The taxi driver knocked on the door a little before noon and Bob picked up his luggage. He hesitated in the doorway for a second, sighed, then closed the door and got in the cab. Twenty minutes later he joined the crowd at Newcastle Central Station awaiting the 12:43 to Bristol Templemeads via Cheltenham. He regretted his choice of jacket as he stood on the cold exposed platform. The wind was getting into every nook and cranny and he wished he was back in that comforting hot shower. He looked up to the station clock as the tannoy kicked in and announced the arrival of his train.

He found his carriage next to the restaurant car and settled in. He picked up the complimentary paper, scanned the back pages. A sharp blast on the guard's whistle and the train gave a jolt, lurching forward. It picked up speed as it left the station and pulled onto the old Victorian railway bridge that spanned the river.

Bob looked out of the window as the train rolled along, watching as the industrial landscape changed. The train left Durham station and he decided it was time for lunch. Times had changed on Great North Eastern Railways. No longer was lunch a near death experience on the National rail network, instead they'd made a real effort with the on board restaurant and Bob had enjoyed several pleasant experiences aboard the train over the last few years. He would choose a decent bottle of wine, his only one this week, he vowed, and stretch three courses out for at least half the journey.

A pleasant looking woman with deep sea green eyes greeted him at the entrance of the restaurant car. She looked more like a stewardess from a bygone era, with her smart, deep red corporate uniform and the pill box hat she was wearing.

"Lunch?" She smiled.

"Please."

"I'm afraid you'll have to share a table, sir. We're very busy today. Is that okay?"

No, it wasn't okay, Bob wanted to tell her. He wanted privacy, a table by the window, where he could read the racing post and watch the rolling countryside pass by, enjoying his glass of wine in silence, alone. He wanted to daydream as he passed the cities en-route and fantasize about the future. He couldn't do that sitting opposite a total stranger, forced into uncomfortable mind numbing pleasantries. Then his thoughts changed tack, what if it was a nice young lady, also on her own. Maybe pretty, maybe looking for some company, maybe looking for someone to show her around Cheltenham prior to meeting her friends the following day. A pretty woman, now that would add to the adventure.

"I wouldn't mind some company," he said.

"Then follow me." She led Bob to the far end of the carriage. "I hope you'll enjoy your lunch, sir."

Bob sat down and looked into the rusty brown eyes of his lunch partner. His fantasy adventure girl had been switched somewhere along the line into a balding, dour looking gentleman, who saluted Bob with a glass of whisky.

"Kevin Kelly's the name, pleased to meet you. That is, if you like whisky and the ponies. Otherwise, I guess I'm not so pleased. So which is it, am I pleased or not?"

"Irish," Bob said, "from your accent. And I assume that's good Irish whisky in your glass." Bob smiled, offered his hand. "I suppose you're going to be half pleased, or half not pleased, depending on your point of view. I love the ponies, but it's a bit early for me to start in on the whisky. It'll be red wine for me, I'm afraid."

"Cheltenham perhaps?" The Irishman took Bob's hand with raised eyebrows.

"Name's Bob Heggie and yes, I'm on my way to the races."

"Grand, Bob, just grand. It's a pilgrimage you understand, been going for twenty years now, meet up with friends from the old country."

"I go every year myself, so I understand."

"Then I'm damned pleased to have your company, even if you aren't drinking the Irish. Just so you're drinking something, that will be fine."

Bob warmed to Kevin straightaway and his good time girl was soon forgotten. The two diners swapped story after story and Kevin came up with more hard luck stories than Bob had ever heard in such a short time. Kevin Kelly was in full flow and Bob lost count as to how many glasses of the good Irish whisky he got through.

"And last year, Bob, oh fuck that was the worst of all. Kicking King. Kicking fucking King."

Bob thought back to last year's festival.

"But Kicking King won the Gold Cup. What went wrong?"

"Everything." Kevin's eyes glazed over and Bob knew

the Irishman was going to tell him a major hard luck story about last year's races and he was on the edge of his seat. There was nothing Bob liked better than a good racing story, hard luck or not.

"Let me guess," Bob said. "You were going to bet on Kicking King, but at the last minute you picked another horse." This was the kind of story he'd heard a lot. He hoped Kevin's was better.

"No, I was going to bet on Kicking King. He's an Irish Horse, after all. Plus, he has the same initials as me and if that wasn't enough, he had the best form in the race by far and the bookies were giving four to one. Can you believe it? The best bet of the year, the best bet of the decade, a racing certainty as far as I was concerned."

Bob raised his eyebrows, signaling to the Irishman to continue.

"The drink, Bob, the bloody drink. It was forty-five minutes before the Gold Cup and I figured I had time for one more glass. You see, the Gold Cup always goes off late, doesn't it?"

Bob nodded.

"Five hundred quid I had in me sweaty little mitts, five hundred quid. I wasn't even worried when the commentator announced they were on the track, because it always goes off fifteen minutes late."

Bob pictured the scene and tried not to smile, because now he knew what was coming.

"I finished the drink and walked down onto the track, I looked at my watch 3:15 exactly and I had a nice warm feeling." Kevin took another swig from his glass. "Then it happened, the race went off on time. On bloody time! Can you believe it? Never in the history of the Gold Cup has a race gone off that quick. I ran around like a headless chicken, trying to get the bet on."

Bob wanted to laugh, but figured it wouldn't go down very well.

"Not one of the lousy bastards would take my bet, not one. Thousands of pounds I've given them over the years and not one of them would cut me a break."

"Unbelievable, Kevin, just unbelievable."

"Yeah, I knew after two furlongs he'd win. I must have been the only sober Irishman in Cheltenham that night." Kevin held up his glass. "Never mind, Bob, let's drink to this year."

"That I'll do." Bob held up his wine glass.

"To success on the track. I hope we both return with thousands in our pockets."

"From your mouth, to God's ears." Bob took a drink.

"To God's ears." Kevin drank too.

The train slowed as they neared Cheltenham and Bob and Kevin sat with their noses pressed to the window like children aboard the seaside express, dying to get in the water.

"Where are you staying, Bob?"

"The Cheltenham Park."

"Wonderful!" Kevin Kelly's eyes lit up. "I'm staying in the Dawn Run, not very far away, we can share a cab."

"Brilliant," Bob said, meaning it.

"And what's more you can join me and my friends for our traditional pre-festival card school. It's been a sort of tradition over the years."

"Oh, I don't think so, Kevin. I was hoping for an early night."

"You'll love it and I won't take no for an answer."

And as Bob looked into his new friend's eyes, he figured that he probably wouldn't.

* * *

Hannah woke on her uncle's sailboat as it rocked in its slip. The bulkheads were painted white with teak trim. The overhead was painted white as well, with brass light fixtures. She wasn't a nautical person, but the boat was plugged into the marina's power, so she didn't have to worry about running the generator, charging the batteries or any of the other chores the sailors on the other boats had been talking about for the day she'd been here.

Bob Heggie's faced flashed across her mind. She couldn't help herself. It must be love, she thought, and that made no sense, because she hardly knew the man. Still, she'd never felt this way before. What if he rejected her? She felt so insecure, but she had to take the chance.

She sat up in her berth, stretched, pushing her palms against the bulkhead. She'd been on *Windcatcher* in the past, years ago, sailing with her Aunt and Uncle, back when her parents were alive, but not since then. Though she'd been invited to use the boat whenever she wanted, she'd always begged off, but once she found out Bob was going to the races, she took her uncle up on his standing offer. The boat was docked in Portishead, less than an hour from Cheltenham. And she even managed to squeeze one of his bank's tickets to the festival out of him. Uncle Harry may have huffed, in his gruff way, saying that the tickets were for valued customers, but he was an old softy and gave up the ticket without her having to plead too much.

She got out of the berth, went into the galley, made a

cup of tea, then picked up her cell phone and started calling hotels in Cheltenham. One hour and thirty-seven calls later, she found that Bob Heggie was staying at the Cheltenham Park, but he hadn't checked in yet, wasn't due till later in the evening, as he was coming on the afternoon train from Newcastle. Now all she had to do was to figure out a way to arrange a chance encounter and let the chips fall where they may.

* * *

Bob got out of cab in front of the Cheltenham Park, smiled at the doorman as he took in the façade of the hotel. This year he was doing Cheltenham the way it was meant to be done. No more bare bones, cheap guest houses for Mr. Robert Heggie. He felt like royalty as he made his way over the black and white tiled entry way.

He had pockets full of dirty money and his sole aim was to clean up as much of it as possible, hopefully in the form of bookmaker's checks. The bookies were only too happy to distribute checks which could be entered into their loss column for the year's tax return. Cash on the other hand could be dispatched into whatever expenses were required and occasionally even missed off the return's income column altogether.

Many bookmakers also operated a client confidentiality policy and extracting information about a punter could sometimes prove very difficult. Even if a bookie did disclose the details of a big win, it would still be classed as income from a legitimate source and the source of funds would be impossible to trace.

Bob wouldn't be greedy, he thought, as he checked in. He would play the system. Betting a thousand to win five hundred wouldn't appeal to many punters, but it did to Bob. He'd set his take home target at twenty thousand, but anything over fifteen would be fine with him, because that, combined with his savings, would more or less give him twelve months income, breathing space for a year.

He took his key from the desk clerk, put his credit card back in his wallet and started for his room. A quick shower before going by the Dawn Run and meeting up with Kevin and his pals.

* * *

Hannah had been sitting in the lobby for about an hour when Bob walked in. She knew the train got in at 6:30 and that it would probably take Bob another fifteen to twenty minutes or so to get to the hotel, but she was so excited about her spying adventure, that she bought a newspaper and made her way to the hotel early.

She just about peed her pants when he walked in, almost didn't get the newspaper up in front of her face fast enough. He walked right on by without as much as a glance. He seemed preoccupied. She was riveted to her seat throughout the check in process. She couldn't have moved, even if she'd wanted to. Once that was finished, she watched as he slung what she assumed was his computer bag over his shoulder and headed toward the elevators followed by a bellman with his luggage.

Now what? Should she go running over there, stop him before he got in the elevator, or not?

Bob said something to the bellman as the elevator door opened. They went in. She got up as the doors closed.

Too late.

She could call him on the house phone. Bad idea, she rejected the thought straightaway. She needed to engineer that chance encounter, but how?

All she could do was wait.

But she didn't have to wait long, less than half an hour later Bob popped out of the elevator and started for the entrance and, Hannah assumed, the taxi rank outside. The instant he was out the door she was up and after him. She got to the entrance just in time to see him get in a cab. She hung back till the cab passed, then she hopped in the first one in line.

"Follow that cab," she said.

"You're kidding." The driver looked on the far side of sixty. A man who had been around.

"Fifty quid plus your fare says I'm not."

"Your wish is my command." He pulled away from the curb, sped up as they left the hotel grounds.

"Careful, don't get too close. I don't want him to know we're following."

"Lady, these cabs all look alike, he's not gonna know."

"Aren't you curious?" she said. "You know, about why I'm following him?" She'd had a story all planned about how he was her husband and how she suspected him of an affair.

"I make it my business to mind my own business, especially when a big tip is involved."

"Thank you," she said.

Ten minutes later Bob's cab stopped in front of a pub called the Dawn Run. Her driver parked right behind and Hannah scrunched down, afraid she might be seen. She dug in her handbag for her money as Bob went into the pub. She'd made up her mind. She was going to stroll in there after him. Where better to have a chance encounter than a pub? Even if it was over half a country away from Newcastle.

* * *

To Bob it seemed most of the pub's patrons were Irish, who had come to follow their horses over the course of the next three days. They were confident, patriotic and money seemed no object. They were for the most part working class men, who would be punting with stakes equivalent to a week's wages. Some bragged they had only come to bet on one horse for the three days and would watch the remaining races without a bet. Somehow Bob didn't believe them. They were good humored, friendly and they all enjoyed their drink.

Strangely enough, not one of them mentioned an English trained horse. Bob found this hard to comprehend. They obviously knew their horses and could tell anyone prepared to listen, the ins and outs of the form book and where their equine hero had had their last crap. However, they were totally discounting the English form book, as if it were a major crime to punt on a non-Irish horse. Bob tried to reason with them several times on the merits of certain British trained horses, but his arguments fell on deaf ears.

"Hello, Bob, over here." It was Kevin. He was with his pals from Galway and they seemed very friendly. Bob soon learned that the older men in the bunch had been coming to the festival for thirty to forty years. They welcomed Bob into their company, seeming to sense he was on his own, a little unusual for Cheltenham.

A little after 9:00 somebody produced a pack of cards

and most of the Irishmen opened their eyes wild with delight at the thought of an early gamble. They didn't bet with coin, notes only.

Bob watched as some of the more drunken race-goers were parted from their money a bit too quickly for his liking. They asked Bob to join the school, but he turned them down. He'd never liked cards.

He also observed that the more sober member of a card school more often than not ended up on top. Stupid decisions and judgments were made in drink. Bob watched a young man named Eric, a red-headed kid who had a facial tick that went wild every time he got a good hand, betting the same amount on every hand he played, oblivious to what actual cards he held. Needless to say, his friends noticed that tick and enjoyed relieving him of his money.

As Eric left the school he vowed revenge the following evening, laughing and joking to save face. Deep down he was gutted, but didn't let it show. His money for the evening was gone. It was hard to tell how much he'd lost, but certainly a lot.

"Hey, Eric," Kevin said as the young man got up to leave the table, "here." He shoved a twenty into his hand. "No more cards, drink only."

"Yeah, drink only." Eric made his way to the bar to watch the game from a distance.

Once again Kevin asked Bob to join in. He felt uncomfortable watching the entertainment from outside and agreed to take Eric's place, against his better judgment. But he told himself he was sober and he was disciplined enough to refrain from dulling his senses with drink.

The dealer, a walleyed man named Conner on the wrong side of sixty, dealt the cards and Bob watched the Irishmen betting blasé. They were getting more drunk by the minute and they were increasing their stakes. Bob adopted a very simple betting strategy, betting low on a poor hand and high on a good one. Ten and twenty pound notes piled up in front of him, but his new friends didn't seem to care. They laughed at each other's misfortune and it seemed they were doing their best to make Bob feel as if he were one of them.

There were no betting rules. Instead, a gentlemen's agreement seemed to be in place to bail out after three or four bets on the final hand. Several of them were waiting for one good run of the cards.

They were ready to pounce.

After about an hour, Connor dealt Bob a full house, Queens over Jacks. He knew no one was likely to beat it. The final betting started, leaving four people in. Kevin, Conner and a young man named Regan, who was going bald before his years, and Bob. It was Bob's call and he raised them twenty.

They all matched and he raised another twenty. Conner dropped, turning over a sad pair of fours.

Bob couldn't believe it. He had bet and lost forty quid on that?

Two left, Kevin and Regan, Bob raised them fifty. The Irishmen held their nerve and he raised them fifty again.

They began to take notice and all of a sudden the atmosphere changed. Bob could see where they were coming from. Johnny English, a stranger, sober, sensible and cash rich, taking advantage of working class Irish lads. They seemed to cool toward him, no longer joking and playing. Was it just because he wasn't playing like a drunken sod, happily losing his cash? Did they only invite him to play because they thought he'd be an easy mark?

He didn't think Kevin was that kind of sort, but then he didn't really know him.

Everyone in the pub seemed to be watching. Regan dropped out and left Bob with only Kevin in competition. Bob raised him a hundred. Kevin was sweating now and seemed stone cold sober. He was probably betting with the money he'd saved over the last year for his Cheltenham holiday and Bob's pockets were full of stolen money. They hadn't set any rules and Bob wasn't about to back down. How far would the Irishman go? Kevin matched Bob's hundred and whispered to his mates. Bob realized he had run out of money. His pals were looking at his cards and considering backing him. He obviously had a decent hand.

Bob was in a quandary and knew now his original decision not to play had been the right one. He wished he could turn back the clock. He raised another hundred and Conner started fumbling in his pockets. He gave Kevin another hundred pounds in twenties to play with and someone cut off the music from the jukebox. How far would Kevin go?

Bob said he was raising by two hundred and he could hear the inward groans of the Irishmen in the background. Regan shook his head and walked to the bar to join Eric, who had been banished from the table.

Four of them had a quiet huddle. Their voices were raised and they looked at the cards once again. In a normal school this was forbidden, but this wasn't a normal school.

Bob could see they thought Kevin had a good hand. It

was worth betting on and there was no turning back. Two were contemplating funding the bet and Conner was hesitant, apparently he was tapped out.

"He's bluffing," someone said in a loud, but deliberate whisper.

They scraped the two hundred together and the men from Galway willed Bob to lose.

Bob looked into Kevin's eyes, imagined how he must feel. If he lost this hand his holiday would be ruined. He'd have no money to bet with for the three days of the festival. Kevin's mates had backed a loser, they just didn't know it. Bob's popularity within the group had slid from top to bottom in a few seconds.

Bob thought hard about where his money had come from. If he were to raise, they couldn't match it and he'd win. But he'd have bought the pot. Somehow that didn't seem right.

"Well, that's about all I'm willing to spend, my good friend," Bob said. "What do you have?"

Once again the friendly banter and buzz returned to the table. The word had gone round the bar and it seemed everyone was watching. The backers looked on, every man from Galway still willing Bob to lose.

"You're an interesting man, Englishman." An old man, who had been watching the game through the haze of a cigarette since the beginning, said.

"Get him a drink," another said.

"I'm not drinking," Bob said

"You are tonight," the old man said and they broke out into raucous laughter. It seems they suspected he could've bought the pot and hadn't.

Within seconds Regan put a pint of Guinness and a

strong Irish whisky in front of Bob. He studied the glass, remembering his vow. The temptation was too great. He took a long swallow. He raised the whisky and took in its distinctive aroma, prior to allowing himself the luxury of a mouthful, letting it slip down his throat. He gasped. It was good.

He looked at Kevin and all of a sudden felt sorry for him. He was still sweating, still gambling with his mate's money. He would be a hero or villain in just a few seconds.

"Well, what have you got then?" Bob said.

His pals had sobered up, too. He turned over three aces and watched Bob, looking down at the cards.

"Nothing else?" Bob said.

"A four and a two."

Bob had won, without buying the pot.

"What have you got, Englishman?" Eric said.

"He's called, Bob," whispered the old man in the corner.

Bob looked at the Irishman's friends. He looked at the old man. Then he turned over the three queens.

Everyone looked at his remaining two cards, face down on the table.

Bob waited a few seconds, smiled.

"Come on, Bob," Kevin said, "what else?"

Bob shook his head

It was Kevin's turn to smile.

"You've got piss all, haven't you."

"Nothing else," Bob said, "fuck all. Congratulations on a game well played."

The bar erupted and the boys from Galway grabbed and pawed at each other as if they'd just scored the winner in injury time.

They swallowed Bob up and thrust more drinks at him. They started singing and Bob lost count of how many men hugged him. They were certainly gracious in victory and Bob wondered what their reaction might have been if he had shown them his true cards and taken their money.

Kevin came up to Bob with a large whisky.

"Get that proper Irish drink down you!" he hailed, intoxication suddenly returning to him. "I knew I had you. What a great game."

Bob's last two cards were still face down on the table. He looked at them, quickly looked away.

Kevin had seen the speed of Bob's eyes. He took the cards, turned them over. The rest of the company were too busy celebrating to notice. The Irishman looked down at the two Jacks, looked puzzled.

"I don't understand."

"Easy come easy go." Bob took the cards from Kevin's hand, turned them face down and tossed them on the table, confident no one else had seen his pair of Jacks.

"But—" Kevin said.

"Don't worry about it," Bob said, cutting him off. "No worries, really."

Bob half thought he was about to offer him the money back, but instead the Irishman offered him a grand smile.

"Attaboy is a horse you want to bet," Kevin said.

"Say again." The horse wasn't Irish, so Bob was surprised.

"One good turn deserves another. Attaboy runs stronger than his stats," Kevin said. "A lot of people are going to be surprised. Don't you be one of them." He winked, touched two fingers to his forehead, then went to join his friends.

Bob took a sip of his drink.

"Well played, Mr. Heggie, you were so close."

Bob swung around as he heard the familiar voice.

"Hannah, what are you doing here?"

CHAPTER FOURTEEN

HANNAH SMILED AT BOB HEGGIE. The moment was upon her, could she fake it well enough to convince him? She couldn't just come out and tell him her feelings. Not until she knew his.

"I was just about to ask you the same thing," she said.

"I come to the races every year. Didn't I tell you?" He looked perplexed.

"No." And he hadn't, she'd found out from Jim Moody that he was going to be on vacation and that he was going to Cheltenham.

"So, what are you doing here? Are you following me?"

"Actually, no." She sighed, here goes. "My uncle couldn't use his tickets this year, so he asked if I wanted one. I didn't really, but he threw in the offer of letting me spend a week on his boat and I couldn't refuse a free vacation, now could I? Especially since he's showing it to a potential buyer next week, so this might be my last chance to spend some time on the boat my parents loved to sail on."

"So, how did the new girl get time off? I can't see Mackenzie letting you have it just because you have a pretty smile."

"Pretty smile? You think so?"

"You're changing the subject."

"You're the one who brought up my smile." He seemed worried, or maybe he was getting irritated by her banter. "Mackenzie is afraid of my uncle."

"What?"

"That's right. My uncle and Lord Harris are golfing pals. They've known each other forever. So when Uncle Harry called Mackenzie and asked if I could have some time off to stay on his boat and go to the races, Mackenzie probably pissed himself in his desire to please."

"So if you wanted a raise, could you get it?"

"Maybe."

"How about your boss, you know me, could you get me a raise?" He was smiling. He was buying her story.

"Probably not." She laughed.

"That's too bad." He was still smiling. "Why don't we have a drink and you can tell me all about your uncle's boat."

"Why don't we just get a cab and I can show you?" She couldn't believe she'd just said that. How forward could she possibly be? She wouldn't blame him if he just walked out.

"Should I get a bottle of wine to bring along?" And still he was smiling, so maybe he didn't think she was a tramp after all.

"That won't be necessary."

By the end of the hour long cab ride she felt as if she'd known him forever. Once started, she couldn't shut him up, but truth be told, she didn't want to. She enjoyed listening to him talk. She'd already known he didn't like his job or his boss and she'd gotten a glimpse as to how much he'd loved his children, but she was surprised at how much he'd been hurt when his wife left him.

She felt a tingle of apprehension when they got to the boat. Bob paid the driver and then the cab was away, leaving them alone on the dock. It was going on midnight, the sailboats on both sides of the dock rocked in their slips. A few of them had their masthead lights on and to Hannah they looked like stars fallen from the sky, weaving and rocking just above the water.

"This way." She started down the dock.

"Big boat," he said as they approached *Windcatcher*.

"Sixty feet," she said. "It was built by an American named Charlie Morgan." She grabbed onto the shrouds, stepped up, pulled herself onto the deck.

"You did that like a pro." He did the same.

"Come on below." She led Bob through the aft companionway into the salon. "Have a seat." She pointed to the settee and he slid in behind a teak table.

"Very nice." He ran a hand across the table top. "I bet there's at least twenty coats of varnish on this."

"At least." She went to the galley, got a couple glasses. "How do you want your rum, neat, with water or with Coke?" She set a stubby bottle of dark rum on the table.

"Pampero Anaversario rum, it's Venezuelan. Uncle Harry says it's the best rum on the planet and it's the only spirit he'll allow on board, so don't even think about asking for anything else."

"I'll take it with ice, no water, no Coke."

"Your wish is my command." She served him his drink.

"Thanks." He put the glass to his nose, inhaled the flavor, took a sip. "Reminds me of a good cognac, flavor's a bit different, but very good."

"I'm glad you like it." She poured herself a glass, slid in next to him. "What should we drink to?"

"Luck tomorrow." He raised his glass.

"Luck." She tapped his glass with hers, took a drink. "Now I have to go to the head and freshen up." And get a grip on myself, she thought. She couldn't believe he was affecting her this way. She wasn't a child, so how come she felt like one?

"Head?"

"You know the bathroom. Everything on a boat has a different name. The kitchen is the galley, the walls are bulkheads, the ceiling is the overhead, the bedrooms are cabins, the living room is the salon." She pointed as she talked. "Left is port, right is starboard, the front is forward, the back is aft. So up there, she pointed forward, is the forward cabin, back there, she pointed aft, is the stately master's cabin or you could call it the aft cabin."

"I know what a head is. I was just caught off guard when you said you were going to freshen up."

"Relax," she slid out from behind the table, "I'm just going to use the toilet. I'm not going to pop back out in a revealing teddy or anything."

"I can only hope." He laughed.

"Keep wishing." She got up, hoping he didn't see the goosebumps on her arms. She was more nervous than she could ever remember being.

* * *

Alone, Bob looked around the boat. The bulkheads were painted white and accented with teak trim. There was a brass nautical clock above the settee opposite, a brass hurricane lamp hung above the sink in the galley and most nautical of all, there was a large overhead hatch above that afforded him a view of thousands of stars on this very clear night. He could hear the faint clinking of halyards against their masts and it sounded magical to him. He could well imagine the Jack of Hearts on a sailboat somewhere in the vast Pacific, battling a typhoon, face in the wind with a grin a mile wide.

"I'm back." Hannah closed the door to the forward berth and went into the galley, where she opened a cupboard and took out a pack of wooden matches. "I'm going to light the hurricane lamp." She lit it.

The moonlight shining through the hatch above made her hair shine. The defined curve of her body sped up his heartbeat. She was breathtaking. He could stare at her forever, but all of a sudden he had other things on his mind. His desire was too strong.

He got up from the table, went to her, brushed her hair from her shoulder, kissed her neck. He inhaled her perfume, afraid for a second she might reject him. Instead she dropped the match into the sink and leaned into him. He wrapped his arms around her, kissed her throat, shivering at the taste of her. She had baby smooth skin.

His desire was palpable.

He eased a thumb into the top of her dress, pulled it down just a bit and licked her collarbone. She was salty with sweat and it was delicious. He had been so long without, but his plans had put any thoughts of sex on the back burner. Well, it was on the front burner now as he was touching her, tasting her. His desire was fierce. His blood was pumping. He wanted to be gentle. He wanted to be rough. He wanted to take his time. He wanted to rip her clothes off. But most of all, he wanted her to enjoy it. He wanted it to be the best experience she'd ever had. He wanted to draw it out, to make it last.

He moved his hands to her breasts, soft and firm at the same time. He felt her nipples beneath the flimsy material of her dress. She seemed somehow delicate. He kissed her neck again and she moaned. He ran his hands down her sides, slid them over her belly, then back up to her shoulders, where he hooked his fingers into the straps of her dress and pushed them down. He licked her left shoulder, then back up to her neck again. He moved away from her neck, looked into her eyes. Her pupils were dilated.

"Are you afraid?" he said.

"No, not afraid. Nervous maybe, a little. I haven't done this in a while."

"Me neither, I'm terrified," he said.

Hannah laughed, a quiet laugh, low, almost a whispered laugh.

"You are beautiful," he said.

"Keep saying that, flattery will get you everywhere."

He put a hand to her cheek, kissed her. He parted his lips and she slid her tongue into his mouth. It was moist and hot. He tangled his fingers into her hair, held her in place as the kiss went on and on, longer than he thought possible, forever was just a word, this kiss was reality, his only reality.

He reached around, found the zipper at the back of her dress, slid it down, shivering a bit at the sound, forbidding, promising and thrilling all at the same time. What a wonderful sound, the sound of a zipper going down. He broke the kiss, wanting to see her as the dress came off.

She slipped it on down. He saw her breasts, threatening to break free from a very skimpy, black lace bra. No wonder they felt so real and fine under her dress.

"Very sexy," he whispered.

"Wait till you see the panties." She was whispering too, but she might as well have been shouting, so quiet had it become.

"Hurry." His heart was throbbing, his eyes were glued to that falling dress.

"Patience." She giggled and sighed. She sounded like a little girl as she slid the dress past her belly, down her thighs.

"Wow." He said aloud. Her panties, frilly though they may be, barely covered her pubic area. They were black like the bra and they were eye catchers. "Those are almost naughty."

"I changed into them when I used the bathroom."

"Not bathroom, head, we're on a boat remember?"

"That's right," she said, "so we'll be retiring to the fore cabin, not the bedroom," she said.

"Not just yet," he said.

In the moonlight streaming through that hatch,

reflecting off her body, she reminded him of a sculptured goddess. Her breasts, pushing against that flimsy and barely concealing bra, were the color of the cream he put in his coffee. He reached behind her, found the clasp and her breast sprang free, her nipples were small and hard. Her belly was smooth and tight, her thighs were magnets for the eyes, her legs were supple and lithe. Her panties hid hardly anything, but just enough. She was sex personified and he ached for her.

"Okay, now," he took her hand, started for the forward berth.

* * *

Bob woke with the sun, feeling better than he had in weeks. He credited the sex. It had been a long time for him. And much longer since he'd had any fun at it. He'd forgotten that it could be fun, playful.

He got out of the berth, careful not to wake Hannah and went into the galley. This was his first time on a boat, but somehow he didn't think they were all this well apportioned. Still, as nice as it was, everything seemed to be in miniature, stove, oven, sink, all smaller than he was used to, however all very functional. The stove top was gimbaled and he imagined that was so it would stay flush as the boat rolled at sea.

He figured out how to turn on the propane, found the wooden matches Hannah had used the night before and boiled water for tea. And while he waited, he thought about this new problem. He needed to launder his money and he couldn't very well do it with Hannah on his arm. And he couldn't ditch her at the races, not after last night.

He could come clean. No, that wouldn't be very smart.

She'd think he was a criminal. She might even call the cops, turn him in.

"Hey, you." Hannah came into the kitchen wearing nothing but an old tee shirt. "Do I look as bad as I feel?"

"You look great."

"Liar." She got the tea out of a cupboard. "I don't think I'm going to make it today. My head feels like it's going to explode."

Bob thought fast. This could be perfect.

"I'm meeting my Irish pals for breakfast before the races. I'd hate to stand them up." He hated lying to her, but it was the only way. "I could go for the first couple races, then come back and check on you."

"Really? That would be nice."

"Then we could do the races together on Wednesday. That's my favorite day of the Festival anyway. It's the Queen Mother Champion Chase Day, all the ladies dress up, have a good time." Bob smiled.

"What is it, what are you smiling at."

Bob moved forward and placed his hands on her slender hips.

"It could be our first proper date."

"We had dinner," she said, "that was kind of like a date."

"Okay, this could be our second date."

"All right then," she said, "a date it is." She kissed him and Bob shivered with the joy of it. She pulled him in, kept the kiss up, used a little tongue.

He broke the kiss.

"Whoa!" He gasped. "If we keep that up, I might not be meeting my pals."

She smiled.

"Seriously, I haven't got time because you coerced me onto a boat sixty miles from Cheltenham. I'll be late for the races if I don't call a cab now."

"Yeah, like you regret it." She laughed.

He looked into her eyes, wondering if he was dreaming. Her hair was messed up, she hadn't removed last night's make up and she was wearing a baggy tee shirt that didn't do her figure any favors. Yet she was irresistible. He didn't want to go to Cheltenham, didn't want to go to the races. He wanted to spend the day with her, get to know her, really know her. But that would have to wait, because he had that money to launder. It had to be done.

Bob got in the cab scheming, planning and regretting the lies he would be telling Hannah later on that evening. He told himself it was necessary if he wanted to spend the following day with her.

"Where to, sir?" the driver asked, interrupting Bob's thoughts.

"Gloucester," Bob said. It was close by. He didn't need to go all the way to Cheltenham, because he wasn't going to actually be betting on any horses, not today anyway.

Once there he wandered around the town center, bought a copy of the racing post and sat down in the Dead Horse Pub near the station.

Not really a scheme he thought to himself, just a simple little accountancy calculation. He was carrying thirty thousand pounds he needed to clean up, which he wouldn't be able to hide from Hannah, not if she was coming with him tomorrow. He could make an excuse, tell her their date was on hold for a while.

No.

He wanted her there with him, in a perverse kind of way he wanted her to be a part of his great adventure. The trouble was convincing her it was possible to win that sort of money on the typical bets of a small time bank manager. It's not as if he could tell her he'd placed a six grand bet on a four-to-one winner. Even a two grand bet on a fourteen-to-one might rouse her suspicion. No, he needed a long shot or a double or even a treble, three big prices to a fifty pound stake. That was more believable.

He dragged out two pints for two hours, then picked up his paper and made his way outside for a breath of fresh air. It was a crisp morning and the sun burned at his eyes, weakened from lack of sleep the night before.

His mobile phone vibrated in his pocket and as he focused on the display he smiled. It was Hannah.

"Hi, just wondering if you'd found your friends."

"I did, I'm with them now," he lied.

"I'll be watching for you on the tele."

"Like you'll pick me out among sixty thousand people." He laughed.

"You never know, I'll be watching anyway, but if I don't see you on the tele, I'll see you later."

Bob spent the next couple hours back in the Dead Horse watching the races on television. He made a note of the winners and the prices of the first two, a three-to-one winner and an even money favorite, not the odds he was looking for to make his fictitious win believable. It was all getting to be to much. Lies and deceit, dishonesty and now figures and odds flying round his brain, so that he could lure Hannah into his scheme, use her to help prove he won the money at the races if he had to.

His mind drifted back to the bank. He wondered what

was happening there now. He half wished he could put it all out of his head, but he couldn't. Were they trawling back through his bank records? Were they pin pointing his exact movements on the day? And, worse still, had they pieced together his visit to head office on the day the e-mail had been sent? A shiver ran up his spine, had the police been brought in? Was he now the prime suspect? Were they getting a warrant to search his home?

He smiled to himself.

They would find nothing.

A welcome relief as a sixteen-to-one winner flashed on the screen. The remaining races gave Bob odds of an eleven-to-one, a two-to-one and an eleven-to-ten favorite. He spent the next few minutes scribbling on a beer mat. Then sat back relieved at the odds returned on his pretend fifty quid treble.

Fifty pounds on a sixteen-to-one winner gave him eight hundred and fifty pounds going into the second leg, and that eight hundred and fifty on an eleven-to-one winner gave him ten thousand, two hundred pounds going onto the final horse. A two-to-one winner would give him a whopping pretend win of thirty thousand, six hundred pounds.

Near enough Bob thought, as he double checked the odds and wrote down the name of the three horses. Just a bit of good acting and a couple of bottles of champagne and he was confident he could carry it off.

However, his confidence started flying out the window as his cab approached Portishead.

"Just drop me off here." He told the driver. "I'll walk the rest of the way."

He needed a few minutes to clear his head. He needed

to remember the names of the three horses. And what names they were, they didn't exactly trip off the tongue. Gaelstrom, Bob Tisdall and Mister Mulligan. He was still getting his tongue around them as he neared the boat. Hannah was on deck, wrapped in a padded ski jacket with a steaming mug of something in her hand.

"Aren't you cold?"

"It's a bit chilly, but I was starting to feel cooped up below."

"Is that coffee or tea in that mug?"

"Coffee, want a sip?"

"Do I?" He pulled himself up, using the halyards as a hand hold.

"Here." She offered him the cup.

"Thanks." He sipped at the coffee. It was strong, just the way he liked it. However, he preferred his with a bit of cream.

"It's kind of nice out here," she said, "don't you think?"

"Yes." He took a deep breath, started in on his lies. "I've had a very lucky day." He mentally crossed his fingers. "Did you watch the races on the tele, like you said?"

"Yeah."

"Do you remember the horses, Gaelstrom, Bob Tisdall and Mister Mulligan?"

"They're kind of familiar."

He took a deep breath.

"I backed them all, a treble, a fifty pound treble."

"What does that mean, exactly?"

He raked his fingers through his hair, took another breath.

"It means I've won a lot of money."

"How much?"

"A little over thirty thousand pounds."

"On three horses?" Her eyes lit up. "How'd you do that?"

"A treble. Your fifty pounds goes onto the next horse, together with what you've won. I won eight hundred and fifty on the first horse and that went straight onto the second at eleven-to-one. By the time the third one set off, it was carrying over ten thousand of my money."

"And it won?" She seemed fascinated now.

"It sure did, though only by half a length. I was pretty nervous during that race, let me tell you. By the time it was all over, I was up by thirty thousand and all for a very lucky fifty pound bet. I can hardly wait till tomorrow."

"You won thirty thousand and you can hardly wait to get back and bet it?" She laughed. "Are you a secret gambler? Are you hooked on it?"

"Only during the Cheltenham Festival and I never allow myself to lose over a thousand pounds. I save up for it. It's sort of my mad week. Some people go to Disney World in Florida, others go on a photo safari in Kenya. Me, I go to Cheltenham."

"But what if you lose your thirty thousand pounds?"

"Actually, I don't count it as mine until the Festival is over and I'm on the train home."

"Speaking of the train home, I won't be going back to Newcastle with you. I'm staying on for another week or two, maybe longer."

"What? I don't understand."

"I told you my Uncle Harry was selling *Windcatcher* and that he wanted me to show it, remember?"

"Yes."

"Well, he wants me to stay here until it sells. If this buyer doesn't buy her, then I'm to stay until the next one does.

"That could be forever. What about your job?"

"I called Mr. Mackenzie while you were at the races and quit."

"I thought you wanted to be a banker. You seemed to have your heart set on it."

"After being around you and seeing how you feel about the job, well the shine has worn off it a bit, besides it's not like I actually need the money."

"Don't tell me you're independently wealthy."

"Let's just say I'm comfortable."

"But you are coming back?" All of a sudden he was worried this relationship was going to be cut short.

"Sure I am." She smiled. "Just not next week."

"That's good to hear." He ran a hand through her hair. "Hey, let's go to town and celebrate my winnings before I lose it all tomorrow."

"I have a better idea, let's stay in." She leaned over, kissed him.

"Yeah, that is a better idea. Let's go below."

CHAPTER FIFTEEN

"I CAN FEEL THE TENSION in your arm, you're pretty excited aren't you?" Hannah said as they entered the race course.

"I get excited every year, but not like this. I save up, allow myself a thousand pounds to bet with. I know that seems like a lot, but this week at Cheltenham is the highlight of my year. And besides, I don't usually lose, in fact I usually come home a couple hundred quid to the good. But after my good fortune yesterday, I have a whole lot of money to play with."

"But—"

"Don't say it." Bob laughed.

"Say what?"

"You were about to say that since I'm almost thirty thousand pounds ahead, maybe I should call it quits."

"Well, maybe something like that."

"I wish I could do that, but I can't. I'd rather lose it all than not play out at least one good day here." He sighed, turned to her, cupped her cheek, smiled. "Especially since this is probably the last time I'll ever come to Cheltenham."

"What? I don't understand."

"I'm a man who has been bogged down in a loveless marriage. I see that now. I have a job I loath, working for a man I loath even more. I have no hobbies, nothing to look forward to, other than the odd football game with my son. I've nothing in common with my daughter, don't understand her at all. I'm jealous of the man who took my wife, who I know I should be glad to be rid of, and the only friend I have is an old man who sells newspapers at the train station and we're not really that close. So, when I come here, for this one glorious week, I'm a somebody, a player.

"Cheltenham has been my salvation, but I don't need it anymore. Today is my farewell, but I want to go away in style. I want to remember this day that I kissed the Cheltenham Festival goodbye."

"Now I really don't understand."

"I don't know if we're going to have a relationship. If we're going to marry and raise a dozen kids or if we're ever going to see each other after today. But I know this. You saved me, brought me back from the abyss. So today, I'm going to gamble with this money too easily gained. I'm going to enjoy the races, the company of a beautiful girl and this wonderful day."

"I can't answer any of those questions right now except one. You're going to see me after today. You are definitely going to see me."

"Really?"

"Kiss me you jerk, then let's go make this a day we'll never forget."

He kissed her.

"So what do we do next?" She looked flushed, happy too.

"We go to the news agent and get a copy of the racing paper. I've studied the form of the horses for several weeks and watched most of the big races. I'm pretty confident of a good return."

He led her toward the news agent, where he studied the paper, pointing out his reasons for liking one horse and why he didn't like another. She was a willing pupil, eager to learn. After having devoured the paper, something he'd only done for Hannah's benefit, because he knew the horses like he knew the back of his hand, they headed for the course.

There was an hour to go before the first race, so they made their way to the bar, where he ordered an orange juice. No alcohol for him today. The punters were loud and raucous, none of them adhering to the same rule. Several already seemed drunk and Bob wondered how many would actually see any racing.

The commentator welcomed everyone and announced the runners for the first race. Bob explained to Hannah that he planned to start betting with roughly two thousand pounds per race, keeping a bit in reserve for the runners he really fancied. The first race had thirty runners and was a bit of a lottery. Nevertheless, he had four horses picked and would back them each way, hoping one, or even two, may just run into a place position.

The race started to a cheer from the crowd, but no one was shouting louder than Hannah. She was really enjoying herself. Bob tried to pick the colors out with his binoculars, but Hannah kept after him for the far away glasses and finally he gave up, gave them to her and listened to the commentary instead.

Disaster! One of his horses had fallen on the first circuit and hampered at least ten others. Several had been brought down and Bob groaned as the commentator announced two of his other horses had also been caught up in the melee. One had been brought down with another so far back in the field the jockey had all but given up.

"Rotten luck." Hannah squeezed his hand as the rest of the pack turned for home.

His remaining horse loomed up into second place, seemingly full of running, with the race at his mercy. Four horses had pulled away from the rest of the field and Bob felt sure of a place and maybe even a win. He started calculating his return as they approached the final fence. His horse had edged into a slight lead and took off high over the fence. It was a spectacular jump that took him a length up in mid air.

Bob watched in horror as the horse stumbled on landing, losing his momentum. The jockey ended up around the horse's neck as the other three challengers passed him. The horse began to gallop again as the jockey found the saddle. Two more horses passed him just before the line and Bob cursed his luck and tore up his ticket.

"Oh no!" Hannah said.

Not the start he wanted, but this was Cheltenham and there were plenty of races to go. However, he carried the same bad luck into the next two races and began to doubt his ability.

"Are you sure you don't want to quit?" Hannah said.

"I'm sure," Bob said. "Thing's will turn around." He smiled.

"How do you know?"

"Because I have you for luck." He kissed her.

The fourth race was a far smaller field and Bob prayed he was right about Hannah being lucky. He'd chosen the favorite and had taken a thousand each way at three-to-one. As the field made their way up the hill toward the finish, the favorite had poached a three length lead. Bob viewed the challengers, his eyes watering as he tried to pick them out without blinking, the biting cold forcing tears to his eyes. The jockeys were all hard at work. Bob's horse gradually pulled clear and in the end won without the jockey going for his whip. The crowd was deafening and the jockey saluted them as he crossed the line.

Bob felt good as he made his way with Hannah to the bookie to collect his winnings. Bob asked him for a check and the bookie was only too happy to oblige. He despatched the check into a zip pocket.

He had five thousand pounds in clean money, ready to be banked tomorrow morning and Hannah had witnessed the whole thing. Bob smiled to himself as he steered her to the bar for a celebratory orange juice. Others were celebrating too. He looked at the happy faces and longed to be part of it. He had five thousand pounds in his pocket, but it had cost him twelve thousand to get. He was a little downhearted, but oh so grateful for the one winner.

He wanted something stronger than orange juice. It felt strange not drinking at Cheltenham, despite his vow. Normally racing and drinking went hand in hand. One wouldn't hurt, he told himself.

"I'm going to have a Guinness," he said, "want one?"

"Little early for me," she said, "but sure, I'll have one too."

He ordered the drinks and cursed himself for being weak as he watched the barman pull the last bit of the thick black stout. He moved the glasses in a circle, leaving the customary shamrock in the froth of the beer. Bob was tense, because in the back of his mind he knew the shit would hit the fan soon. But as he reached the bottom of his glass, his paranoia faded a bit.

Then his cell phone vibrated. It was Jim Moody. He asked Bob if he wouldn't mind placing ten quid on Attaboy in the sixth race.

"I'm not a bookie." Bob laughed, but he took notice, because this was the second tip he'd had on that horse.

"Come on, I'm stuck here at work and all hell is breaking loose, be a sport."

"Okay, I'll make the bet." He paused. "So, what's going on?"

"The money hasn't come back."

"You're kidding?" Bob tried to sound surprised.

"No, I'm not and even worse, the place is crawling with head office directors and bank inspectors."

In a way Bob was pleased. He'd waited and agonized over this moment, had feared it and yet now that it had arrived, he felt relieved. It was out in the open. But while he had controlled the operation and felt comfortable doing so, now others were going to be pulling the strings.

"Mackenzie looks bloody awful," Jim said. "He says he hasn't slept well since the exercise, or whatever it was. He claims he knew something was up." Bob listened to the details. Jim didn't mention an inside job, nor did he mention any suspects. He wished Bob luck and asked him not to forget the bet, then hung up.

"Someone from work?" Hannah asked.

"Yeah, Jim Moody. He says the money hasn't come back."

"He called to tell you that?"

"Not specifically. He wanted me to make a bet for him."

"Oh."

Back on the racecourse, Bob was ready for another round of betting. He watched the runner's parade for the fifth race. He struck two five hundred pound bets and watched with disappointment as both runners finished down the field. By the time he and Hannah returned to the parade ring, some of the runners for the sixth race were already walking around it. The noise from the expectant crowd, the elegance of the horses walking the ring and the jockey's colorful silks made him tingle with excitement. It was what horse racing and Cheltenham were all about.

He was about to take a look at the horse he'd picked for the race, when he spied number thirteen, Attaboy. Two tips, he'd be crazy not to check out the horse. As he led Hannah over for a look, he saw the lad leading him stop to check Attaboy's hind quarters. Bob watched as the lad felt and prodded at the muscles of the thoroughbred's back leg. The lad signaled the trainer, who made his way over with a worried look. Now they were right in front of

Bob and Hannah.

"I think Attaboy's lame, Guvnor," the stable lad said. "Stiff as a board. We can't run him."

The trainer looked gutted. Months of preparation and planning wasted. He'd seen the stiffness too and agreed with the lad's analysis.

"Withdraw him. I'll let the stewards know."

Bob took Hannah by the arm, led her away.

"Can you wait here? I forgot to make that bet for Jim."

"Sure," she said. "I won't budge an inch."

Bob couldn't believe it. He had to act fast. He had accidentally stumbled on a golden opportunity to turn dirty money into clean. Backing a non-runner was a no brainer. Hand over several thousand pounds in cash and receive a bookie's check on announcement of the withdrawal. Simplicity itself.

He hurried, almost running toward the bookmakers. The horse was a big price and the first bookie refused his ten thousand pound bet. If only he knew, he would have taken the bet. Bob froze in horror as the public address system crackled into action. They would announce the withdrawal any minute. He had to hurry.

"Would the jockeys please mount for the next race."

Bob breathed a sigh of relief, but only had minutes to spare. He rushed to the next bookie showing ten to one.

"Ten thousand on Attaboy, number five please."

The bookie looked at Bob in apparent disbelief, but soon realized his serious intent as Bob pulled a bundle of pounds from his inside pocket.

"Just a second, sir."

He picked up his cell phone and punched in a number. The few seconds his colleague took to answer seemed like forever. Bob expected the PA system to kick in any second.

"Thank you, sir." He took Bob's money.

On his way back to the parade ring and Hannah, the loudspeaker clicked into action.

It had worked.

Bob felt smug and waited to hear the withdrawal, ready to return back to the bookies for his check.

"Ladies and Gentleman we have an announcement about the eighth race."

Bob smiled, saw Hannah, waved.

"Because of an injury there will be a jockey change."

Bob couldn't believe what he was hearing. No mention of a withdrawal.

He hurried toward the parade ring. The jockeys were on board their mounts. That is, everyone except the lame duck. He breathed a sigh of relief and got to within earshot of the party gathered together. A group of six assembled round the horse. The trainer, stable lad and the expectant, but disappointed looking owners. They lifted a worried looking jockey onto the horse.

"Give him one last chance," the trainer said.

Bob watched as the jockey completed a full circle of the ring.

"Just a little stiffness, but it seems to be easing. He might be okay by the time we get to the start."

"We can't run him if he's not right," the stable lad said. And he should know, Bob thought. He'd probably cared for and nurtured the horse all season.

The owners were half smiling again, clinging to a faint hope, but the trainer still looked unsure.

"Withdraw him, withdraw him," Bob muttered under his breath.

"What are you saying," Hannah said. She hadn't been paying attention.

"Nothing." He sighed. "I made Jim's bet and I think I might have made a mistake. Jim sounded so confident that I bet ten thousand on the horse."

"That's an interesting system," she said.

"Well mine hasn't been working very well." He gave her a weak smile, looked out at the jockey who seemed keen to go.

"We can always withdraw him at the start if it doesn't get any better Guv," the jockey said.

Bob listened in horror as the trainer agreed.

"Okay let him take his chance."

"Oh, now I see," Hannah said. "You bet that horse." She gave Bob a funny look. "That doesn't seem to have been very smart."

"Maybe not," he said, "but Jim seemed so sure." He hated lying to her. He felt bile creeping into his throat, choked it back down.

"Are you all right?"

"Yeah, I'm fine," he lied. "Easy come, easy go."

They went from the parade ring round to the front of the course. Then made their way to the top of the grandstand, where they could view the preliminaries at the start. Bob was still hopeful of a withdrawal.

He focused in on the runners with his binoculars. Found Attaboy's colors, studied his action, not a bit of stiffness to be seen and the horse didn't appear lame. His action was smooth and relaxed. The trainer looked at the jockey. The jockey gave the thumbs up and the starter climbed the rostrum. He lowered the binoculars in despair as the horses formed in line.

"They're off!" the commentator cried and the crowd roared.

Bob could hardly bear to look. He glanced at the selection page only to find his forced bet hadn't even made his first five. He usually assessed all the horses on the form and the race conditions. He took into account the trainer form and the horse's jumping ability. He awarded marks in each area and generally placed his money on the top two horses. All in all it was a reasonably successful system that more often than not showed a profit at the end of the race day.

The runners settled into the race and the horse he'd selected, based on his system, eased into an early lead. He thought of the sickening scenario should the horse win. Ten thousand on a horse he didn't even fancy and bugger all on a winner he did. He couldn't look and he couldn't stay any longer.

"Let's watch it in the bar," he said.

"Fine by me," Hannah said. "I could use a drink."

They made their way to the bar as the runners approached the first fence. The bar wasn't quite so busy. Most of the punters were outside, following the race live. He ordered a couple of pints, then forced himself to look at the monitor. His original selection had now taken a four length lead out of the field. By the time they turned for home, Bob had nearly finished his pint. Three fences to go and he searched for the horse carrying his money and found that it was running well. It had settled into third or fourth and was looking comfortable, much to his surprise.

"Come on, Attaboy!" Hannah said.

Bob looked back at the leader, who was now eight lengths clear. As he took off over the fence his front legs didn't leave the ground. He ploughed through the fence and even though he managed to stay on his feet, the jockey catapulted over his neck.

The crowd shrieked in horror and the favorite's backers cursed their luck. Suddenly Bob was in with a chance.

"Come on, Attaboy," Hannah said again, louder.

He kept his eyes on the screen and prayed under his breath. Attaboy was in the leading pack of four or five and looked sure of a place in the first three and he cursed his judgment for not backing the horse each way. Five thousand each way on a ten to one shot, second or third would have meant a good return.

They cleared the second last and still each horse was in with a chance as they approached the last.

"Come on, Attaboy, come on, Attaboy," Hannah chanted.

The crowd was cheering now, shouting, willing their horses to the front. Bob joined them as his horse went second. The lead jockey was hard at work with the whip. Attaboy's jockey hadn't asked the horse a question and glanced behind. The other two had dropped away and Bob shouted at the jockey to let him go. Just as he did the jockey reached for the whip and slapped the horse around his hindquarters.

Bob waited for the response, Attaboy still had two lengths to make up. He waited while the jockey slapped him again. And once more he pleaded for a reaction. And he got it, but not the one he wanted. Attaboy didn't like it and veered away from the whip, drifting across the course. The noise of the crowd was at a crescendo now as the winning post loomed close. A hundred yards to go and

Bob screamed louder, but not as loud as Hannah.

"Come on, Attaboy." Hannah was out of control.

People in the bar were looking at them, but Bob was past caring. He was watching ten thousand pounds disappear down the drain.

Suddenly the jockey stopped hitting the horse and Attaboy found a straight line once again. The jockey pumped with hands and heels and Attaboy responded. He was a length down, half a length, then a neck. The two horses flashed past the post and the angle made it impossible to select the winner.

The judge called a photograph.

Bob's heart was beating fast and he could feel perspiration on his brow. Several people were watching him as he left the bar, Hannah on his heels.

An Irishman asked him who he was on.

"The winner," Bob said as he passed.

Bob felt sure he had won. It was just something within him. He was convinced. It was meant to be. He measured the scale of his win. Ten thousand on a ten to one winner. A hundred and ten thousand returned.

The minutes passed and he began to doubt himself.

The public address system kicked in.

The judge has called for a further print.

More agony, more stress. He waited.

Hannah was biting her nails.

"I need another drink," she said.

"Me too," he said.

They made their way to the Guinness tent. It was heaving, six deep at the bar, not pushing, not shoving, patient people waiting for their glass of porter. Bob and Hannah joined them. Just as they reached the counter the judge's decision was announced.

"And the winner is—" he kept the crowd in suspense and dramatically announced, "Number Fifteen, Attaboy!"

Some race-goers leapt into the air. Some hugged each other and others tore up their tickets in despair. Two friends close to Bob shrieked with delight and barged through to the bar, promising their friends and others around them free drinks.

No shrieking from Bob. No jumping around like a lunatic. No free drinks for anyone. He waited patiently until he caught the bargirl's eye.

"Two pints of Guinness please."

She handed Bob the drinks. He passed one onto Hannah and they walked over to a half empty table. His throat was hot, sticky and a little sore from his effort during the race. He cooled it with a large gulp of the Guinness. He savored the remaining half pint and got up with a slight wobble.

He felt light-headed and out of control.

"Are you okay?" Hannah said.

"Never better." He started toward the overbearing grandstand, leading Hannah through the throng, looking for his bookmaker as he mentally thanked Kevin. Had it not been for his good fortune in meeting the Irishman on the train, and then doing him the good turn at cards, he never would have gotten that tip, never would have bet on Attaboy.

"I'm afraid it'll have to be a check, sir," the bookmaker said.

"That's fine." Bob nodded, then asked, "Can I have my stake back in cash?"

"No problem," the bookie said.

Bob held his hand out as the bookie counted ten bundles of a thousand pounds. People were taking notice and he felt uncomfortable. He took two fifty pound notes from one of the bundles and handed them back to the bookie.

"A drink for the boys," Bob said.

"Thanks, sir." He shook Bob's hand. "All the best to you now, enjoy your winnings."

Bob led Hannah away, feeling good, despite thoughts about the bank and the music he'd have to face when he got back. He still had over twenty thousand in his pockets. He couldn't go back with all that cash. Depositing that kind of money in his savings would make him their prime suspect, if he wasn't already.

The latter part of the day was turning damp, with a fine drizzle in the air. By the time they got back to the racecourse, they were cold and wet, so they took refuge in the bar and Bob was pleased to see a log fire in the center of the room. They ordered coffee and sat at a table near the fire.

He took stock. His heart told him to bet like he was made of money. His head told him not to be so greedy. He listened to his heart and checked over the racing paper, searching for an obvious favorite. One bet, twenty thousand on a sure thing.

Of course there was no such thing as a racing certainty, but the Irish banker, Running Scared, running in the last race looked good. The Irish wouldn't hear of it getting beaten. It had broken course records all season in Ireland and hadn't put a foot wrong. That was good enough for Bob, he'd bet the twenty thousand on Running Scared.

Almost immediately the adrenaline began to kick in. He felt confident, a little light headed perhaps, but looking forward to the excitement and the buzz he would get from the race.

"Do you want to come with me while I make my bet or would you rather wait here?"

"Let's see," Hannah said, "go out in the cold and damp to watch you make a bet or sit here by the fire till you get back. I choose the warm fire." She laughed.

"Okay, I won't be long." He left the bar.

The runners were at the start and it was a strange sensation, walking past the bookmakers and not placing a bet, but this wasn't the race he was interested in. He saw the bookie he'd used earlier and wondered what sort of affect his big win had had on the man's day. He didn't look very happy.

Bob decided to watch the end of the race in progress from the winning post, then he'd make his bet. He leaned over the fence and strained to pick out the runners and their jockeys as the horses closed on the finish. The noise of the crowd drowned out the commentary as the horses thundered home. From his position he couldn't tell who was in the lead, but the jockeys were hard at work, each believing they had a chance of winning.

They pushed, pumped and sweated for all they were worth and, as they approached the winning post, three of the horses, Dead Ringer, Night Witch and Hurricane Dream were neck and neck. Bob had a clear view of the line and as the three magnificent animals flashed past the post, Night Witch, the horse nearest to him, stretched his neck out as he crossed. To Bob's eyes he'd won by the narrowest of margins.

The jockeys turned their mounts, not knowing the outcome. They were exhausted and their breath was visible on the cold afternoon breeze as they made their way back toward the grandstand, the horse's breath almost synchronized with their rider's.

The judge called for a photograph. It had been a terrific race and Bob felt privileged to have witnessed the finish from such a good spot.

His curiosity got the better of him as he walked over to the bookmakers, who were betting on the result. He hadn't considered a bet of this nature, but decided to take a look at the odds anyway. Betting on a photo is the only bet a bookie will take after the race has started and usually it's a suckers bet, because the bookies oftentimes have a man on the line and are certain of the winner, at least in their own minds, and therefore will only take a bet on the horse they believe has lost.

Strangely enough Night Witch wasn't the favorite with the bookies. They seemed to be favoring Hurricane Dream. Had he got it wrong? Had they got it wrong? He decided to test one of the bookies, knowing he wouldn't accept a large bet if he had any doubts.

"Twenty thousand on Night Witch please."

The bookie seemed shocked and looked at his colleague. They huddled and whispered to each other.

"You can have five thousand." He seemed nervous, not as confident about the result now.

Just then another punter came in with two thousand for Dead Ringer. The bookie took his bet and seemed a little happier. More bets were coming in now and it seemed the punters were favoring Dead Ringer, while the bookies apparently still liked Hurricane Dream. Was he the only one who thought Night Witch was the winner? Now he was beginning to have doubts, but he didn't want to lose face.

"Come on, sir." The bookie smiled. "I'll take an even five thousand."

Bob cast his mind back to the finish of the race. He was convinced of the result, close, yes. But he was still sure of the outcome.

"Make it ten thousand and you can have my money," Bob countered.

"A little too rich for my blood." The bookie lost his smile and several punters began to get involved.

"Go on, take his money!" one of them shouted.

"You call yourself a bookie?" another said.

The bookmaker collaborated with his friend once again and after a few seconds agreed on the bet. Bob handed over the cash and as soon as the bookie put the money in his satchel the result was announced.

"Ladies and gentlemen the winner of the seventh race is number two, Night Witch."

The bookie was gutted as several of Bob's fellow race-goers congratulated him and slapped him on the back. They goaded the bookie and at one stage Bob thought it might turn nasty. Thankfully everybody calmed down and the bookie beckoned Bob around to the back of his board, where his clerk was counting out the money.

"A check would be better," Bob said, knowing the bookie would prefer it that way. He couldn't believe his good fortune. It seemed everything was going right. He felt indestructible.

Then his phone vibrated.

Mackenzie's name was on the display.

Damn, just as he was beginning to forget about the bank, the raid and the imminent police interrogation. He felt a shiver worm up his spine and his fingers went numb as he fumbled to answer it. He went into acting mode, forcing himself to smile and acting like he meant it.

"Hello, Mr. Mackenzie, how are you? I'm a little pissed, but other than that, I'm feeling pretty good." Bob wasn't lying.

"Glad you are, Bob, things are a little shaky at this end," Mackenzie said.

Bob ignored him, knowing what was coming next and trying to delay the inevitable for as long as possible.

"I'm having a very good Cheltenham. I've won thousands, sir."

"That's right, you're at the races aren't you?" He wasn't interested and didn't inquire about Bob's good fortune. Bob wondered if anything he'd said had registered. It was typical of the man. When Mackenzie won two pounds on the Grand National, he made bloody well sure everyone in the branch knew about it. Bob had won nearly a hundred and fifty thousand and the man didn't give fuck all. "Are you back next week, Bob?"

"Not if I keep winning like this." Bob couldn't help himself, he had to say it.

"The police are interviewing all the staff." Again Mackenzie hadn't heard him. "I'm afraid it's official now. I was right, the money is missing and they suspect an inside job. You're the last man to be interviewed."

Bob kept quiet, taking it in.

"They've even interviewed me." Mackenzie sounded like a whipped dog. "It wasn't very pleasant, I can tell you. They accused me of everything they could think of, even making up the bloody e-mail. The inspectors are in as well, going over everything, looking for anything out of place, anything at all. They've interviewed all the staff."

"Except me."

"Yes, except you, because you're on vacation. But don't worry, you can handle their questions. I have every confidence. But I wanted to tell you everyone is sworn to secrecy. Anyone mentioning the raid to anyone at all will be sacked, forfeiting all pension rights. They've made us sign declarations to that effect." He went on, depressing Bob even further with every detail. "Your interview is scheduled for 9:00 on Monday, don't be late."

"Thanks, sir, I'm having a wonderful holiday, the break is just what the doctor ordered." Bob couldn't believe how his emotions could change so quickly.

"What? Oh, I'm sorry. I didn't mean to spoil your day. Are you having a good time? Don't suppose you've won have you?" He just confirmed he hadn't heard a word Bob had said.

"A hundred and fifty thousand, sir."

"Very funny, remember, 9:00 sharp on Monday." With that he hung up.

Suddenly Bob didn't feel very well. Thank you very much, Mr. Mackenzie. He cursed himself for allowing the man to get to him, but as much as he was upset about what Mackenzie had said, he hadn't told Bob anything he hadn't been expecting. It shouldn't have bothered him. Besides, it could have been much worse. It could have been the police on the phone and not Mackenzie. He wasn't in the clear yet, but at least it didn't look like he was their prime suspect.

Fortunately he'd cleaned up most of his money,

because Cheltenham had just lost it's appeal. It was time to be getting back. He wanted to see the children, catch up on the time he'd missed. And he wanted a nice evening with Hannah before he left. He'd take the dogs out to the moors over the weekend, maybe climb a hill or two, clear his head, then go to bed early on Sunday and get a good night's sleep in preparation for the battle ahead.

It was going to be a battle, because in his heart of hearts, he knew they'd already suspected him. The break in at his house told him that. Someone had been looking for the money, there was simply no other explanation.

CHAPTER SIXTEEN

HANNAH SAT IN THE COCKPIT, reflecting on the last few days. Had she gotten Bob Heggie out of her system. No, if anything, he was planted inside her deeper than before. Was it love? She shivered as a stiff wind blew up the mouth of the Severn. She should have chosen a thicker sweater instead of the thin one she was wearing.

She looked toward the North East. She could just make out the outline of the Severn Bridge in the distance and for a second she wished the river continued onward in the same direction for another two hundred and fifty miles, so she could sail on up to Newcastle.

She was going to miss him, that she knew. Their special few days were over. He'd gone on the afternoon train and she didn't know when she'd be seeing him again.

* * *

Bob woke just as the train was pulling into the station at Newcastle on Sunday evening. He'd called ahead and Debra was going to meet him at the house with the children. It was dark, wet and very grey, but his hometown station looked warm and inviting. He pulled up his collar, protecting himself from the elements and went out to the taxi rank. He was feeling good again and any thought of the bank and Mackenzie had been pushed aside by images of the children.

The taxi pulled up at the door and the dogs barked at the strange car. He saw Elisa looking out the window as he got out of the cab. He paid the driver, then saw Cameron at the window as well. He barely got through the door before Cameron draped himself around him. He had to pry him off and he would only let go at the mention of a present. Debra stood back, a blank look on her face.

Cameron's eyes lit up at the sight of the football Bob had picked up at a sports shop in Cheltenham. He was more worried about the gift for Elisa.

"Oh, Daddy, I just love it." She put the jacket on. "It's so sophisticated."

"When did you get such good taste, Bob?" Debbie said.

"Just a dormant quality, I guess." He smiled, pleased Elisa liked the jacket. He'd bought it at one of the hotel shops. The woman assured him his daughter would love it and apparently she'd been right.

"Well, as long as we're trying on coats, I think I should put mine on and get going."

"So soon?" Bob said, secretly happy she was leaving. It seemed he no longer enjoyed her company the way he once did.

"I feel a bit uncomfortable here now."

"I don't see why."

"Well, it's not my house anymore now, is it? Anyway, Steve and I are going out for dinner, then the theatre, we won't be too late."

"Elisa and Cameron can stay over, I'll drop them in the morning."

"That'll be fine," she said and left.

* * *

Bob got up early, the kids were still asleep. He'd only had them one day this week and for that he was grateful to Debra. He sighed. If he hurried he could have a walk with the dogs and do some thinking before she came to pick them up for school.

He smiled to himself. He was growing quite close to those old dogs, the dogs he'd never particularly liked. They heard him on the landing and greeted him at the bottom of the stairs. They seemed to sense a run across the fields.

Outside in the crisp air, he started to think about the upcoming interview with the police. He wondered what the copper would look like. Perhaps there would be two interrogating him, maybe even a good cop, bad cop scenario.

He knew the questions they'd probably ask. He'd gone over them time and again. He knew what answers to give. He knew to be short and to the point. He needed to be careful, to concentrate on keeping his mouth shut. He needed to be calm and collected.

He was good at that.

As long as he concentrated and kept his guard up, he'd be all right, they had nothing to connect him with the crime. No evidence. He went over the questions and answers again during the train into town.

He walked up the high street toward the bank in plenty of time for the interview. He was wary as he neared the bank. He remembered back to the day of the raid and even then he hadn't experienced a feeling such as this. He was excited, confident and perversely, looking forward to a fight.

That's what it would be, a fight, a competition between him and them, a competition which would ultimately make or break his life. High stakes. A competition Bob had to win, because he wouldn't last in jail. He knew that. He needed open space, the fields, the moors, the mountains and above all he needed his children. And just maybe, he needed Hannah too. He would get none of that banged up in a cell. He tried not to think about it. He was determined that wouldn't be the outcome.

He went into the bank with a bounce in his step, greeted the cashiers with a smile, but the atmosphere was thick. No one wanted to be there. People were pointing fingers at one another and Bob could just imagine the gossip in the restrooms. They'd all been interviewed, just Bob to go. He went over to Jenny MacPartland.

"And how is our head cashier this morning?"

"Not so bad." She looked awful, apparently the police interviews and the realization that the crime was real had taken their toll.

"How about you, did you have a good week?"

He'd rehearsed the next bit well.

"Jenny, I had just about the best week of my life, but I must swear you to secrecy." He lowered his voice to a whisper. "Would you pay these checks into my bank account when we open?"

"My," she said when she saw the amounts.

"I had a little run of luck at the races. But I don't want anyone to know."

"It's a lot of money," she said.

"And it's our secret," he said. "If word gets out, everybody will be wanting to borrow money."

"How'd you win so much?"

"I was very, very lucky. I'll tell you the details later."

"I can't wait," she said and Bob was sure she couldn't wait to tell whoever would listen to her. She was the biggest gossip in the branch. It's why he'd picked her.

"Remember, it's a secret."

Mackenzie interrupted them.

"Are you ready, Bob? The police are waiting. Might as well get it over with, eh?"

"No problem, sir. Where are they?"

They were using Mackenzie's office as their interrogation base, as it was the most comfortable in the building. No doubt Mackenzie had offered it and no doubt he would be keeping an eye on the proceedings.

Bob wondered whether they suspected any involvement from Mackenzie, after all he was the man at the top. He'd signed the letters and authorized their circulation. No, he'd probably come over well in the interview, a nervous bumbling man not capable of organizing a piss up in a brewery, let alone a well-planned scam. No, they wouldn't suspect him, suspicion would fall on his right hand man.

Bob went to Mackenzie's office and found two policemen sitting over in a corner. Someone had brought in an extra desk for the occasion. The two coppers got up and greeted Bob.

"I'm Detective Inspector Philip Bowen." He held out his hand. He seemed too young to be a detective. Bob thought he was in his twenties. He had short cropped, blonde hair, shaved at the back and sides. He carried far too much weight and already he was perspiring in the room's warm atmosphere. He wore a dark suit and darker tie.

"Glad to meet you." Bob shook his hand.

"And this is my partner, Detective Chief Inspector Kevin Stainbridge. Stainbridge was a man with thin graying hair in his mid-sixties or so. He wore a garish checked sports jacket, with an open neck shirt and badly ironed black trousers that had seen better days. He offered his hand and Bob shook it.

A bank inspector sat in the far corner. He had been part of a team that had carried out an inspection at one of the branches a few years ago. Bob couldn't remember the man's name. But that was all right, because the man didn't welcome Bob, didn't look up. He stayed seated, staring at a clipboard, pen at the ready.

The scene was set.

Three against one.

"Can we call you Robert?" Stainbridge said.

"I prefer Bob, but you can call me anything you like." Bob smiled.

"Bob it is then," Bowen said as he beckoned Bob to

take a seat.

"This won't take too long," Stainbridge said. "It really is just routine. You understand that we need to interview everybody?"

Bob nodded and wished they'd been telling the truth. He knew this wasn't going to be like the other interviews they'd conducted here, but for the first few minutes the interview was pleasant. No good cop bad cop, only two good cops.

They asked how much Bob knew about the up to date situation and he explained he had been on a week's holiday and knew very little. He told them Mr. Mackenzie had notified him that the money hadn't turned up and that there was suspicion an insider may be involved.

He detected an attitude change.

"Not quite correct, Bob," Bowen said. "We know an insider is involved." He emphasized the word know. "We can trace it right back to a dodgy e-mail. An e-mail that was created by someone or somebody working within this branch, or possibly head office. We don't know who it is yet, but it's only a matter of time before we find out."

"The e-mail letter I distributed?" Although Bob knew they would discover the e-mail, it still unnerved him. "I don't understand."

"Dodgy, Bob. Made up. Fictitious," Bowen said. "We interviewed the director who allegedly wrote it and we're satisfied he knew nothing about it."

"Do you know what that means, Bob?" Stainbridge added. "It means somebody else created it, somebody else sent it and the person who sent it is our thief. The insider who is looking at the inside of a prison cell for a twenty year stretch."

His words filled Bob with dread, as they were intended
to do, but he remained silent through a long pause, a
stalemate. The game had begun. Bob longed to open his
mouth and defend himself, but he was determined not to
speak first.

"Nothing to say for your self, Bob?" Bowen broke first
and Bob had won the first round.

"Like what? You know I printed out the e-mail. It's
my job."

"Very convenient, isn't it?"

"What, my job? Yeah, it'd be convenient if I was your
insider, but I'm not."

"Did you create it, Bob?" Bowen said. "Perhaps on
your computer at home and then bring it in and load it
onto a PC here?"

"I guess you don't hear so well."

"What do you mean?" the young copper said.

"One, I told you I'm not your insider. Two, I told you
it was my job. The message came from head office. Yes, I
printed it out and took the copies in for Mr. Mackenzie to
sign. I do that every morning."

Stainbridge sighed.

"Well I hope for your sake it did come from your head
office."

They fell silent again. They wanted Bob to reply, to
waffle and to trip himself up.

He didn't. He looked at Mackenzie over at his desk on
the far side of the room. The man was pretending to work,
but was listening to every word.

He glanced at the bank inspector, who was looking at
him and the man put his eyes back to his clipboard.

The two coppers stayed silent. Bob imagined them

willing him to start talking, praying he would start rambling.

It wasn't easy, but Bob stayed silent again.

"Have you anything to say, Mr. Heggie?" Again Bowen broke first.

"Any chance of a cup of tea?"

The bank inspector dropped his pen and Bowen hammered his first onto the desk. Bob thought he detected a slight grin from Stainbridge, but perhaps he was mistaken?

"You're taking the piss, Bob," he said, raising his voice.

Bob wanted to laugh, but kept a straight face. He wanted to tell him he'd just won round two.

"Let's take a break," Stainbridge said. "Get him a cup of tea, Phil."

"One sugar," Bob said.

The young copper glared at him, then stormed out of the room.

"Look, Bob," Stainbridge said, voice barely above a whisper, "we just need to know where the e-mail came from and who created it. We know you printed it out and DI Bowen is fairly certain it came from within this branch. We have a computer expert at head office checking all the hard drives in the computers. If he reports back it wasn't sent from there, the suspicion falls on you. We will also be checking the hard drive on your computer and we will know sometime today where that e-mail came from. It'll be better for you if you tell us the truth now."

Bob didn't answer the good cop and the bad cop came back into the room with a tray of Polystyrene cups.

"I've told him about our computer man at head office, Phil."

"Thanks, Phil," Bob said as the younger man handed him his tea.

"What do you think of that, Bob?" Bowen was glaring at Bob, apparently annoyed at Bob's familiarity. "Within hours we'll know where that e-mail originated." Now he looked smug. "Where it was sent and where it was created, but more importantly, who created it."

"It came from head office, I know for a fact," Bob said.

"And do you want to know what I think, Mr. Heggie?" He paused for effect, then lowered his voice to a whisper as he leaned across the table, "I think you created it."

Bowen leaned closer.

"Have you anything to say, Bob?" Bowen raised his eyebrows

Bob looked at him straight in the eye.

"You forgot the sugar for my tea."

The young copper snapped, sweeping his hand across the desk, knocking the tea to the floor. The hot liquid spilled across the table and a little of it hit Bob's trousers. It was the kind of break Bob had been hoping for. He screamed out in pretend pain, loud enough to be heard throughout the branch.

"You've assaulted me, you clumsy oaf. I'll sue you and your bloody force. You'll regret this and I won't answer any more of your bloody questions."

Bowen looked shocked at Bob's outburst. Stainbridge jumped up, started wiping Bob's trousers, apologizing for the action of his colleague. Mackenzie was also on his feet, shocked and stunned at what the copper had done, but more surprised at Bob's outburst. He rushed over to him.

"Bob, Bob, please be calm, please keep the noise down, remember where you are."

"Remember where I am?" Bob whipped off his coat, threw it on the table, continuing his amateur dramatics. "I know where I am. I'm in a bloody bank, not a third world prison cell." Bob felt he was overdoing it and pretended to calm down a little. "I didn't expect to be assaulted here. I thought I was just answering a few questions."

"I'm sure Bob would be happy to answer your questions, after a little break." Mackenzie said to DCI Stainbridge, trying to take control of the situation.

"I'm going to go and get cleaned up." Bob pushed his chair back, got up and left the room. He went into the toilet to wash himself down. He knew the others would follow and he took off his trousers and put them under the hand drier. He scratched his leg with his nails, creating a red mark. Sure enough, Mackenzie and Stainbridge followed behind after a few seconds.

Bob pointed to his leg.

"Look at that, scalded."

The two men looked at the red mark and the old copper looked disconsolate.

"I hope you realize, Mr. Mackenzie, that you're my witness to this. I want a full written signed statement from both you and the police, then it's straight to my lawyer."

Mackenzie and the copper looked at each other.

"Two statements or I'm done answering questions."

"All right, Bob, whatever you say." Mackenzie sighed.

"I'm not sure I can do that," Stainbridge said. "After all it was an accident. He didn't mean to splash the tea on you."

Bob put his trousers on before the red mark faded and stuck to his guns.

"A written statement or no questions answered."

He went back to his office and after a few minutes Mackenzie came in with his coat. He handed it to Bob along with a signed statement, verifying Philip Bowen had knocked over a cup of tea that had fallen into Robert Heggie's lap. It went on to say that Mackenzie had witnessed a scald on his right leg.

"And the other statement?"

"I'm sorry, Bob, but they're not prepared to offer one. It would need to come from their supervisors and you know the red tape involved in that sort of thing. Mr. Bowen has said he will apologize though."

Bob refused at first, but Mackenzie kept at him till he agreed to accept Bowen's apology. Mackenzie telephoned through to his own office and after further discussions, Bob went back to the makeshift interview room.

Stainbridge looked relieved and Bowen looked embarrassed. The young copper knew he'd made a major cock up and had betrayed his so-called professionalism. His apology was short and to the point and every word appeared a struggle.

"Okay, Mr. Heggie? Can we go on now?" Stainbridge said.

"Sure."

They took up their positions and Mackenzie went back to his desk.

"We have the results from the computer expert," Bowen said. "Would you like to say anything before I go on?"

"I could have saved you the bother, the e-mail I printed out came from head office. It definitely did not originate from this branch."

"You're right." Stainbridge heaved a sigh. "It was sent

from the receptionist's computer at head office.

"So it's a head office job then?"

"We didn't say that," Bowen said. "We still have our suspicions."

"But it was sent from head office." Bob raised his voice and leaned across the table. "I don't work there and it wasn't created on my computer. Why on earth are you still asking me questions? Can I go and get on with my work now?"

Stainbridge intervened.

"Would you have any objection if our computer expert came home with you tonight to check on your home computer?"

"He can come right now if he wants," Bob said, "and I'll have half a day off for the privilege."

They seemed surprised at Bob's reaction. Although they'd found the computer he'd sent the e-mail from, they hadn't found the computer that had actually created it. They'd checked Bob's work machine and hadn't found anything there. The next natural place to look would be on his home computer. Did they really think someone would be that stupid? He'd created the original message at an Internet café.

They coppers seemed surprised at Bob's suggestion that the computer expert go to his home straightaway. But they had to take him up on it, because they couldn't take a chance he might dispose of the evidence if he already hadn't. Besides, from their point of view, Bob could be bluffing.

"Any objections if I come along?" Bowen said.

"I don't mind. The more the merrier."

The policemen offered Bob a ride, evidently expecting

they'd be able to carry on the interview along the way, but Bob declined, said he'd take a cab. The last thing he wanted was to be cooped up in a car with them. If it made him appear guilty, so be it, because he wasn't going to answer questions to the back of their heads. He wanted to see their eyes when they questioned him.

The computer man was waiting in Bob's driveway when they showed up. The policemen had followed the cab, apparently not wanting to let Bob out of their sight.

"Please feel free, gentlemen, our computer is upstairs in my daughter's room, my PowerBook is in the study. Take your time."

They came in and straightaway the dogs charged them, barking and snarling. The coppers and the computer man sought refuge as they huddled in the hallway, where the dogs had them cornered, Hamish taking a hold of Bowen's trouser leg.

Cassius stood back, baring his teeth, daring them to move.

Bowen shouted at Bob to call them off and after a few seconds he commanded the dogs back into the kitchen.

"I don't know what that's all about," Bob said. "They've never gone after anybody before."

"You should keep the damn things locked up in the kitchen," Bowen had gone white, was shaking and that didn't make any sense, then all of a sudden, it did.

"Anyway, no harm done," Bob said. "They're as gentle as lambs. Wouldn't harm a soul. Unless, of course, that soul broke into my house one night when they were locked up in the kitchen and they couldn't get at him then." Bob bore his eyes into Bowen. Bowen looked away and that was all the proof Bob needed. They were on to him, had been right from the start if they'd gotten a warrant to search his house that quickly. He was going to have to be very careful.

"Would anyone like a cup of tea?" Bob said, playing the gentleman host. He wanted to go after Bowen himself. Searching a house is one thing, trashing it is another altogether. Bob wasn't going to forget this.

Stainbridge shook his head and then they went about their business, wary of further canine disturbances. After about twenty minutes they left, leaving Bob alone. He'd survived the first day of questioning and learned that he'd been their prime, probably their only suspect right from the beginning.

He'd also learned that Bowen had it in for him. There was no doubt about that. He imagined him working late, pouring over the files, examining every detail. Searching, racking his brain, going over the interview notes word by word. Bob didn't like him, didn't trust him, but conceded he may perhaps be a bit brighter than he had at first thought. He likened him to a young Mackenzie, immersed in his profession one hundred per cent, the way Mackenzie had been, before he got lazy. He pictured Mackenzie in his mind, then Bowen. Yeah, he could picture Bowen in forty years time, same features, receding hairline and a slightly upturned nose.

He spent the rest of the night with a bottle of wine and his thoughts, before going up to bed and drifting off to sleep, where he tossed and turned the night away.

CHAPTER SEVENTEEN

ANOTHER EARLY-MORNING WALK and another early-morning train brought Bob into the city center just after 8:00. He bought his usual paper from Tom, who seemed edgy and unhappy, not his usual self.

"Something wrong, Tom?"

"They're sacking me." He appeared on the brink of tears. He went on to tell Bob he was being replaced by a vending machine. "Don't know how I am going to survive. No one is going to hire an old man like me."

"I'm so sorry." And Bob meant it. He felt terrible about what was happening to his friend.

"They didn't give me any notice. No severance pay or any redundancy. Finished next week. Can you believe that? Twenty bloody years I've sold their papers and never missed a day."

A queue was building up behind them.

"Never missed a day, rain, snow, winter, summer, colds, flu, whatever this old life has thrown at me, I've always been here. Now they just tell me to piss off."

Bob moved aside as Tom sold a few papers. He tried to console him and reassure him something else would come along, but in his heart of hearts, he didn't believe anything would.

"The pretty people, Bob, they get all the breaks in life, the good jobs."

"You're talking rubbish again, Tom. I didn't believe you the last time you said it and I don't believe you now."

"Think about it, Bob, you're interviewing two people with identical qualifications. Who gets the job? Miss Ugly or Miss Pleasant-on-the-eye? Think about it."

Bob watched as a well dressed, thirty-something man took a paper from Tom. Good looking, nice suit, expensive shoes, a good profession, no doubt about it. Then another customer, different this time, a man in his fifties, a scar down the left side of his face and a bent nose from a fight he lost way back. He smiled at Tom with a toothless grin and a weather beaten face. Bob took notice of his clothes, grubby, soiled waterproof, a hole in the left shoe and his trousers held up with beat up old belt.

"You see, Bob, I'm right aren't I?"

"Two people, coincidence that's all."

"Pretty people, Bob, pretty people, you watch 'em, watch 'em close and you'll see I'm right."

After leaving Tom, Bob headed for the bank. As he walked in he was surprised to see a slight change in personnel. The two coppers, Stainbridge and young Bowen were waiting the next round of games, but along with Mackenzie was a new face, yet a face that was vaguely familiar.

Mackenzie introduced him to Lord Joseph Harris, a board director and the name he had coincidentally chosen to use on his fake e-mail. He had seen his picture on company publications and newsletters and the man greeted Bob in a reserved, but confident manner. Bob was puzzled by his presence and felt the numbers against him were getting more uneven.

"So, Bob," Stainbridge started, here we are again. "Back from head office with some interesting information."

Bob didn't answer.

"We found out that you knew Tracy's password, so you could have accessed her computer."

"I don't know her password."

"She says you do," Bowen said. "She says you needed it to access her computer when she worked for you."

"It's been five years since she worked for me," Bob said, "and to the best of my knowledge she never told me her password. I least I don't remember her telling me. Christ, I can't even remember the password I used last month, much less somebody else's from a half a decade ago."

"You went into her e-mail, stuck a disc in her machine, copied it and sent it to yourself," Bowen said, ignoring Bob's explanation.

"And the moon's made of green cheese," Bob said.

"And do you know something else, Mr. Heggie," Bowen said, "you were in head office the day the message was sent. You took the girl out for lunch and hung around afterward for your train."

Bob wanted to stay silent, but now they were getting too close, he had to say something. He told himself to keep his answers short.

"Coincidence."

"I don't think so," Bowen, still the bad cop, said. "You sent the message on her computer that day, didn't you?"

"Never touched her computer that day."

"Eureka!" Bowen shouted. "Another lie."

Bob looked at the young copper. He was looking confident. It was a confidence that made Bob wary.

"We have something else, Bob," Stainbridge said, stepping in.

Lord Harris looked up from his notepad for the first time, interested at the latest revelation. Again Bob kept silent.

"Fingerprints, Bob. Fingerprints on Tracy's computer. Your fingerprints."

"And you've just said you never touched it," Bowen said, eyebrows raised, waiting for an answer.

And Bob waited, still playing the silent game. He waited for the amateur to crack. Bob's professional training on interview skills would win the day. The police thought they had him and they sat back, waiting for a confession.

Lord Harris and Mackenzie looked smug.

Bob decided to disappoint them all. He went on to describe his visit and interview at the head office the week prior and how he took the opportunity to look at his messages at Tracy's desk.

"Ask her." Bob said. "She even suggested it."

"I would suspect that the young secretary went off to the powder room leaving ample time for you to send the e-mail," Bowen said, again ignoring what Bob had said. "The disc had already been prepared, you wouldn't even need to type anything out, three or four clicks and that was that."

Bob sighed with a slight grin tilted at Bowen. Deep down he was jittery at how accurate Bowen had described the sequence of events. Lord Harris sat ramrod straight in his chair, chewing at his glasses. He sighed too. Mackenzie had a blank look on his face.

"And, apart from the prints, the one thing that convinces me, is your absence from the branch during the entire raid and how you magically appeared very briefly at crucially convenient moments. We have timed the raid and done an exercise that proves you could have carried it out and had sufficient time to hide the money somewhere and be back in Mr. Mackenzie's office just after 9:00."

Another sigh from Bob.

Another sigh from Lord Harris.

"We know," Bowen continued, "that you changed in the public toilets at the bottom of the high street."

Lord Harris looked curious now.

"What do you mean, you know?" Bob was curious too.

"More prints, Mr. Heggie." Bowen smiled wide and Bob disliked him even more.

Lord Harris gasped.

"Fingerprints in the toilet. Your fingerprints." Bowen was obviously pleased with himself.

"Then we have evidence to charge him," Lord Harris said.

"You think?" Bob turned to Stainbridge. "Do you

want to tell them or shall I?"

"I will." The old copper shook his head. Then to Lord Harris. "It's not evidence, sir, not really. It's hardly a crime to use a public convenience."

"Depends what you're doing in there!" Bowen said through gritted teeth.

"Go on, Mr. Bowen," urged Lord Harris.

"After leaving the toilet, he would have had a good ten minutes to hide the money and still have time to make Mr. Mackenzie's office when he did."

"And where do you suggest the money could be then?" Bob said. "In my office? In my desk?"

"There are several places you could have gotten to in that time, like the bus station, the train station, a sports center where you could have stored it in a locker."

"Or a car or an accomplice or both," Lord Harris said.

"I'm trying to figure out how you'd present this to the judge," Bob said, "but I just can't seem to get my head around it." Bob continued, mimicking the upper class tones of an old school tie judge. "So you are saying constable, he is guilty because he took a piss in a public toilet."

"You've enjoyed taking the piss out of us, Heggie," Bowen said, "but I think you did it. Oh, I know all the evidence looks circumstantial now, but we're going to put it together. We're going to nail you and you're going to go to prison."

"How can you put something together that isn't true?" Bob said.

"Because I think it is true." Bowen was turning red. "I think you've been very clever. CCTV cameras everywhere, but only one video of you in the clown mask. A video of you coming out of the station with your newspaper as you said during your first interview. Almost too convenient, as if you wanted to be filmed."

Lord Harris seemed to be getting impatient.

"Could I have a word alone with Mr. Heggie?" Stainbridge said.

"If you think it'll do any bloody good." Bowen got up, left the room.

Lord Harris and Mackenzie left as well, leaving the old copper and Bob on their own. Stainbridge switched off the recorder.

Bob looked across the table at Stainbridge, who twiddled his thumbs and gazed upward. The detective sighed, then looked back at the chief suspect.

"You don't really think it was me do you, Stainbridge?" Bob said.

"I don't know. Detective Bowen certainly thinks you did it. He's not planning on interviewing anyone else. Lord Harris does as well. I'm not so sure. But you should know the whole bank hierarchy thinks you're the one."

"And that's why you wanted them out of the room, so you could tell me that."

"No, I just wanted to give Bowen a minute to cool down. Things were starting to get out of hand."

"They can't be serious." Bob shook his head.

"Oh, they are," Stainbridge nodded, "believe me they are. We've got instructions from them not to let it go. However, I'm an old copper who can't find any hard evidence, circumstantial only, that's all we've got. The physical profile of the robber doesn't match you either. We've studied the CCTV cameras and we haven't found a single item to connect you with anything. You may have been very clever and the force would probably have let you go by now." He sighed, rubbed his eyes and all of a sudden Bob wasn't convinced of his sincerity.

"But?" Bob said.

"But the bank isn't having it," Stainbridge went on. "They're convinced you're the one who did it."

Bob latched on to his words.

"What do you mean the force would have let me go?"

"Sorry, Bob, this interview is over."

"I'm getting a bad feeling here," Bob said. "A real bad feeling. You know, like you're not who you say you are."

"Bob?"

"Don't Bob me, I'm Mr. Heggie to you, Stainbridge. Now tell me what's going on."

"As I said, the interview is over." Stainbridge left the room, leaving Bob alone with his thoughts.

And his thoughts were running wild, shooting here and there and finally settling on the fact that these guys weren't police at all. He didn't know just what Stainbridge was, but a Detective Chief Inspector he was not, of that, Bob was sure.

So if not police, what? Private investigators probably. Hired by who? The bank, of course. But why? To fool Robert Heggie, that was certain, but there had to be more. And then, like a lightning strike on a crisp night, Bob figured it out.

The bank wanted to keep the raid from the real police.

But why? Five hundred thousand pounds missing and the bank didn't want the police involved, that didn't make any sense.

Bowen came in and told Bob they were breaking for an early lunch.

Bob headed for the Grapes to kill an hour, the problem gnawed at his mind the way Cassius gnawed at a bone.

He was disappointed that Old Tom wasn't at his usual table.

Jackie and Peter didn't look their normal selves either, particulary Peter, who had fallen off a ladder and broken both wrists. He was plastered on both arms up to the elbows. It looked as if all he was fit for was holding a glass of beer and he wasn't even very good at that, balancing a half-pint between forefingers and thumbs.

Jackie went on to describe the accident and more.

"I have to wipe his arse for him. Fifty years old and he can't even do that. What a life, no wonder we spend it in the pub." They laughed and Bob pictured the scene.

After a little more time in the pub, Bob headed back to the bank. If he had his way, he'd stay away forever, but he was going to have to get through the sessions with the detectives, if he want to be really free.

The interview started up again at 2:00. Stainbridge and Bowen sat across the table from Bob, ready to begin the next round. Lord Harris and Mackenzie took up their old positions in the corner of the room.

Bob wondered whether Stainbridge had mentioned anything to his younger colleague about their conversation. He still couldn't get his head around the bank not bringing in the police, or was it a trick they were playing on him?

What would the Jack of Hearts do? Bluff, that's what he'd do. The Jack would bluff and so would Bob Heggie. Better to find out sooner, rather than later, what was going on anyway.

Bowen started by repeating the allegations and going over his suspicions of Bob's involvement, the e-mail and the fingerprints. He took Bob through every stage of the operation, at times so accurate it was eerie.

Bob stayed quiet, listening and waiting.

"We can go over this from now until doomsday if we want, Heggie, but it'd be better for everyone if you confess, so we can all go home. We know of your involvement and we have even more proof we haven't disclosed yet. We won't let this go, we know you did it."

"Then charge me," Bob said, voice calm.

"What?" Bowen said.

"You heard me. Charge me, take me to the lock up. That way you can go home."

"We may just do that very soon."

"No, Phil," Bob said. "Charge me now or get out of my life."

"Don't push me!" Bowen said.

All of a sudden Lord Harris and Mackenzie seemed much more interested, but Stainbridge looked embarrassed.

"I am pushing," Bob said.

Bowen looked unsure of what to say next. Bob decided to beat him too it.

"What force are you with, Phil?

Bowen looked surprised. Stainbridge did not.

"What are you on about?" Bowen said.

"What police force? You should be able to tell me that. I'm about to get up and call my lawyer. He'll want to know who I'm dealing with here."

Bob reached for the phone.

Lord Harris jumped to his feet, grabbed the phone

from Bob.

"You're not calling anyone." Phil slammed his hand on the desk.

"Then I'm leaving. I'll nip round to his office. It's just round the corner." Bob got up

"You're not going anywhere. Sit down!" Bowen leaned over the table.

"On my worst day the likes of you wouldn't be a challenge," Bob said, voice very calm now, calm but threatening. "And this is one of my better days. I'd like nothing better than to find you between me and that door."

"Bob?" Mackenzie said.

"Shut up!" Bob glared at him and for once Mackenzie appeared at a loss for words. He turned back to Bowen, whispering to him through clenched teeth.

"Come on, Philip, your call," Bob said.

Bowen was trembling, turning red, his mouth half open.

"What's the matter, the real police reject you?" Bob said. "Did you have dreams of being a copper when you were a little boy? You liked the smart uniform?"

Bowen clenched his fists. Bob had hit a nerve.

"Come on, pretty boy." Bob was running on an adrenaline high.

"Enough!" Lord Harris shouted. "This interview is over!" He looked at the two investigators. "Gentlemen, please leave the room."

"What do you mean?" Bowen said. "We've got the bastard, we know it's him."

"Come on, Phil," Stainbridge said, "let's go."

"You too, Mackenzie," Lord Harris said.

Mackenzie looked shocked, because of Lord Harris's informality or being asked to leave the room, Bob wasn't sure. Probably both. Mackenzie gave his chief executive a pleading look, then followed Stainbridge and Bowen out of the room.

Lord Harris took Stainbridge's seat opposite Bob.

"Okay, Mr. Heggie, first of all let me apologize for the hostility and let me tell you from now on everything is off the record. I'll be honest with you, if you're honest with me."

"They're not coppers, are they?" Bob detected an air of desperation, a wish to conclude this as soon as possible.

"You're right, they're not policemen." Lord Harris rubbed his jaw, sighed, apparently attempting to show real honesty.

"So what are they?" Bob said.

"They're from a private investigation firm. They're supposed to be pretty good at what they do."

"They are?"

"Well, they're pretty damned expensive and I'd have to say they were worth it, quite incredible what they've unearthed really, very interesting." Lord Harris went on to tell Bob how they had pieced together how the job could have been done. He was accurate in almost every detail. He went on to describe Bob's exact moves on the day of the raid. The private investigators had timed everything and were sure they had had it right, right up to where Bob had changed in the public toilet. They had everything, except where he'd hidden the money.

"That's all speculation," Bob said, "based solely on circumstantial evidence, which I'm sure, if you tried hard enough, you could pin on other suspects."

"You're the only one in a position to have been able to carry it out. Furthermore, no one can remember seeing you during the raid. You conveniently made an appearance just before and just after the event. You disappeared on holiday the week after the raid and returned making large deposits in your bank and building society accounts."

"I won that money at Cheltenham and I can prove it. Not only did I deposit bookmaker checks, but someone who works with the bank was with me when I made the bets and won the money."

"I don't care, I know it was you, the investigators know it was you and if we involved the police, they would come to the same conclusion."

"So, if you're so sure, why not call the real police and be done with it?"

"Perhaps the time has come to bring them in, Mr. Heggie. I'm not sure we can take it any further internally."

Bob felt a shiver slide up his spine. His stomach was queasy. He fought to remain calm, struggled to stay silent and once again that strange uneasy feeling came to him.

"You've been clever, Mr. Heggie." Lord Harris smiled. "The height and build of the robber doesn't match your profile and even though we have some fingerprints, there is no CCTV evidence and, despite having searched your house and home computers, we haven't a shred of anything that would stand up in court. Only circumstantial evidence as you said." He raised a hand to the side of his face, massaged his temple.

"So, what you're saying," Bob said, "is that you have nothing to go on, no evidence and nothing to charge me with, yet you're still convinced it was me?"

Lord Harris nodded.

"I want to call my lawyer. I think it's time this was out in the open."

"No, Mr. Heggie. No lawyers, no police, no publicity. The bank can't afford it."

"What did you say?"

"The bank can't afford it."

"That's what I thought you said." And suddenly it came to Bob. "If word of this got out, the bank would be a laughing stock at this simple breach of security by a low ranking bank official."

Lord Harris stayed silent. Bob was starting to feel better, because now he knew he was unlikely to be charged. The bank didn't want the publicity. What a drop in the ocean Bob's paltry five hundred thousand was in the grand scheme of things.

"No Police, Mr. Heggie. The directors feel if news of this gets out, not only would we be ridiculed, but the price of our shares could drop by as much as ten percent. The money stolen would look like small change. However, if we had an instant conviction, a quick fix, the market traders would take a more sympathetic view."

"What do you want then?"

"In a word, Mr. Heggie, a scapegoat." He paused for a few seconds, he pulled of his glasses, placed them on the table in front of him, "or perhaps two."

Bob couldn't believe what he was hearing. Was he going to go scot-free? That's what Lord Harris seemed to be saying. He also seemed to be aging right before his eyes. The man's face was twisted in anguish, the full responsibility of the bank resting on his shoulders. The pressure was beginning to show.

"What if I don't want to be a scapegoat? I've got

children. I wouldn't want them growing up thinking their father was a thief."

"You won't be labeled a thief." Lord Harris seemed to cringe. "We need to make an example of a couple of the senior managers." He some papers in front of himself. "Senior managers of the branch where a serious breach of security has occurred, you and Mr. Mackenzie. We're suspending him. He doesn't know yet, but we are. You'll be suspended too."

Mackenzie, suspended? Bob was beginning to like what he was hearing.

"I'm not so sure what your saying? I'm not thinking straight. How can this benefit the bank?"

"We don't want this to get out, Mr. Heggie, at least not the fact that any money has been stolen. Gone missing for a few hours we can handle, but stolen, no." He picked up a pen and began to shade in some of the letters on the bank logo at the top of the pad.

"I'm still not understanding you."

"Mr. Heggie, if it gets out, if a so called training exercise has gone so drastically wrong, the media will have a field day. Finance and banks are already fair game in the press and the public will lose confidence in us. And it'll be worse if we bolt the stable after the horse has gone and that's why we need to take action now, before it leaks out. Prompt action, a swift decision, that's what we want.

"So, you sack the two men at the top?"

"Yes, but not for stealing any money, not attempting to defraud the bank, but for gross incompetence during the training exercise."

"So, you're sacking me then?" Now Bob really liked what he was hearing. Mackenzie and himself sacked. If that's all they wanted, he was ready to cooperate.

"I'm afraid so, Mr. Heggie." Lord Harris sighed, the pen shaking in his hand. "And of course you'll return the money, that's non-negotiable. If not, the police come in."

Bob didn't expect the last condition. All of a sudden, he didn't feel so good.

"But I didn't do it. How can I give back the money if I didn't take it?"

"Mr. Heggie," Lord Harris, raised his eyebrows, not for the first time, "remember our pledge of honesty." He started tapping his fingers on the desk.

"Tell me about it again."

"Okay, here it is, I repeat, we will pension Mackenzie off and you will be sacked for gross incompetence and breach of security. You won't lose your pension as long as the money is returned. Think about it. It's a great deal for you. After all, we know you want out anyway."

Bob wanted to kiss the man. He wanted to jump up and tell him how wonderful he was and that he would accept his great get out, but he stayed silent. Bob didn't trust him. It was all too easy. As soon as he returned the money he was vulnerable, because then they would have the evidence to convict him. Lord Harris was lying. Bob was sure of it.

"I'd love to walk away from the job, because you're right, I don't like it here. In fact, I like it a lot less after meeting you, but how can I give the money back, if I don't know where it is?"

"For God's sake, man," Lord Harris jumped to his feet, "what do you want from us?" He paced round the room, looking at the ceiling, swinging his glasses round in circles. "We know you did it. Couldn't have been anyone else. Give the money back and you can walk away."

"Assuming, for argument's sake, that I did it, why in the world would I accept your deal? No wage and eighteen years to wait for that pension?" Bob waited for a response, he got none. "You would need to do better than that, a lot better. You're going to have to sweeten the pot or I'll be going to the press. I'm sure one of the tabloids would pay handsomely for this little story."

"Oh. I see. You're wanting a little pay off," Lord Harris sounded disgusted. "Something to buy your silence. A nice little earner, I believe they call it."

"I'd rather call it redundancy," Bob said.

"You want redundancy, Mr. Heggie? To save your face, perhaps your reputation?"

"Just like Mackenzie," Bob said.

"Okay, you've got it. We'll make you redundant, say two years salary. That good enough for you?"

"Yeah, sounds good." Bob couldn't believe the amazing transformation of events.

"Now at last we're getting somewhere." Lord Harris seemed pleased.

"Well, I'm glad it's settled," Bob said, but he knew it hadn't been.

"And the money?" Lord Harris said.

"What about it?" Bob said.

"Where is it? When do we get it back?" His eyes had that same pleading look his dogs gave him when they wanted a treat.

"You still don't get it, do you?" Bob said. "I'll be your scapegoat. You can say anything you want about me. You know I want out. And I'll take a redundancy package if it gets me out of this godforsaken bank, but God as my witness, I don't know anything about the money. If I had it, I'd give to you, but I don't, so I can't." Bob had never been a religious man.

"Look, Mr. Heggie," Lord Harris paused, bit his lip, started up again, "tell us where the money is and we have a deal."

"You really are hard of hearing, aren't you?"

"Please, Mr. Heggie, this is your last chance. Redundancy and the money returned, the whole incident brushed under the carpet. No further investigation, no more interviews."

Bob didn't utter a word and Lord Harris had his answer.

"All right, have it your way." Lord Harris crossed over to the other side of the room, picked up his jacket and left.

For an instant Bob thought about running after him, but he didn't. So close, yet so far.

He stayed in the room for a few minutes, wondering what he could have done differently to clinch the deal. A deal he wanted, a deal he could not have dreamed of just a few hours ago. Finally he got up, left and headed toward the train station and home.

CHAPTER EIGHTEEN

BOB WAS PAST CARING and thought he was likely to be suspended anyway, just like Mackenzie. He felt for the man. All those years devotion to the bank, then cast out. His professional reputation ruined. Bob's fault.

He tried to take some positives from the day. He still had the money in the bank and Lord Harris' meeting had convinced him that, while they had figured out how he'd probably done it, they didn't have any proof.

As the train got closer to home he began to cheer up a bit, but he couldn't get his worst case scenario out of his mind. Would Lord Harris turn everything over to the police?

His cell phone rang, he didn't recognize the number.

He answered and identified the public school tones of Lord Harris.

"Another meeting tomorrow, Mr. Heggie, and I suggest you bring a lawyer, as we're going to charge you."

Bob pressed the end button.

He watched the countryside flash by for a few minutes, thinking, wondering, then deciding that maybe it was time for him to get himself lawyered up, as they say in America. Easier said than done, he thought, because he didn't know any lawyers. He'd never needed one. He hadn't had so much as a parking fine in twenty odd years. Well, he'd find one in the phone book as soon as he got home.

He thought about Hannah. She was probably watching television on the boat. He missed her, wished she was with him now. But, on the other hand, he was glad she wasn't here to see what he was going through. By the time she got back, it would all be over, one way or another.

As soon as he got home he fed the dogs, then got out the phone book and picked a lawyer at random. Within the hour a young man rapped at his door. The guy was a kid, Bob thought, hardly old enough to wipe his own backside, but he had a wise man's inquisitive eyes and that settled Bob, this was the lawyer for him.

"I'm Quincy, James Quincy, but call me Quincy. I don't like Jim and James sounds too formal."

Bob invited him in and outlined his problem.

"I need to know the truth," Quincy said.

"You mean whether or not I did it?"

"Well, yeah, that's what I mean. You want me to defend you, I gotta know."

"What do you think? Do you think I'm guilty?"

"It's not important what I think, but yes, after hearing you out, I think you did it. I don't care, mind you, I just want to hear it from you. No secrets between us, that's the deal if you want me in your corner."

All of a sudden Bob didn't like this young man very much. He imagined Quincy defending murderers and child killers, trying his best to get them acquitted, yet knowing they'd committed the crime. He imagined Quincy's satisfaction at the not guilty verdicts and he imagined him picking up a fat check as his guilty clients returned to society to commit further crimes. It sickened him and he had no hesitation in lying to the man. After all, he'd lied to Hannah, so there was no way he'd tell Quincy what he'd done.

"I didn't do it and that's the honest truth. I suspect my boss. I think he's trying to shift it on to me."

They talked for over an hour and Quincy reassured Bob proving the charges would be very difficult, especially since he was innocent.

"People don't become bank robbers overnight. Besides, that's why they've offered you the redundancy package, because it's an impossible case to prove."

"I feel a lot better now," Bob said.

"And you can keep feeling better, unless, of course, they have something we don't know about, or unless there is something you haven't told me."

"No, with God as my judge, I've told you everything." And for a second time that day, Bob used God to add truth to a lie.

* * *

Bob took the Harley to work, parked it at the station in

Newcastle, where he met Quincy just after 10:00. He hadn't bothered going into work, as he considered himself suspended, even though he hadn't been told officially.

The young lawyer greeted him and suggested they have a coffee prior to the meeting. They sat in Starbucks and chatted for about half an hour. Quincy raised several points relating to the likely charges and once again asked Bob whether he was keeping anything back and once again Bob lied.

Quincy paid for the coffee and Bob was a bit surprised about that.

"Don't worry," the lawyer said, "it'll come out in your bill."

They set off for the bank with Quincy talking the whole way, probing, searching. He shut up only when they reached the bank, then he adopted a methodical, subdued approach. As they neared the steps up to the bank from where he had been shot all those weeks ago, the raid came back to Bob. He'd carried it off. It had been absolutely faultless, perfection. But he wondered now, if he could, would he turn back the clock?

When they walked through the banking hall several of the staff looked over. Jim Moody spotted him, waved and smiled. Bob returned his signal, appreciating his token gesture of support.

The first thing Bob noticed in the interview room was the unfamiliar, unfriendly faces. Lord Harris was still taking center stage, already positioned at the table, his hands on his briefcase. However, a well-heeled young man with a more expensive looking briefcase sat at Harris's right. He peered at Bob over his gold rimmed glasses, his facial expression giving nothing away. And two large, well-built, middle-aged men flanked him. They were dressed in cheap suits. It seemed to Bob as if they were pretending, posing, trying to threaten. And another stranger was sitting at Mackenzie's desk, notepad at the ready. The entire presence intimidated Bob.

Quincy sat in one of the two vacant chairs and motioned for Bob to take the other.

Lord Harris switched on the tape recorder. He didn't stand on ceremony, he got straight to the point.

"Interview beginning." He gave the time and date, named everyone present.

Bob didn't listen. He had a lawyer now. He decided to float above it all, let Quincy handle everything.

"Mr. Heggie," Lord Harris said, "are you willing to reconsider the deal placed on the table late yesterday?"

"My client knows nothing about any raid, robbery or any missing money," Quincy said, "so I'm afraid he's in no position to help you."

Bob felt a sigh building, didn't let it out.

Lord Harris took off his glasses, used them to motioned to the smart young man on his right. The man pushed his briefcase toward the center of the table, clicked open the gold catches and pulled out a two page document.

"We'll give your lawyer a few minutes to read over this, then we'll reconvene," Lord Harris said.

Bob cut in.

"Aren't you supposed to tell me the charges?" Bob said. "That's what they do on TV."

Lord Harris looked at him with an expression Bob hadn't seen before. The bodyguard like figures gave Bob blank stares, impassive, cold.

"It's not a charge sheet, Mr. Heggie," Lord Harris said.

"I don't understand."

"We're not charging you."

"Come on, Bob," Quincy said. "Let's talk about this outside." He stood up and Bob followed. He didn't need to be told twice.

Bob directed Quincy to his office. It seemed strange sitting in the old chair, a chair he would most likely never sit in again.

Quincy spent a few minutes studying the document, smiling every now and again.

"What is it? What do they want?" Bob was confused, impatient.

Quincy held up a hand.

"What are they doing to me?" Bob said.

"Bob, please," Quincy looked up, frowned. "I'm nearly finished, just be patient." After what seemed an eternity, he looked up again, smiled.

"What is it? What do they want?"

"They're sacking you," Quincy said and it took a second or two before Bob realized what he'd said.

"I don't understand?" It wasn't what Bob had been expecting.

"Sacking you, showing you the door. Not enough hard evidence I imagine. Not enough to take to court anyway."

"No charges?"

"None," Quincy said. "They're sacking you for misconduct and negligence."

"I don't know if I like the sound of that." Bob closed his eyes for a few seconds. He wanted to jump for joy, but he didn't want Quincy to see him happy about getting the sack.

"And there's more. They're buying your silence."

"Now that I don't understand," Bob said.

Quincy went on to explain the document. Bob was sworn to secrecy under his current contract not to disclose any information relating to any security issues involving the bank to the general public.

Nor could he disclose any information that might jeopardize or harm the bank. The official secret statement had been reworded slightly to emphasize that this also included the media and television. In return for his signature agreeing to this, they agreed to drop any ongoing investigation and in effect brush the whole incident under the carpet. They would also continue paying his salary twenty-four months from signature.

Bob clenched his fists. He was free. Free from the shackles of the bank and free to continue with the rest of his life.

"A scapegoat, Bob," Quincy said. "That's what they want and it seems they've found their man."

"No charges?" Bob mouthed to himself as he gave Quincy a grin.

"You seem happy. I don't get it. Twenty odd years, unblemished record, they sack you and you're smiling. It's a clear case of unfair dismissal."

Bob bit his lower lip to keep from laughing.

"You did it, didn't you?" Quincy said.

"If I did, it's a secret I'll take to the grave."

"You lied to me."

"Hey, you're a lawyer, you should be used to that."

"Pity you can't write a book about it."

"Yeah, pity."

Back in the interview room Quincy handed the document to Lord Harris, who seemed relieved as he asked if he and Bob could have a few minutes alone.

Bob nodded that it was okay and Quincy and the others left the room.

"Return the money," Lord Harris said as soon as they'd gone, "and I promise we'll leave you alone."

"How many times do I have to tell you that I didn't take it?"

"By courier, in a bin, drop it off at my house in the middle of the night if you wish, anything."

Bob shook his head, trying his best to look annoyed, but he was afraid he wasn't pulling it off.

"I'll have you followed for as long as at takes if you don't, Mr. Heggie. That's a promise." He raised his voice, not quite a shout. He was furious. "I'll have you watched night and day. I don't care how much it costs. As soon as you pick up the money, I'll have you."

"Your Lordship, I'm just a simple banker with an ex-wife, a couple kids and a pair of dogs I don't like. Why in the world would you ever think a guy like me could rob a bank?" He turned away from Lord Harris, left the room, waived to Quincy and the others on his way and left the bank without looking back.

As he reached the bottom of the steps, he turned and looked up at the lackluster building. A light drizzle had started and dark grey clouds hung over the town, making it look even more depressing than it actually was. The rain wet his face and he blinked it out of his eyes.

"I've beaten you." He turned and walked away.

The relaxing environment of the Grapes suited Bob. He ordered a Guinness and the window cleaners, Jackie and Peter came in as the barman was pouring it. Bob caught the barman's eye and ordered them each a drink as well.

They looked tired and Jackie seemed subdued. Their current working arrangements were taking their toll and Peter's arms were bothering him. Bob spent a few minutes talking to them, but then a few of their friends came in and pulled Jackie away for a game of darts and Peter drifted along with them, leaving Bob alone at the bar. But he didn't mind. He had plenty to think about.

Like that threat Lord Harris had made. Would the man really have him followed? Bob didn't want to believe it. He'd hoped Lord Harris would have had a higher opinion of the kind of mind that could pull off such a daring robbery right under their noses. After all, only an idiot would pull off such a successful scam, then go and visit his money.

But after another drink, Bob started thinking about the money. The thought of four hundred thousand pounds lying in a station locker preyed on him. He couldn't leave it there, he'd worked too hard for it. He'd lost too much sleep and ultimately his career and livelihood because of it. It was sitting there, waiting, begging to be collected. It seemed to be calling to him and Bob longed to answer its call.

All he had to do was to open the locker, push in an empty rucksack, fill it, and walk away. Less than a minute, and he wouldn't need to take all the money. Perhaps about a hundred thousand, maybe a little more. He could leave the rest for a year or two.

One thing made it dangerous. One thing worried Bob above all else. What if they really were watching him? He looked around the Grapes. Nobody unusual, just the regulars. If they were going to watch him, they obviously hadn't started yet, probably because he'd left the bank in too much of a hurry for them to get organized. Nothing like the element of surprise.

Still, even though they weren't watching, he couldn't be too careful. He needed some kind of disguise. He got up, joined the boys at the dart game.

"Jackie, I have to go out for a bit, do you mind if I borrow your coat?"

"No worries, mate." Jackie pulled off the sheepherder coat, handed it to Bob.

"You mind if I borrow the hat as well."

"You can borrow it." Jackie pulled off his Bushman hat, "but it's a genuine Akubra and I've had it a long time. It means a lot to me."

"In that case, maybe I better not borrow it."

"Nonsense." He handed the hat over. "Just promise you'll buy me another if anything happens to it, 'cuz I can't afford another one right now."

"You got a promise," Bob said.

With the long brown coat and the Bushman hat, Bob felt sort of like an Australian Indiana Jones. He went to the bar and grabbed a look at his reflection in the mirror hanging behind the cash register. He looked daring and dashing. He didn't look like Bob Heggie. Even his own kids would pass him on the street without a glance.

Outside he checked the street. Nobody watching the Grapes, nothing unusual. He started off toward the station, stopping a couple times to check behind. He saw no one.

The station concourse was busy when he got there,

full of travelers and commuters going about their business. Bob crossed the open area in front of the timetable, weaving between the commuters checking the schedules and went into the gentleman's toilet on the far side.

He locked himself in a cubicle and waited for ten minutes.

It was another precaution. He pictured his walk to the station. He'd seen no one, of that he was sure, but it couldn't hurt to be extra careful.

He left the toilet, looked left, right. There were people hustling about, but no one seemed to be watching. No one looked suspicious or out of place. He walked the perimeter of the station and strolled toward the stone entrance leading to the street.

And saw Old Tom.

"Tom, I thought you got the sack?"

"Got my old job back. It appears somebody keeps filling the coin slots with Super Glue." Tom ran his eyes up and down, settled them on Jackie's hat. "Trouble is I don't know how long it will last. They're bound to come up with something. So I'll be out of a job again, soon enough." Tom sighed. "And anyway this Super Glue is bloody expensive." He fumbled in his coat pocket and showed Bob a glimpse of the tube.

"You're smarter than the average man, that's for sure." Bob laughed.

"And you, how come you're out of uniform?" Once again, Tom ran his eyes up and down Bob's attire.

"I've got some private business to take care of and I didn't want to be recognized. If you know what I mean."

"I don't, but from the looks of you, I'm thinking you should be careful."

"I'll do my best, Tom."

"I don't guess you'll be needing the evening paper then?"

"Actually, Tom, I do." He handed over a five pound note and Tom gave him a paper. "Use the change to buy me a drink later at the Grapes."

"Thanks, I'll look forward to it."

A queue was building up behind them.

"You've got customers. I'll talk to you later."

"Remember what I said, be careful."

"Yeah." Bob turned away, headed for the locker section.

It was quiet, two or three people were going about their business, fumbling with the keys and the stiff locks on the heavy metal doors.

Bob strolled on through, trying to look casual as he made his way to number twenty-eight, his new lucky number. He glanced behind and saw that he was out of view of the main station concourse. Nobody there could see him. He waited, pretending to access a message on his cell phone. At locker twenty-six a young girl, a student most likely, struggled to remove a large framed rucksack. Eventually she managed to pry it out and tried to lift it onto her back. She tied it around her waist and left.

Now he was alone. It couldn't have worked out better. It seemed the gods were smiling on him. He fumbled for the key in his pocket with sweating hands, found it. He looked around again at an empty scene. He looked back at the locker and moved toward it. He keyed the lock, but the door wouldn't open.

Something was wrong, it didn't feel right.

He checked the locker number. Twenty-eight. Right

locker. He tried again and this time the key turned. He pulled open the door with a rapid heartbeat. The rucksack was there. He started to reach for it, but something held his hand. He froze. He couldn't pinpoint what was wrong, but something wasn't right.

He looked around again. And again he saw nobody. He was being paranoid. But sometimes, he told himself, paranoia was a good thing. He eased the locker door closed and turned the key. He almost ran from the enclosed area. All of a sudden it had become claustrophobic and it was suffocating him.

He sighed with relief as he mingled with the throng of people once again. Everything had been perfect. Why couldn't he carry out such a simple task? He had to try again, had to give it another go. He needed to prepare himself and he sat at a table outside of the station café. He held his paper up and pretended to read. All the while scanning the open station square.

What was he worried about? Why was he being like this? Just do it, he told himself, walk to the locker, take out the money, walk away. He was about to get up and do just that when he caught sight of someone who sent cold daggers knifing up his spine.

He'd lost the smart corporate suit and replaced it with jeans and a baggy tee shirt. He had on a baseball cap and sunglasses. Nevertheless Bob recognized him. It was Bowen. Now he knew why he'd felt so uncomfortable. He watched the man from behind his newspaper.

He wondered whether Bowen had seen him go into the left luggage enclosure and he wondered if he had the sense to put two and two together? Why not? They'd timed Bob's movement during the raid and the station was the obvious place to hide the money. Bob had been stupid. Bowen didn't have to follow him. All he had to do was hang out here and wait for Bob to fall into his trap.

He watched Bowen for a few minutes, studied his movements, but the man gave nothing away, yet he was clearly looking for someone. He hovered by the left luggage department and then he disappeared out into the street. It wasn't a hard decision to call off the day's mission. Bob got up and left the station, heading to the park. It was still drizzling, threatening to come down harder, but Bob didn't care. He needed to think.

He set off up Grainger Street, away from the station, turned left at the monument and made his way to the park. Nothing like putting the city behind him for awhile to clear his head. At the park he took the footpath to the lake. Oftentimes he'd seen fishermen trying their luck when he'd taken this walk during his lunch breaks, but with the day as gloomy as it was becoming, he didn't think he'd find anybody there today.

The sky was quickly turning, first a solid grey, now getting dark. He wandered for a few minutes and found himself in the heart of the park. He found a bench by the lake, made himself comfortable.

He could barely make out the island in the center of the lake as a grey fog was rolling in. He looked out over the trees on the other side of the water and could just see the outline of the football stadium that dominated the landscape. It was as if he were cut off from the outside world. In a few seconds the fog obliterated the view of the stadium, where he'd seen so many games. The island too was fading away.

He looked over the lake. As he'd suspected, there were

no anglers, no lines in the water, today. No tourists plodding about. He felt as if he was in one of those Jack Priest stories Debra liked to read so much. A black and white world where nothing is real and nobody gets out alive.

The depressing sky was depressing Bob. He went over to the jetty, leaned against the rail. From here he could still make out the island. Funny, he thought, he'd wandered through the park so many times, yet had never taken a boat out to the island. He'd always wanted to, but never had. Now that he had the time, he vowed he'd do it someday soon.

He saw movement on the lake. A swan swam out of the fog, her long neck curled sort of like a question mark. Bob couldn't take his eyes off her. The graceful white bird lifted his spirits. All of a sudden he felt better as he watched her glide over the pond, like him, oblivious to the fog.

She squawked and Bob felt his heart in his throat as something slammed into the white bird. Half her side was blown away, the water turned crimson as the bird jerked in the violent throws of death.

"Next one is for you, Mr. Heggie!" Bowen's voice boomed out of the fog.

Bob froze.

"Move and you're a dead man. Do you understand?

"Yeah." Bob shook a bit, scared.

"Did I give you a fright, Heggie?" Bowen shouted out.

"You could say that," Bob said, not sure where Bowen was.

"Guess you don't feel so well without your fat lawyer," Bowen said, voice loud, but not a shout anymore. He sounded like he was off to Bob's left, but the way the acoustics were around the lake, he couldn't be sure.

"I feel okay," Bob said, stalling for time, hoping he could keep Bowen from shooting again.

"Doesn't feel so good when you don't have the upper hand, does it?" Bowen sounded even more threatening than he had earlier. "You thought you were so cleaver in that interview room. So cool. You planned well, but you made one mistake."

"Since I didn't do it," he said, still clinging to his story, "I couldn't have."

"Don't act like I'm an idiot, Heggie." Bob wished he could see the man. "I know you did it and I know you stashed the cash somewhere. Not your house, though, we know that, don't we? I'm betting in a locker at the station, so I was waiting around and funny thing, I saw you walk out of there in that stupid disguise. That was your mistake, Heggie, going to the station in that stupid hat."

Bob thought his disguise was much better than the getup Bowen was wearing, but he wasn't about to say so. Instead he said. "If you know so much, why don't you call in the cops?"

"Me, call in them? Not on your life. I gave years of loyal service to the people of this city, risking my life. I was a good cop, but they let me go, said I was unstable. Imagine that, unstable."

"Yeah, Imagine that," Bob muttered, then said aloud, "What happened?"

"None of your fucking business," Bowen shouted, "that's what happened." Unstable was kind, the man sounded demented.

"And now my career as a private investigator is over,

thanks to you."

"What are you talking about?"

"You made me look like an incompetent amateur during that interview. They're laughing at me and it's your fault!"

The man was a nutter. Bob was in trouble. He strained his eyes into the fog, trying to figure out where the voice was coming from. He looked around, searching for an escape route. There was none. He was out in the open, exposed. If he made a run for the trees behind, Bowen would have him before he closed half the distance.

"I'm gonna need that money, Bob."

"How many times to I have to tell you? I didn't take the money." Bob thought back to that day when the robber came out of the National. That's how he felt now. He just didn't want to take it anymore.

"Either you give me that money or I'm going to put a bullet in your brain."

It was time to bluff.

"Then I'm afraid you're just going to have to do it, because I didn't take the bloody money."

"I'll kill your wife and kids after." A shiver racked through Bob. Bowen had called and his cards were pretty good.

"You wouldn't, you couldn't." He had been stupid and now he was in serious trouble. Bowen was toying with him, of that Bob was certain. And when he was done, he planned on leaving Bob in the same condition as that poor swan, a corpse in the lake.

"The money for your life, Bob. Simple as that."

Bob was about to shout out again that he didn't know what Bowen was talking about, when he heard a thud off to his left.

"Run, Bob!" Hannah came charging out of the fog. "I hit him from behind and got his gun." She was panting, out of breath as she blazed past Bob and on into the trees. She had a long barreled gun in her hand. "Hurry!" she shouted.

CHAPTER NINETEEN

"DOWN!" Hannah shouted to Bob as she dropped to her stomach, squirmed around on her belly, pistol pointed in the direction they'd come from. Her hands were shaking, she couldn't help it, couldn't stop it. She was so scared.

Bob hit the ground next to her. His funny looking hat flew off. He seemed awkward in that long coat. Why was he dressed like that?

"Are you all right?" she said. He was breathing fast, but he didn't seem out of breath.

"Yeah, yeah." He nodded toward the gun. "You know how to use that?"

"I don't have a clue." She was still shaking, but now she was starting to get it under control. "But how hard could it be. You just point and shoot."

"Give it to me."

"You ever shoot a gun before?" She handed it over.

"Yes." He checked out the pistol. Then he started unscrewing the silencer from the barrel.

"What are you doing?"

"Taking off the silencer. These things get less accurate the more they're used." He put the silencer into his coat pocket. Now the gun didn't look anywhere near as menacing.

"Silencer?"

"Yeah, it muffles the sound of the shot, but after a few rounds they screw up accuracy. Something you don't learn in the movies."

She stared out into fog, couldn't see a thing. She shivered.

"Why was he shooting at you?"

"He thinks I robbed the bank." He reached out for the hat, grabbed it, put it on.

"He what?"

* * *

"I didn't." Bob pointed the gun out into the fog. He was a little disoriented, but he thought he knew the direction Bowen would be coming from. And he'd be coming, gun or no gun, of that Bob was sure. Bowen wasn't the kind of man who gave up easily.

"So why does he think you did?" Hannah said. "Why was he following you?"

"He's got a one track mind." Bob took his eyes out of the fog, looked into her eyes. Why was she here, sprawled out on the cold ground with him? "I thought you were going to stay back with the boat until your uncle sold it."

"The man came, said he wanted it, so my job was done. I took the train back and just as I got into the station I saw you in that getup and then I saw this man following you."

"How'd you know he was following me?"

"He seemed to be signaling somebody and he was watching you. Even so, if you wouldn't have been in disguise, I wouldn't have thought anything about it. But since you were dressed so out of character, I thought I'd follow along too. Just curious, I guess. I hope it doesn't get me killed." She laughed. It was forced.

"Shhh, I thought I heard something." Bob strained his ears, trying to pick something up out of the fog. "Just the wind, I guess."

"So, why are you wearing that getup?"

"To avoid the man who's been following me, of course. His name's Bowen. The bank hired him and Mackenzie's put him onto me. Personally, I think Mackenzie stole the money. I didn't at first, but the way he's been pointing the finger at me has made me change my mind." He sighed. He was doing the best he could, lying on the hoof. That had never been part of his plan. And getting shot at in the park had never been part of the plan either. He almost wanted to give up, tell her the truth and give the money back.

No, that was not a good idea. If he came clean, she'd never speak to him again. And now, all of a sudden, he realized she was more important to him than the money back in that locker.

They couldn't stay like this forever, waiting for Bowen to come for them. He was going to have to do something.

"I'm going to go out there and settle this," he said.

"What?"

"Don't worry," he said. "I know what I'm doing. I can take care of him."

"Then why were you disguised, trying to evade him?"

"I'll avoid a fight whenever I can, but once a bully gets in your way, you have to take a stand or he'll make your life miserable."

"He tried to kill you."

"But we've got his gun now, so his advantage is gone. I've seen into his eyes. I know what he's made of."

"He's big."

"I've handled big before." He looked into her eyes. "I was involved in a lot of close combat in the first Gulf War and those were brave men, fighting for their lives. This Bowen is nothing like that. He's just a weasel trying to make some easy money."

"An awfully big weasel."

"Yes, and that's why I'm going to leave this with you." He handed the gun toward her. "This is a Star nine millimeter automatic. It's a good gun. Spanish made. All you gotta do is what you said, point and shoot."

"You're crazy!"

"I'll call out to you, so you'll know it's me coming back. If anybody else comes through here, shoot."

"No, this is a park, anybody could come along."

"In this weather?" He started to get up.

"Stop!" She grabbed his arm.

"Don't worry, I can handle myself."

"I'm sorry, but I have to ask. Did you take the money? Are you in anyway responsible for this?"

"I'm not." He got up. "Now I have to go and put an

end to this."

* * *

Hannah shivered with the cold and the fear as Bob disappeared into the fog. Did she believe him? He answered quickly, seemingly without guilt. She looked at the gun in her hand. It was shaking. Could she shoot someone? She didn't think so. She started to set the weapon down, changed her mind. Though she loathed it, it was the only security she had right now.

No, she had Bob Heggie. He was out there trying to find that madman who was behind all this. He was far more capable than she ever would have thought. She'd performed pretty well herself. She'd seen the man shooting at Bob, almost stumbled upon him in the fog actually and, without thinking, she'd charged up behind him, snatched the gun out of his hand and saved Bob's life. She should be proud of herself, she'd done a real Lara Croft kind of thing.

So how come she didn't feel like Lara Croft? How come she was so frightened? She heard something behind her.

Footsteps.

It wasn't Bob, he'd gone off in the other direction. Either it was somebody else or it was that Bowen person.

She tried to flatten herself against the cold earth, because she knew it wasn't somebody out for a stroll in the park, not in this fog. It was that guy who had been following Bob. She was sure of it.

"I'm coming for you, Heggie!" the man shouted.

* * *

Bob heard Bowen shout out and chills ripped up his spine, because it sounded as if he was behind him and Hannah was back there. He moved through the trees, making as much noise as possible to try and draw him away from Hannah as he headed toward the sound of Bowen's voice.

"Don't shoot! It's me," he called out as he moved toward Hannah. She was flat on the ground. He almost missed her, the fog was so thick.

"Bob," she said as he passed.

"It's all right," he said. He was going to kill Bowen for putting her through this, for frightening her so much.

"It doesn't seem all right."

"Come on, you have to get up." He tugged at her arm as she got up and pulled her toward the undergrowth. He cursed under his breath as the leaves crunched beneath them. It was no good, he might as well be waiving a torch at Bowen.

"Stay here, don't move."

"Where are you?"

He didn't give her time to finish as he moved back toward the direction where he thought the man was. Him or me, he whispered to himself. Him or me. He peered through the trees, straining to focus through the dark and the fog, he looked for a shadow or a sharp movement, anything, then he'd be on him.

Then a lucky break. A twig cracked off to his right and the bulky figure of his pursuer showed through the trees, lumbering out of the fog. And he was coming toward him. Something flashed in his hand.

He had a knife.

Now the advantage swung in Bowen's favor. Almost on top of him now, Bob pressed against the tree, blending in with the shape of it. As Bowen drew level Bob stepped forward and swung at his throat. He misjudged, connecting instead with his breast bone. Pain shot up Bob's shoulder as Bowen fell back into the bushes, choking for breath. He was up in a second and lunged at Bob with the knife. Bob whipped his head back as the blade flashed by his face. He grabbed hold of Bowen's shoulder, pulled up hard, swept a leg swept across the man's ankles. Bowen crashed to the ground and, as he scrambled to get up, Bob jumped on his back, wrapped an arm around his throat.

"Move and I'll break your neck."

Bowen struggled, but Bob had him in a firm grip. Bowen thrust the knife around, trying to end it, but Bob slammed a fist against the knife hand, grabbed a fistful of Bowen's hair, jerked it back, snapping Bowen's neck with a quick crack, then recoiled as Bowen's bowls cut loose. He got up, stepped away from the body, started back to Hannah when he heard someone rustling through the trees. He dropped to the ground next to Hannah, pointed the gun at the sound.

"What's going on?" she whispered. "It sounded like you were killing each other."

"Bowen's dead, but there's someone else out there."

"Oh, God."

The rustling stopped. It had to be Stainbridge. And if Bowen had had a gun, then Stainbridge would have one too. The situation was going very south, very fast.

Bob heard him moving through the trees again. It sounded as if he was moving away.

"Maybe he's leaving," Hannah said.

Bob wished that were so, but he knew better. Stainbridge wasn't going to go away. Bob had seen the kind of man he was. Experienced, calm, the kind of man who had been around. The kind of a man who wouldn't let his partner go un-avenged.

He couldn't kid himself. A hot head like Bowen he could handle, had handled. But Stainbridge was a horse of a different color. He and Hannah were in trouble.

"I don't hear him anymore," Hannah said.

"But he's out there."

"It's a big park," she said. "If we stay put, he'll never find us."

"I think you're right. Eventually he'll go, then we can get out of here."

"Yeah, and forget all this."

"It won't be so easy to forget," Bob said, thinking of Bowen dead out there in the fog.

A scream pierced the air. It was the most agonizing sound Bob had ever heard.

"Why would he scream like that?" Hannah whispered.

"I think he found his partner's body."

Bob started to get up, gun still in his hand.

"No, stay down." She grabbed his arm, held on tight.

"It came from over there," Bob pointed with the gun toward the direction of the lake. "That's where the body is."

"This is not good," she said.

"I think now is a good time to think about getting out of here," he said.

"Maybe we should wait a bit longer, make sure," she said.

Bob didn't want to wait. He had no desire to tangle with Stainbridge. The sooner they were out of the park, the better. He thought about the money in that locker. It wasn't worth this.

"No, I think we should get out of here while the going's good." He got up, held a hand down for her.

"All right, you win," she took his hand and Bob pulled her to her feet.

"Which way?" Bob said. They were shrouded in fog. The park was quiet. Bob felt like he was standing in the Twilight Zone.

"I don't know," she said. "That way, I think." She pointed.

"It's as good a direction as any."

Bob started off with Hannah so close behind he could feel her breath on his neck. He pushed his way through a copse of trees. They were so close together he almost felt as if he were breaking trail in a dense jungle.

He slipped the gun into the deep pocket on the right hand side of Jackie's sheepherder coat, but he kept his hand in the pocket, kept it around the gun.

At least Stainbridge couldn't see any better in the fog than they could. He wouldn't be able to find them in this. No one could.

A shot rang out, the noise dynamite loud, shattering a low hanging branch just to Bob's left with a thunder cracking sound and once again Bob and Hannah dropped to the ground. Bob pulled the gun from his pocket as still another shot boomed through the fog.

"How'd he find us?" Hannah shouted.

"Don't know, move!"

"Yeah!" Hannah crawled on her belly, soldier style, away from the wounded tree, Bob right behind, Jackie's hat brim inches from the girl's feet as they slipped and slithered over the damp earth.

Another shot rang out, another tree hit.

"Shit, that went right over my head!" Hannah said.

"Move it! Move, move, move!" Bob urged.

But Hannah wasn't the kind of girl who needed to be told, already she'd picked up the pace, snake crawling faster than he'd thought possible.

He struggled to keep up with her. It seemed like they'd been crawling for hours, though he knew it had only been seconds. His elbows ached, his forearms were sore, his right hand was tired from holding up the gun, which now seemed made of lead.

She stopped.

"What's wrong?"

"Fence."

He crawled up alongside her. The fence looked temporary, chain link, about six feet high, probably built to keep park patrons out of a construction site or an area they were renovating.

"We either go over it," she said, "or go left or right and try to get around it, or go back the way we came."

"Let's wait here a second." Bob listened to the mist and heard nothing. "I think we lost him." He put the gun back in his pocket, unclipped his mobile phone from his belt.

"What are you gonna do?" she whispered.

"Dial 999."

"No, I don't like that idea."

"Why not?" He started to punch in the numbers.

"No." She grabbed his hand. "You left a dead man back there, remember?" She was very intense. "And I don't fancy spending the rest of my days in prison."

"Yeah, I didn't think of that." He held his fingers.

Prison if he completed the call, maybe worse if he did not. However, he'd done what he'd done to save himself and Hannah from getting shot by Bowen. But she was right, nobody would believe him, especially after they found out about the missing money and his part in it. And they'd find out.

"So, no coppers, right?" she said.

"No coppers." Bob clipped the phone back onto his belt. "I think we're safe here anyway. If we just sit tight and stay out of sight, eventually this guy will have to leave."

Another gunshot rang out, a bullet ripping into a piece of the chain link, cutting it in two.

"Over the fence," Hannah screamed out.

"I'll give you a boost." He put his hands together, fingers linked.

"Thanks." She stepped into the stirrup, he helped push her up. "I'm caught." She said. She was stuck on the top, the fence digging into her belly as she tried to flop over.

Another shot.

Bob stuck his hands under her stomach, shoved and she was over, falling to the ground with a thud as he scrambled up. He hadn't climbed a fence like this since childhood, but his hands and feet had long memories. He flopped over the top in much the same manner as Hannah, hitting the ground hard.

Another shot.

He was on his feet in an instant.

"Come on, get up!" Once again, he pulled her to her feet.

Another shot.

He pushed her on ahead, charging into the clearing fog. He'd felt adrenaline rushing through his veins in the past, but nothing like this. This was no adrenaline rush. This was adrenaline fear.

He ran on using up that unforgiving minute Kipling had made famous, breathing like a train out of steam, but it looked to him like Hannah could go on forever. He struggled to keep up, struggled to keep himself between the gunman and Hannah.

"The tree," Bob said, hoping she would see the wide tree off to their right.

"Yeah." She turned toward it.

They hurried around the tree, Bob panting hard. He needed to catch his breath. After a few seconds, he started to think about the man who was dogging them. Stainbridge had a reason for revenge. He'd lost his partner.

"Hey, I know where we are!" Hannah said, interrupting his train of thought. "The exit's that way." She pointed and he hoped she was pointing true.

A half minute that seemed like a half century later, they were at the gates and almost safe. Bob heard a siren off in the distance. His heart was beating like it never had when he'd under fire in Iraq. Safe, he wanted to be safe, and he wouldn't be as long as he was out here. the Grapes, he'd feel safe if they could get there.

Not permanently safe, because Stainbridge would probably try again, but for a day, only a day, he wanted, needed safety. Tomorrow he'd try and get on top of the situation. He'd get a hold of Stainbridge and see if they could work something out, cut a deal.

"Not far now," he said.

"But too far for you, Bob Heggie."

It was Mackenzie. He had a gun in his right hand and in his left he was holding what looked like a small version of a television antenna, the kind you used to see on house after house before cable and satellite TV.

Bob frowned, what was he doing here?

"Hands where I can see them. You too, young lady."

Bob couldn't believe it. He'd been so sure it had been Stainbridge dogging them, trying to kill them. Not Mackenzie. Why would he do that? Surely not for the money, the man was wealthy.

"You thought you could get away in the fog, didn't you?" Mackenzie shook the antenna. "But you couldn't fool the Yagi tracking machine."

"How?" It was all Bob could think of saying. He was stunned.

"Phil bugged your cell phone when you threw your coat down that day you pretended you were scalded." Mackenzie threw the antenna at him, but it fell short. "You thought you were clever, didn't you? So smart, stealing the money and getting them to fire me." The man looked like he'd been crying. His hands were shaking. His lower lip was trembling. He was angry. He looked insane.

"It's Mr. Mackenzie." Hannah started to move toward him.

"Stay where you are, young lady," Mackenzie said. "I'm an ace shot, Bob will tell you. Champion of my gun club."

"I don't understand," Bob said. He never would have figured Mackenzie would do something like this. He was a crack shot and a pistol champion, to be sure, but he was a coward too. Too cowardly for what he was up to now. At least Bob would have thought so, right up until he saw Mackenzie with the gun.

"What, Bob? What don't you understand?"

"You, out here, with Bowen?"

"His name wasn't Bowen. That was part of the act. His real name was Mackenzie."

Bob gasped.

"Yes, now you get it. He was my son from my first marriage and because of you, he's dead."

He wanted to shout out that he'd only been defending himself. But he could see the state of mind Mackenzie was in, he could see it in his eyes. Besides, in a way he was right. Everything was his fault. The e-mail, the raid, everything. If he wouldn't have robbed the bank, Mackenzie's son would still be alive. Of course, if Mackenzie hadn't treated him like something you'd scrape off your shoes all these years, he never would have taken the money in the first place.

"I still don't understand. You, your son, with guns, shooting at me for a lousy four-hundred thousand quid that I didn't take. Even if I did, it doesn't make any sense."

"It's not about the money!" Mackenzie shouted. "It's about what the Japanese call Face. You walked all over mine, made me look like a fool. Nobody does that."

The siren he'd heard earlier seemed to be getting closer, but he didn't think it'd get to them in time. He was going to have to charge Mackenzie. It was the only way he could give Hannah a chance to get away. He was about to shout at her to run when she gasped.

"My heart." She grabbed her chest, dropped to her knees. "Help me," she croaked as she fell on her face, taking Mackenzie's eyes off Bob for just long enough.

Bob wrapped his hand around the automatic, fired with the gun still in his pocket, catching Mackenzie in the chest, the sound ripping through the still mist. Mackenzie went down, body jerking.

Bob dropped to his knees.

"Hang in there, Hannah, I'll get you a doctor."

"I'm fine." She looked up at him with a tight smile. "I just thought you needed a distraction."

Bob pulled out the phone, punched in 999.

"What are you doing? Don't you remember our conversation back there by that fence?" She pushed herself up, grabbed the phone, shut it off. "Look at this mess. The cops come and we are in an awful lot of trouble. They'll put us away faster than I can blink, and I can blink pretty fast. They'll bury us deep and we'll never get out."

"Yeah, I suppose you're right."

"Suppose?" On her feet now, she went over to Mackenzie's body, picked up the gun. "Look at this, it's a gun! This is England and the coppers don't like guns, in case you didn't know." She pointed to Mackenzie. "Plus we got this dead guy here and the other one back there. Two dead bodies, plus the guns. If we don't get out of here now, we are big trouble."

Her outburst hit home.

The siren was getting closer still, louder.

"Stick this in that other pocket." She handed over the gun.

"All right." He did it, felt weighed down.

"Come on, we gotta go," she said.

And he followed her out of the park. Ten minutes later they were at the Grapes, listening to more sirens as police car after police car roared by.

"Why are we here?" Hannah wanted to know.

"I have to return this hat. I borrowed it from Jackie. Plus we have mud and muck all over ourselves. We look as if we'd been rolling around Leazes Park. In fact, if I was a copper stumbling on that scene up there, the first person I would look for would be someone fitting our descriptions."

"I suppose you're right." She nodded.

"We'll give Jackie back his hat, then maybe have a stiff drink. I don't know about you, but I need to calm down."

"I'm with you there."

He took off the hat as he made his way to the bar where he ordered a Jameson, he was about to ask Hannah what she wanted when she ordered one too.

"I'm surprised," he said.

"Why?" She smiled. "You didn't think a girl like me could appreciate a fine Irish whisky?"

"I don't know what I thought."

"There's a lot about me you don't know."

"How long do you think it'll take me to find it, this stuff I don't know?"

"A very long time."

"I've got as long as it takes." He clinked glasses with her, downed his shot in a quick gulp.

He saw Old Tom come in the bar.

"On your own, Tom?" Bob asked.

"Just waiting for the lads."

Bob introduced Hannah. He took her by the hand. It felt good in his and she gave him a squeeze. A shiver ran the length of his spine.

"I think maybe Hannah is my girl friend."

"Yeah, I guess I am." She nodded, then said, "I have to

go to the loo."

Bob followed her with his eyes till she was inside the lady's restroom as thoughts and concerns flooded into his head, but he tried to replace them with thoughts of the future. A future with Hannah.

"I've been keeping an eye on your bike," Tom said, bringing him back to the present. "I wouldn't have too much to drink if you're riding that monster home."

"What?"

"The motorcycle I saw you park over at the station this morning."

"You don't miss a trick, do you?" Bob laughed.

"I sure don't. I know everything that goes on in that station. I won't be there much longer though, I've accepted that now."

The sadness was evident in the old man's eyes. He wanted to console him, wanted to reassure him and yet ask him what was so special about a poorly paid job in a cold rail station.

"Cheer up, Tom, something will turn up."

"Like what, a lottery win?" Tom shook his head.

"Maybe this will help." Bob handed over the key.

"What's this?"

"It's a key to locker twenty-eight at the station."

"What's in there?"

"A lot of money, Tom." Bob smiled, he'd won a good bit at the races, had his house, which was almost free and clear. He didn't need that money and besides, one way to make sure Hannah never found out about it was to get rid of it. And he couldn't think of a better way.

"I don't understand."

"It's money I'm not supposed to have, money that has

to disappear. Money I don't ever want to hear about again. Money that could get me locked away for a long time if it ever came to light." Bob held his hand out. "I'll need your word that you'll never connect me with this money."

"How much money?"

"I told you, a lot."

"You have my word." Tom shook his hand.

"We'll have to invent a reason for you having it. Then we'll never speak of it again."

"I think me brother in Dublin is about to die and leave me a little something," Tom said.

"That would be good." He checked the bar, no sign of Jackie or Peter. "Something else, I've ruined Jackie's coat, could you see that he gets a new one?"

"No problem." Tom checked out the state of the coat. "I'll take care of it."

Bob caught Hannah out of the corner of his eye, coming toward the table.

"Well old pal this is it, you will look after yourself won't you? I don't think I'll be down here very much now that I'm unemployed."

"I'll miss you." Tom extended his hand. "But I don't understand why you're doing this for me."

"Just think of it as a little present for you and the boys, courtesy of the pretty people."

Just then Jackie and Peter burst through the door.

"You guys aren't going to believe this," Jackie said. "There's been a shootout at Leazes Park!"

The fog had lifted a little by the time they climbed onto the bike. More than ever Bob felt like the Jack of Hearts, with the guns in his pockets and Hannah behind. He smiled to himself. He knew of a tree out in the moors he was going to have to be visiting very soon, because it was the perfect hiding place for a coat with a hole shot through its pocket and a pair of guns that needed to disappear.

Hannah wrapped her arms around him, squeezed and shouted above the noise.

"Something tells me this is going to be a bit cold."

"I'm afraid so."

"Have you ever wondered how wonderful having a bike like this would be in a warmer climate?"

"I dunno, I suppose we could give it a try."

"Sounds good to me." She squeezed tighter.

As Bob gunned the machine out onto Neville Street an ambulance with blue lights flashing and siren wailing flew by them.

Too late, Bob thought. Too late.

THE BOOTLEG PRESS CATALOG

RAGGED MAN, by Jack Priest
ISBN: 0974524603
Unknown to Rick Gordon, he brought an ancient aboriginal horror home from the Australian desert. Now his friends are dying and Rick is getting the blame.

DESPERATION MOON, by Ken Douglas
ISBN: 0974524611
Sara Hackett must save two little girls from dangerous kidnappers, but she doesn't have the money to pay the ransom.

SCORPION, by Jack Stewart
ISBN: 097452462X
DEA agent Bill Broxton must protect the Prime Minister of Trinidad from an assassin, but he doesn't know the killer is his fiancée.

DEAD RINGER, by Ken Douglas
ISBN: 0974524638
Maggie Nesbitt steps out of her dull life and into her dead twin's, and now the man that killed her sister is after Maggie.

GECKO, by Jack Priest
ISBN: 0974524646
Jim Monday must rescue his wife from an evil worse than death before the Gecko horror of Maori legend kills them both.

RUNNING SCARED, by Ken Douglas
ISBN: 0974524654
Joey Sapphire's husband blackmailed and now is out to kill the president's daughter and only Joey can save the young woman.

NIGHT WITCH, by Jack Priest
ISBN: 0974524662

A vampire like creature followed Carolina's father back from the Caribbean and now it is terrorizing her. She and her friend Arty are only children, but they must fight this creature themselves or die.

HURRICANE, by Jack Stewart
ISBN: 0974524670

Julie Tanaka flees Trinidad on her sailboat after the death of her husband, but the boat has a drug lord's money aboard and DEA agent Bill Broxton must get to her first or she is dead.

TANGERINE DREAM, by Ken Douglas and Jack Stewart
ISBN: 0974524689

Seagoing writer and gourmet chef Captain Katie Osborne said of this book, "Incest, death, tragedy, betrayal and teenage homosexual love, I don't know how, but somehow it all works. I was up all night reading."

DIAMOND SKY, by Ken Douglas and Jack Stewart
ISBN: 0974524697

The Russian Mafia is after Beth Shannon. Their diamonds have been stolen and they think she knows where they are. She does, only she doesn't know it.

TAHITIAN AFFAIR: A ROMANCE, by Dee Lighton
ISBN: 0976277905

In Tahiti on vacation Angie meets Luke, a single-handed sailor, who is trying to forget Suzi, the love of his life. He is the perfect man, dashing, good looking, caring and kind. She is in love and it looks like her story will have a fairytale ending. Then Suzi shows up and she wants her man back.

BOOKS ARE BETTER THAN T.V.

A Few Acknowledgements

In addition to my wife, children and parents, I'd also like to thanks all the people who I've looked up to during my life, though they may not have realized it. And I'd also like to mention my Uncle Robert, my cousins and their children, too numerous to mention. And too, I'd like to thank my great friends Davey Valentine, Andrew Gilbert and Gary Jackson. And lastly, I'd like to thank my friend Thomas Purvis who put me onto Bootleg Press.

Ken Scott
Newcastle, 2005

Made in the USA